Praise for
Skid

"I'm always happy to get a new Rene Gutteridge book in my hands, because I know her characters, story, and dialogue will make me smile. *Skid* had me smiling all the way through."

—JAMES SCOTT BELL, best-selling author
of *Try Dying* and *The Whole Truth*

"*Skid* is my favorite installment so far of Rene's Occupational Hazards series! It doesn't get any better than a zany cast of characters aboard a transatlantic flight. This is a fun, wild ride with devious humor. I loved it!"

—CAMY TANG, author of *Sushi for One?*
and *Only Uni*

"Oh, the hazards of being a Hazard! Before reading the first page, I knew *Skid* would deliver its promised funny adventure at the extraordinarily capable hand and pen of Rene Gutteridge. Reading *Skid,* you feel like you're on the plane with the characters. It's a joy to be along for the ride!"

—CHERYL MCKAY, screenwriter of *The Ultimate Gift*

skid

skid

a novel

Rene Gutteridge

WaterBrook
PRESS

SKID
PUBLISHED BY WATERBROOK PRESS
12265 Oracle Boulevard, Suite 200
Colorado Springs, Colorado 80921
A division of Random House Inc.

ISBN 978-1-4000-7159-3

Published in association with the literary agency of Janet Kobobel Grant, Books &
Such, 52 Mission Circle, Suite 122, PMB 170, Santa Rosa, CA 95409-5370.

Published in the United States by WaterBrook Multnomah, an imprint of The
Doubleday Publishing Group, a division of Random House Inc., New York.

WATERBROOK and its deer design logo are registered trademarks of WaterBrook Press.

Library of Congress Cataloging-in-Publication Data
Gutteridge, Rene.
    Skid : a novel / Rene Gutteridge. — 1st ed.
       p. cm. — (The occupational hazards)
    ISBN 978-1-4000-7159-3
  1. Air pilots—Fiction. 2. Flight crews—Fiction. 3. Travelers—Fiction. I. Title.
    PS3557.U887S55 2008
    813'.54—dc22

                                              2007050280

Printed in the United States of America
2008—First Edition

10 9 8 7 6 5 4 3 2 1

For Sean, who makes my heart soar.

HAZARD

PERCY MITCHELL HAZARD was born January 7, 1940, in Dallas, Texas, and passed away June 8 at the age of 65. He was born to Gordon and Ethel Hazard and raised in Austin, Texas. He was baptized at the age of fourteen at Christ the Lord Church. He married Lucy Boyd in 1962 and shortly thereafter moved to Plano. He worked as the manager of a feed store for two years before becoming a computer manager at the unemployment office. A dedicated and hard worker, he spent twenty-eight years of his life there until he was replaced by a computer and became unemployed. Determined to provide for his family, he and Lucy started their own successful clown business, The Hazard Clowns, entertaining children and adults alike. Many people knew him only as Hobo, but his family and friends knew him as a loving and kind man, full of wisdom and laughter. He is survived by his children: Mitchell, 26, married to Claire; Cassie, 24; Hank, 23; Mackenzie, 22; Hayden, 20; Avery, 18; Holt, 16. He will be greatly missed but is now safely in the hands of his loving Father in heaven. Funeral services will be at Chapel Christian Church on Tuesday at 10:00 a.m.

HAZARD

LUCILLE "LUCY" MARGARET BOYD HAZARD was born February 15, 1945, in St. Louis, Missouri, to Gilbert Boyd, a pastor, and Wanda, a homemaker. She was raised in Louisville, Kentucky, where she spent most of her life until her family moved to Austin, Texas, where she met and married her husband, Percy. She had a long and distinguished career as Inspector 49 at Hanes until 1992, when the company was forced to downsize to 42 inspectors. As her husband lost his job three weeks earlier, they decided to start a clown business. Along with running The Hazard Clowns, this special woman homeschooled all seven of her beloved children. She went to be with her Lord on June 8. She is survived by her children: Mitchell, 26, married to Claire; Cassie, 24; Hank, 23; Mackenzie, 22; Hayden, 20; Avery, 18; Holt, 16. She died happily alongside her husband and will be laid to rest next to him at Resurrection Cemetery. She will be greatly missed by her family who adored and loved her. Funeral services are Tuesday at 10:00 a.m. at Chapel Christian Church.

Chapter 1

T his is going to be a tough crowd."

Forty children gathered on the large concrete patio that overlooked an acre of gardens, while three high-strung adults swung their arms in big, round motions, trying to get a grip on the situation.

"Now, kids, the clowns are *afraid* of loud noises, so we have to be quiet," tried the mother of the six-year-old with more friends than a politician.

"Great," Mack said under her breath. "That's what they need. Motivation to stir the waters."

Hank only nodded. He was in his mime costume already so he couldn't speak, but he didn't have to. Their task was clearly laid out in front of them. A bead of sweat trickled down his temple, smudging his makeup. He was glad they stood in the shade of the house.

Despite the black "blinky" marks on either side of her eyes and the wide, red clown smile, Mack's expression turned sour.

"What mother invites *forty* six-year-olds to a birthday party?" she moaned. "Did you hear what they did last year?"

Hank shook his head.

"The father built an actual pirate ship here in the backyard, with two decks and pirates in costumes. It even made cannon sounds."

Hank thought that sounded cool.

"I heard the kids made the adults walk the plank."

Birthday parties had come a long way. They did a lot of them, but usually it was just one or two of the Hazards making an appearance, and the parties consisted of ten or so children. This woman had hired the entire family. Now they knew why.

Hank's sister Hayden stepped out the back door and stood next to them, surveying the children below.

"You okay?" Mack asked her.

Hayden tried to smile, but Hank knew it was getting to her. Their oldest brother Mitch, the ring leader—literally—had the stomach flu and wasn't sure he could do a cartwheel without vomiting. Hayden had volunteered to step in and help.

"The makeup is making my skin itch," Hayden whispered.

"Didn't you put on that lotion first?" Mack asked.

Hayden sighed. "No. I forgot. I've also forgotten exactly what I'm supposed to be doing. It's been a while."

Hayden had stepped down from performing when they'd realized she wasn't an anxious child, just terrified of clowns. It had taken years to discover this, but once they got an official diagnosis, her parents allowed her to work in the office, booking events and keeping track of bills.

The family business did well, especially in the warm months. They had everything they needed and plenty left over, which they donated to children's hospitals, always making special, exclusive clown appearances when they delivered the check. The children couldn't get enough of it.

At least *those* children. The ones squirming on the patio didn't seem quite as enthusiastic.

While Hayden, Mack, and Cassie discussed what kind of act they would have to throw together to get these kids' attention, Hank marveled at the beauty all around him. The house stood three stories high, with exquisite stone work, a marble banister that could be seen through the front or back window, and what seemed like two hundred feet of flower gardens.

A rich, deep green lawn rolled from the steps of the patio like lush carpet. Bright pink and red roses climbed white lattice walls, while full arches of ivy framed paths he wanted to explore. A gazebo peeked through the foliage.

His parents had taught him the dangers of loving money. They lived off what they had and never borrowed a dime for anything, including the van they used for transportation to all of their performances. The siblings were paid good wages for their work, and Hank never felt he had anything to complain about. Yet standing in what seemed like an oasis, he couldn't help but wonder what it would be like to live with this kind of luxury. His gaze moved to the outdoor fireplace that crackled nearby. It wasn't nearly cold enough for a fire, but he supposed the slightly cool breeze could justify it.

He tuned back in to his sisters' conversation.

"Great time for Mitch to get sick," Mack sighed. "He's the one with the best magic tricks. We're going to have to make a pig fly to impress these kids."

"We don't have to impress them," Hayden said. "Just entertain them. A lot has changed, but at the end of the day, kids still love to be entertained."

"Hayden, it's been a while since you've done a kid party. They're not that easily entertained, and their attention span is all of about three seconds."

Hayden turned to Hank. "Maybe Hank could do some of those magic tricks with the smoke bombs. Kids like bombs, don't they?"

Hank smiled. The smoke bomb trick was usually a hit. But it involved some time and he wasn't sure they could sit still that long.

Cassie gestured toward the mother who had finally managed to get all the children to sit down. "Look how beautiful she is. I wish my hair would do that. It *would* do that if Dad wouldn't have a cow about hairspray. You can't even see it, but somehow he always knows when I'm wearing it." Cassie actually whimpered. "Did you see her nails?"

Mack turned to her. "Cassie, you've got to focus. We have to be on today. This is the first time Mom and Dad have taken a vacation—well deserved, mind you—and we promised them we would handle everything. We've got to pull this off, or they might never leave the house again."

Mitch came out, trailed by the two youngest of the Hazard family, Holt and Avery. A pea soup–colored skin tone bled through his chalky, white makeup. "Are we ready yet? What's the holdup?"

"Forty six-year-olds who won't sit still," Mack said. She pushed on her clown nose. "This is going to take some muscle. Are you okay? You look terrible."

"I just can't jump, roll, bend down, or raise my hands over my head."

Mack scowled. "Great. You can stand there and wave, then."

"We've got plenty of lawn," Cassie said. "Maybe Avery and Holt can do their acrobat routine first. Get things rolling. Literally."

They rolled around like bowling balls. Hank nodded in agreement.

"Good idea," Mitch said as he held his stomach. "Is it hot out here? I feel hot."

"Mitch," Mack said, "go lie down in the van. We can handle it. The last thing we need is you throwing up on kids whose clothes cost more than we're making today."

"No. Mom performed three days after her hysterectomy. I'm in, just not in an excitable sort of way." Mitch raised an eyebrow as Mack frowned. "We're supposed to be bright and cheery."

Mack adjusted her nose. "Yeah, yeah. I'll turn it on when I need to."

The mother in charge of the party clapped her hands, and in a voice sounding as though royalty had just arrived, she introduced

the clowns with, "Children, I give you...THE GREATEST
SHOW ON EARTH!"

Hank suppressed a smile. That was one way to set them up
for disappointment.

Avery and Holt bounded onto the lawn from the patio, back
handspringing their way across the grass with as much grace as
Olympic athletes, but it brought little reaction from the kids, who
sat slumped on the concrete basketball court, half of them picking their noses, the other half picking on the kid next to them.

Hank saw Holt look over, desperation in his eyes. He grabbed
Avery and whispered something to her.

Oh no.

"Mack!" Hank whispered.

Cassie's eyes widened. "Why are you talking?"

"Listen to me—"

"You're breaking the cardinal rule of miming! You must never
talk while in—"

"They're going to do it!"

"What?" Mack whispered back.

Hank pointed toward Avery and Holt, who were lining up on
the far end of the lawn. "The thing they learned three weeks ago."

Cassie, Hayden, and Mack all turned toward the lawn.

Hayden gasped. "No! They're not ready. They haven't even
done it without spotters yet!"

But it was too late. Sprinting simultaneously, Holt and Avery
began with a round off and two back handsprings.

Hayden grabbed Hank's arm and squeezed her eyes shut, her hand over her mouth.

"I can't believe they're doing this," Mack said. "They don't have enough experience—"

With their arms stretched toward the sky, they both jumped off the ground and did double back flips. Then, without a pause, Holt knelt, Avery stepped on his knee, and Holt rose and lifted her above him. She lowered her feet onto his shoulders, then took his hands. Slowly, beautifully, her feet left his shoulders and she balanced perfectly on Holt's hands, upside down. They hardly swayed.

Hank glanced at the crowd. The parents began to clap loudly. A few kids joined in. A red-haired, freckle-faced kid sneered, "So what? At the *Fear Factor* party I went to last week, a kid had to eat real worms."

"I can't believe they did it!" Hayden said as Holt and Avery took their bows to intermittent clapping.

Hank glanced back at the sound of Mitch's cell phone ringing. Mitch slipped into the house to answer it.

Mack moved next to Hank. "We're on. We're doing the magic sequence, right? With the bouquet of flowers and the disappearing stuffed rabbit?"

Hank looked sideways at her. "We're starting with Plan X."

"This is no time for jokes. And why are you talking?"

"I'm not joking."

"Of course you're joking. And talking. You never talk."

"I'm not. Joking, I mean." Hank watched the fidgeting children.

Mack adjusted her cowboy hat and folded her arms. "If this gets back to Mom and Dad, they're going to be mad." She smiled. "But this could be fun. Come on."

Hank and Mack skipped toward the children. Hank waved as Mack shot her pretend gun and rode her pretend horse. With choppy steps and stiff arms, Hank ticked along the front row as a robot. Unfortunately, all he heard was snickering and crude remarks that would have sent him to the bathroom for a dose of soap on his tongue if he'd ever said them.

Hank often played the sad mime, and today it wouldn't be a stretch. These events were getting harder and harder. Two years ago, they'd added firecrackers to the routine. Mitch, who did most of the magic tricks, attended a magic convention in Las Vegas to learn some of the trickier maneuvers. Short of bringing in circus animals, there wasn't much more they could do to get kids' attention.

Battling sugar highs and low attention spans, the Hazards had come to realize they were no match for Donkey Kong, or whatever it was kids played these days. Last year they'd attempted to modernize their clowns by including Darth Vader, who Hayden swore was made scarier than the movie version by the addition of the red smile they painted across Mitch's face. They also tried the Teenage Mutant Ninja Turtles, but they assessed that the premise didn't work well because the concept of ninja turtles was stupid.

Add rainbow hair and a honking nose, and you pretty much have a freak show.

Hank was about to begin the bouquet trick when a blond girl on the front row, her hair cascading down her back in soft ringlets, stuck out her tongue. Hank turned to Mack, and they locked eyes. It was time.

In her cowgirl twang, Mack clapped her hands and said, "Boys and girls, listen up. I want you to be very quiet. The mime has something to say."

"Mimes don't talk, stupid!" a kid from the back yelled.

"This mime does. But in a very special language."

Hank made miming motions. Mack pretended she didn't understand at first, but then she said, "Ooohhh. I get it. He's thirsty. He says he can't talk unless he has something to drink. Who can go get him a drink?"

"I will!" A girl popped up and ran to the birthday table. She returned with a can of soda.

Hank motioned for her to open it. She did and handed it to him. The children watched as he guzzled it as fast as he could, making sure to let some dribble out of his mouth and onto his shirt. Mack narrated the situation. "Perhaps his words fall out of his mouth just like his drinks!"

A few people chuckled. Mostly the adults.

Suddenly, with big motions, Hank reached upward, stretching his whole body. Then he made horrible gasping noises. Mack rushed up to him. "Are you okay? Are you okay?"

A few of the parents stepped forward, but Hank stopped, stood perfectly still, and shot one finger into the air.

Dead silence.

Bingo.

Swallowing one more bubble of air, Hank opened his mouth and let a big one rip, followed by several smaller ones. A total of seven rapid-fire burps echoed in the silence. All forty of the kids' mouths hung open. And then loud, clamorous laughter burst through the quiet pause as the kids yelled, "Do it again! Do it again!"

Hank was winding up for round two when Mitch suddenly appeared, wigless and holding his honking nose. "I'm sorry, folks. I'm sorry." He waved his hand to hush them. "We're going to have to stop our show. I'm terribly sorry." Mitch looked at Mack and Hank and gestured for them to follow him. He walked quickly through the back door of the home and through the huge foyer toward the front door, with Hank and Mack trailing behind him.

Mack sighed. "Mitch is overreacting. I'll handle this."

"It was my idea."

"No offense, Hank, but you're not very good at standing up for yourself."

Hank resented that. Mack was tough, but a little overbearing. All his life Mack had been the one who stood up for him, but she would never give him a chance to do it himself. She didn't even think he was capable.

Hank grabbed her arm and stopped her right before they

went out the door. "I can speak for myself," Hank said, tugging at his white gloves.

Mack studied him. "You know how Mitch can be. He doesn't back down when it comes to his opinion."

"Thanks to a virus, he wasn't the one having to come up with an opening act to entertain children who own stock in Toys "R" Us. Sometimes you just have to use what you've got."

"I agree. But you're going to get lectured, and he's probably going to throw in something about taking advantage of Mom and Dad's not being here."

"I can handle it."

Hayden hurried toward them. "Come on. Mitch wants to talk to all of us."

By all of us, Hank knew it was going to end up being *him*. He knew Mitch must be serious, though, because he interrupted a performance.

They rounded the corner and saw Mitch standing in the large brick driveway. His wife, Claire, stood next to him. She hadn't been at the party earlier and Hank wondered why she was here now. Mitch didn't look good. Sick. And…sad? Hank had expected anger.

Hank drew in a breath, hoping his courage wouldn't slide down the drain of self-doubt. "Mitch, it was my call, okay? I had to do something. I know it's crude and Mom and Dad wouldn't have approved, but—"

"They're dead."

Hank's carefully chosen words came to a screeching halt at the tip of his tongue. Distantly, he could hear the squeals and giggles of the children playing in the back property.

"Who?" Mack asked.

Mitch didn't say it, but the tears dripping down his cheeks did. With each moment that passed, another of Hank's siblings began to cry. But he just felt numb.

"You're talking about Mom and Dad?" Mack finally asked.

Mitch nodded, trying to compose himself.

"No! This can't be true!" Cassie wailed.

Hank's other siblings wiped their tears, staring at Mitch, who took several attempts to find his voice. "In a hot tub."

Claire usually let Mitch do most of the talking, but she took his hand in hers and said, "We just received a call from the hotel where they were staying in Las Vegas. It was an unfortunate accident. A man playing a guitar was serenading them. He tripped over the extension cord to some kind of lighting, and well... they..."

Mitch stood a little taller and cleared his throat. "They died instantly. Together. They were apparently holding hands"—a sad laugh escaped—"and drinking piña coladas."

Hank had certainly felt pain before, but not the lack of pain. Not the lack of any emotion whatsoever. He wanted to cry, but he couldn't. He wanted to talk, but there were no words. All he could do was stand there and try to logically process the entire thing, but even logic wasn't available. It was as if every gear in his body had stopped turning.

Their attention shifted to the sudden clicking sound behind them. The mother of the birthday boy marched toward them, one hand on her hip, the other pointing a finger sternly at their faces.

"What do you think you're doing?" she demanded. She stopped, then stomped one high-heeled boot onto the concrete. "You can't just walk out! I paid a lot of money for you! Do you know what is happening out there? They've gone crazy! They're running around, jumping off things, swinging from things, throwing things. Get in there and do your job!"

Hank tended not to err on the side of anger. That was Mack's trait, and she was good at it. At the moment, he wasn't really *feeling* anger because he couldn't feel anything, but in his mind, he took a swing at this woman and knocked her backward. Before he could play out his thoughts, though, he found himself lunging toward Mack, who'd reacted exactly the way everyone expected her to. It took four of them to keep her at bay.

"Who do you think you are?" Mack yelled, but regained her control when Mitch told her to get it together. Adjusting his red suspenders, Mitch stepped in front of them and addressed the woman.

"Ma'am, we've had a family emergency."

The woman's fierce scowl lifted, but only slightly. She glanced over each of them and then turned her disproving expression back to Mitch. "Then I want a full refund." She whirled and headed for the front door.

"Ma'am," Mitch said. "Wait."

"What?"

"We'll do it."

"Mitch!" Mack protested. "What are you talking about?"

Mitch looked at the woman. "Just give us a moment, okay?"

"Fine, but make it quick." Her eyes grew wide. "I think I smell something burning!" She hurried off as Mack pushed her way in front of Mitch.

"Why would you say that?"

With tears still lingering in his eyes, Mitch put a gentle hand on Mack's shoulder and gazed at each of them. "You know their motto. The show must go on."

A quiet determination set in. Everyone knew this was what their parents would have wanted. They'd always taught their children to persevere and not give up. They'd taught them a deep work ethic and showed them what it meant to work hard even when it wasn't convenient or easy. The Hazards had watched their parents work no matter what.

Mack's jaw jutted forward. "Let's do it for Mom and Dad."

They all nodded. Cassie pointed out that they needed to reapply their clown makeup and went to the van to get it.

Mitch put his arm around Hank. "You okay?"

"No."

"Can you do this?"

"Yes." Hank turned to Hayden. "Holler at Cassie. Tell her to get the flamethrowers ready. Apparently this crowd likes fire."

Chapter 2

Six years later

T he normal, slow burn of a cigarette was accelerated by the fact that Bob Worton wasn't supposed to be smoking in his office, the bathroom, anywhere on the fifth floor, or within fifty yards of the building. He also wasn't supposed to smoke in his home or the car. That meant that Bob had learned to press his lips firmly onto the cigarette, suck five times like a kid slurping up a glass of soda, and have nicotine in his system in less than forty seconds. The smell lingered, but he'd happened upon a wonderful thing called a Yankee Candle in the department secretary's office, specifically the apple spice scent. Making his office smell like a bakery did wonders for hiding the evidence. He explained away the white haze that lingered a foot from the mildewed ceiling of his office by mentioning the ancient air duct system.

The truth of the matter was that he'd been caught smoking at least eleven times and had yet to be fired for it. And he knew why. Nobody wanted this job, and nobody wanted to find somebody who wanted this job. So everyone willingly looked past the fact that Bob smoked in his faraway office, previously a janitor's closet

five minutes from the coffee machine. He'd tried to quit once, and
on a Tuesday at four, in the men's bathroom, his boss had politely
asked him to start back up.

Flicking an inch of ash off his cigarette, he scrubbed the end
into an ashtray, which he then slid into his desk drawer. Flipping
through the file folder on his desk, he paused a moment on the
form labeled *Job History.* He regarded the young man across from
him, who sat with both feet on the floor, knees pressed together,
hands flat on his knees. His hair was cut short and parted to the
far left, swept to the side like he'd just arrived from 1957. Then
there was the suit. Bob couldn't remember the last time he'd seen
anybody around here in a suit.

The guy who'd applied for the job earlier that morning wore
a stained polo, slacks that looked like they'd been wadded up in a
drawer for months, and hair that hadn't seen the useful side of a
brush in what appeared to be days. The man before that had just
been fired by the FAA. He wore a tie, but it didn't make the chip
on his shoulder look smaller.

The ex-FAA guy was the most promising applicant until this
young man arrived. He'd phoned Bob personally, asking if the
position was already filled. Even though Bob told him it was, Mr.
Hazard had asked if he could arrange a meeting in the afternoon.

Mr. Hazard now cleared his throat twice. Turning on the fan
by his desk to get the air rotating, Bob stood and opened the door
to let the smoke out. "Mr. Hazard—"

"Please, Hank, sir."

Sir. Bob kind of wished he'd held off on the cigarette and made a better impression. Apparently that wasn't needed, though, because this kid seemed intent on good impressions no matter what kind of impression Bob made. Falling into a chair crankier than Bob off nicotine, he pulled out his center drawer and used his eye drops.

Hank sat quietly. Attentively.

Blinking until his eyeballs were sufficiently coated, Bob leaned forward and engaged him. "Hank. I'm a little confused about your, uh, job history. Can you explain to me exactly what line of work you've been in?"

"I worked in my family business for a long time, since I was young. We owned a clown company. I was a clown. A mime, actually."

If it hadn't been typed out in front of him, Bob would've thought they were speaking in metaphorical terms or that Hank was about to tell a wildly inappropriate joke. But there it sat, on his résumé. What could he say? People made their living however they must. He was a prime example. Two heart attacks and one hundred forty extra pounds later, Bob wondered if he would have been happier had he been a clown. He liked clowns.

"And then it says here you were a mechanic."

"Yes sir. I like cars."

"I see. But then it says you... I'm sorry, I'm not sure I quite understand this."

"I worked with the Las Vegas police department on a task force called VIPER. We brought down a huge drug ring."

"So you're a police officer?"

"No, my sister is. She was working undercover, trying to break up an auto theft ring. They needed people to work in a fake body shop they set up to catch people coming in to sell illegal parts."

"I thought it was drugs."

"Turned out it was. They were using minivans to transport them."

"Minivans."

"Yes."

"And now you're here. Why are you here?"

"I flew on an airplane for the first time on my way out to Las Vegas to do the undercover job. I loved it. Every moment of it."

"Well, that's a new one."

"What, sir?"

"You just don't hear that anymore. People liking to fly. People hate to fly. But they hate driving thirty hours across the country more, so they fly."

The young man sat still, as if he didn't have the ability to fidget. "How could anyone hate to fly? When we lifted off the ground and my stomach quivered, I looked out the window and I couldn't believe how fast we were going, you know? How small the world became suddenly. Giant trees looked like little..." Hank's words trailed off as his cheeks flushed. "I'm sorry. What I'm trying to say is that I think I would be good at this job. The newspaper said something about flying. I like to fly. I thought it might be a great fit."

Bob tried to lean back in his chair, but it stuck and flung him a little to the left. He wanted another cigarette, but frankly, this kid looked like he'd never seen a vice he needed. The kid probably didn't even use a pacifier when he was a baby. Bob's mother constantly complained he'd never become a self-soother. He could self-soothe. He just needed a little help.

There was something strange about Hank. He was very calm, self-confident but not cocky, quiet when he needed to be, pointed with his words, a certain innocence in his eyes.

Throwing a couple of gum balls in his mouth, Bob said, "Okay, Hank, look. I'll be honest with you. Things aren't going well at the airline. It's my unfortunate luck to get the job of finding out why. Before 9/11, we looked at whether it should be peanuts or pretzels, whether we should give them the entire can of soda or pour it into a glass with ice. We wondered if our rival's decision to serve half-and-half was going to outdo our packet creamers, so we added flavored packet creamers." Bob let out a long sigh. What he wouldn't give for the old days, when offering inflight music and earphones caused their sales to skyrocket in the fourth quarter.

"Well, you can't go wrong with amaretto." Hank smiled.

"True enough. But these days, Hank, nobody likes to fly. And they really don't like to fly on our carrier. For a year now, we've been planting our people on competitors' airlines, trying to figure out what they do better and why. We've sent them onboard with measuring tapes to see how far the seats reclined. We once hired a chef to figure out how they were getting their meat to taste so fresh. We've investigated the reason the flight crew switched from

polyester blouses to knit polos. They put olives back on their sal-
ads, so we started offering crouton packs. You name it, we've done
it." Bob spit out his gum. The sugar was gone. "And at the end of
the day, Hank, we're still behind. 9/11 will be a shadow over all
of us forever, which makes croutons seem inconsequential, if you
know what I mean."

Bob rose from his chair and put a knee into its side, causing
it to pop and shift straight again. "I've been thinking a lot about
this. We've sent guys to scout out what's going on elsewhere, and
we've gained a lot of knowledge. Last week we found out our
main competitor's flight attendants wear three-inch heels. Who
knew that could be important, right?" Bob took a toothpick out
of his pocket and bit down on it. "The thing is, you can try to
look at other people all day long, but at the end of the day, you
can only look at yourself."

"That sounds like good business advice."

"I learned it in marriage counseling right before my divorce."
The toothpick split, and Bob tossed it in the trash.

"Sorry about your divorce. That must have been painful."

Bob's finger plunged deep inside his ear and dug for earwax
just like his ex-wife hated, then slowly emerged, wax-free. "What?"

"I'm sorry that happened to you. I'm very blessed to have had
parents who stayed married for a long time. They actually died at
the exact same time. That was a few years ago."

"Lucky them. I mean, that they were married." And dead.
The finger found an itch at his hairline. "Was it a…uh…clown
accident?"

"No. Electrical shock in a hot tub."

"Right…okay…" Bob grabbed his baggie of sunflower seeds off his desk. "Anyway, we've always hired from inside the company for jobs like this. People willingly applied to see what was going on outside our little world. But now we're having a hard time. It's just that people don't want to rat out their own people. We've been through a lot, and nobody wants to go pointing fingers. We need somebody who will be objective. You don't have an emotional tie to this company, so you can give me a clear assessment of what's going on inside our aircrafts."

"A spy."

Bob thought a moment, but decided it was probably the best word. He'd come up with a job title that sounded politically correct and integrated the words *marketing* and *assessor*, but at the end of the day, the guy was going to be James Bonding it at forty thousand feet.

"I watch the employees, see if they're doing their job, right?"

Bob tried to smile through the wad of seeds in his cheek. "It's a little more than that."

"Well, what more can I do on an airplane except sit there?"

Bob sat down again, sizing up the guy who claimed he went undercover in Las Vegas. Clearly, he wasn't seeing the big picture.

"Hank, it's easy to be a good employee when passengers sit there and aren't a bother. It's more difficult when people get demanding. You're going to need to be a very high-maintenance passenger. The things you have to go through just to board an airplane these days are causing more people to be in bad moods.

You're going to be the guy who is never satisfied. Blankets. Pillows. More pillows. Hotter food. Colder drink. You get the picture."

The young man appeared to be thinking this over.

Bob leaned forward. "Hank, you seem like a very fine young man. The moment you walked in, I could tell you were taking this interview seriously. You said it yourself, you love to fly. You do some fine work here, and who knows what kind of doors might open for you in the airline business."

This perked him up. "It would give me an idea what this industry is really like."

Bob smiled and nodded, though it was all he could do not to burst this kid's idealistic bubble. This industry would never, ever be the same again. He'd been doing it for twenty-five years. 9/11 changed everything.

"Hank, you've got a very important job. We've got to find a way out of this slump we're in. Thousands of jobs are at stake." He finally gave up, spit the seeds into the trash, and lit a cigarette, trying to fan the smoke away. "If we don't figure out how to beat the competition, we're going to have to file bankruptcy. We've got analysts combing over everything from gas consumption to ticket prices. My job is to find out about job performance on the aircraft, which has now become your job. I want you to take scrupulous notes about everything you hear and see. You're going to watch everyone. Listen to the flight attendants talk. How is the captain's tone when he's addressing the passengers from the cockpit? I want every detail covered, Hank."

"I'm hired?"

"You're hired."

"I thought someone else had the job."

"You're a better fit and, quite frankly, seem to be a better human being. That's got to qualify you in some regard. You seem to be a hard worker, Hank, and that's what I need. You've done some time working undercover, so in my book, that qualifies you for this job."

Hank popped to his feet and stuck out a hand. "Thank you, sir. Thank you very much."

Bob shook it, then handed him his papers and ticket. "You leave tomorrow for Amsterdam."

"I'm going to another country?"

"That's right. Transatlantic Flight 1945 to Amsterdam. You'll have a one-night layover, then will come back. You do have a passport, don't you? That was in the job description."

"I do. Seven years ago we planned to go to an international clown training event in Spain. It didn't work out, but I still have the passport."

Sighing, Bob put out his cigarette. "Make this count, Hank. You do a good job and it's nothing but up from here." Unless they filed bankruptcy, of course.

"Mr. Worton, God bless you. I mean that."

"Son, God doesn't bless people who need a pack a day just to get out of bed in the morning."

"You're only trying to fill a void in your life. God loves you, sir. Don't ever doubt that."

Doubt it? He had never even heard anyone say it to him. He glanced at the cigarette, still smoldering in the ashtray that lay in the open drawer to his left. In the smoky room of life, Hank Hazard seemed to be the lavender air freshener he'd happened upon yesterday in the break room.

Bob Worton smiled mildly, but inside, he really, really hoped what Hank said was true.

Chapter 3

I 'm sorry, sir. Your flight has been cancelled."

Sweat poured down Jake Van Der Mark's face, noticeable even to the expressionless woman on the other side of the counter. He couldn't stop glancing over his shoulder. A long line of people, weighed down by luggage and unfortunate luck, waited behind him.

Jake wiped his face with the sleeve of his shirt, and the woman's face expressed her disgust.

"It's hot in here," he mumbled. "Look, I need to get on a flight to Amsterdam. I have to."

She didn't seem inspired by his desperate plea. "Sir, we're doing all we can to get our passengers onto another plane, but we don't have anything leaving tonight, and we're very booked tomorrow."

"Then put me on another airline." He didn't raise his voice. He knew irritating the desk agent wasn't going to win him any points. "It's just very important that I get to Amsterdam. Quickly."

"Sir, we have a flight leaving tomorrow evening at—"

"No! I mean…no, um, ma'am, I'm sorry, it's just a family emergency. I need to get there."

Her fingers clacked against the keyboard. "I can offer you a voucher for—"

"I must leave in the morning. No later."

Sweat dropped from his chin onto the counter, and the woman, who kept antibacterial gel next to her computer, couldn't keep her nostrils from flaring with disapproval. Jake had always prided himself on his ability to take advantage of situations, which was the reason he was in this predicament in the first place. And there was no reason not to take advantage of a woman and her germ gel.

Gasping loudly, he sneezed and didn't bother to cover his mouth. Wiping his nose with the back of his hand, he tried a little wheeze and said, "Sorry. I've been sick with the crud. It's been brutal. Stomach cramps, a bronchial cough that sounds like death, and then there's the chills and the fever and the diarrh—"

"I can get you on a flight going out at 6:00 a.m. tomorrow."

"I'll take it."

She squirted her hands with gel, typed something in the computer, and printed out a piece of paper.

"Thank you."

"You have no checked baggage?"

"No."

This raised a curious eyebrow, which lowered again when Jake gave indication that another sneeze might be coming. He stopped, but she still felt compelled to squirt her hands. "All right, then. You're set. Next, please." She grabbed a can of Lysol from under the counter and sprayed the germ gel bottle.

That was a rare kind of mistrust of the natural, biological order of the universe.

Not that he could speak to mistrusting things at the moment.

Clutching his black leather duffel bag, Jake hurried away from the counter. Like an uncontrollable twitch, he looked over his shoulder, quickly scanning the crowd for anybody who looked like they could kill him. The only person glaring at him was a little old lady who seemed happy to glare at anyone. He stood for a moment, watching the people nearby. Everyone moved past with no concern for him, so he ducked into a long line of phone booths. He retrieved his credit card and paused, flipping it through his fingers. Was it wise to use a credit card? Could they trace it?

Maybe. But only to this airport. And if they were intent on killing him, they probably knew that information already.

But they could get her phone number. Jake closed his eyes, trying to think it through. That could be easily attained too. If they wanted it, they probably already had it. Taking a deep breath, he glanced outside the booth and then unfolded the small piece of paper he kept in his jacket pocket. He swiped the card, punched in the international code, and dialed.

It took several long moments for him to be connected, during which he wondered if he was the biggest idiot the world had ever seen. Until seven days ago, Jake Van Der Mark hardly cared about money. He was barely making a living, but making it nevertheless, flipping burgers during the day while at night he played his electric guitar in a band he hoped would hit it big sooner rather than later. Three years and four "almost" contracts since they started, they still played weddings and bars. But it was fun. His entire life he'd wanted to be in a band. He was living his dream, just not in a profitable sort of way. They'd had several close breaks, and their lead singer, Toby, had a passion for their music and vision. That alone kept him flipping burgers for the sake of the greater cause.

The phone finally began to ring. Four rings. Five rings. Six—

"Met Idya Van Der Mark."

"Um…hi…Idya?"

"Met wie spreek ik?"

"Idya…it's Jake."

"Jaap. Het is midden in de nacht! Waarom bel je midden in de nacht?"

"Idya, please, you must speak English. Remember, I can't understand a word of—"

"It's a shame, Jaap. A real shame your parents never instilled your Dutch heritage. I don't understand it. Not a bit of it."

"Yes, um, well…listen, there's been a delay. The flight I was scheduled to arrive on was cancelled, and I—"

"Call me *Oma.*"

"Oma?"

"Our blood is in each other's veins. I believe the word is 'granny' in English, Jaap."

"It's Jake."

"It's Jaap. It's on your birth certificate."

"I've never gone by Jaap."

"Another real shame. And it's a real shame that your parents couldn't find the time or money to bring you over to see me. Do you know that? They sent pictures once or twice a year. We should've met long before now." They'd never talked over the phone because his parents told him when he was young that she couldn't speak English. Turned out she could, very well, just not very happily.

Jake tried a deep breath. This wasn't a family reunion, at least by normal standards. And he didn't really want to talk about his parents.

"Please. Just listen to me. I'm flying out in the morning. I leave at—" He almost gave her the rest of the flight information, but then decided against it. Just in case somebody was listening. Man, he was getting paranoid. But he had every reason to be, and to let his guard down now would be foolish. "I'll call you when I arrive in Amsterdam. How is that?"

"Jaap, you don't sound good. You sound flustered. Not good at all."

Jake's hand tore through his hair. "Look, this is no small thing." He lowered his voice. He hoped she could hear him over all the airport noise. "Do you know how much I'm risking here for you?"

Her voice turned coy. "For me, Jaap? Ahh, don't kid yourself. You're in this for you, too, are you not?"

That was the *only* reason he was in this. How could he get this woman to understand how dangerous this was? Diamond couriers are very specialized. Only a couple security companies in the entire world will do it. Most security companies wouldn't dream of going into the gemstone courier business. The cost of insurance on the stones is almost equal to their wholesale value. The thieves in the business are very good at what they do and very seldom caught. Diamond couriers have a very high mortality rate.

And this was just what he got off the Internet.

Somehow he managed to find himself at the receiving end of an offer he couldn't refuse. His eighty-three-year-old grandmother, whom he'd never met or even spoken to until seven days ago when she called, had five diamonds stolen...by a boyfriend. They were not insured and she had, unbelievably, kept them safe for years underneath her mattress in her home.

The boyfriend managed to escape to America, but he underestimated what Idya Van Der Mark was capable of. Within three weeks he was caught and the diamonds recovered.

Unfortunately for her, no government agency in the United States or in the Netherlands would take responsibility for the diamonds' transport back. And according to Idya, the security companies wouldn't touch it for any amount of money. Too risky, they said. No kidding, Jake thought, as he stared down at his left hand, which shook like he'd just downed eight cups of espresso.

That's when she'd called him. She promised him two of the five diamonds as an inheritance if he would return them safely to her. It was a deal he was too stupid to pass up apparently, because at the moment, the diamonds were duct-taped to his belly in a tiny black satchel.

"How do you know that I won't just take the diamonds and run?" Jake asked her over the phone the first time they spoke.

In her taut Queen's English, she said, "Jaap, you are a Van Der Mark. Van Der Marks have nobility and character. This has gone back through many centuries."

Jake couldn't say too much in return. He hadn't really thought about his roots. He knew he'd come to America as a baby, brought over by his parents, who were both Dutch. His mother held on to more of the Dutch accent than his father, but by the time he was old enough to care, he was an American and never thought twice about his heritage. Though his grandmother was seldom mentioned, from what he gathered, his mother had a falling out with Idya, her mother-in-law, which caused enough of a strain that they moved an entire ocean away. They sent cards on all the right holidays, but other than that, she was a vague notion far away across the sea.

When his father died, Jake wondered where he came from. When his mother passed away, leaving him with no siblings, cousins, or family to speak of, he felt lonelier than he ever had. But sometimes family comes in other forms, and as far as he was concerned, the Rubber Band had become his family. He spent most of his time with them anyway.

"I have to go now. I don't know who might be watching."

"Nobody is watching you, Jaap. You told me yourself that the arrest didn't even make the newspaper."

"It made the newspaper. One small blurb, but it made it." Jake hoped that nobody had read it or cared. It was buried deep on page ten with, of all things, the obituaries.

"Don't let this get the best of you," she said. "You're going to be on an airplane in a few hours. What can happen on an airplane?"

It wasn't the airplane he was concerned with. It was the few hours *before* boarding that was about to give him hives.

"I'll call you when I land. Good-bye." Jake hung up the phone and wiped his palms on his jeans. Closing his eyes, he wondered if he was the stupidest man alive.

Maybe.

But if he got his inheritance as planned, he would also be pretty stinkin' rich. Rich enough to quit his day job and buy all new equipment for the band. They were in desperate need of new amps and a drum kit. The thought of new amps was enough to celebrate with a Cinnabon.

A soft purple hue bled into the deep blackness of what had an hour earlier been the dead of night. Perry Watts tiptoed his way across the dewy grass onto the long concrete driveway on the west side of the house. Trash cans lined the curb of the neighborhood, and in the distance, trash-truck sounds reminded him that even this early he could be spotted, no matter how black his turtleneck was.

In the backyard, hunched behind a gigantic flowerpot, Perry

examined the house and found a single light on. Probably a bedroom light. He could only guess when the man rose in the morning, but judging from his work habits, Perry assumed it was early.

Looked like he was right.

He waited a few minutes, and soon the kitchen light came on. On the curtains a shadow moved back and forth. He thought he could smell burnt toast.

Perry turned, his back sliding down the flowerpot. He held his hands against either side of his head. "What are you doing?" he whispered. "This is crazy."

Brief moments of anxiety caused him to second-guess his plan, especially since the first plan failed so miserably. It shouldn't have failed, but it did, and now he'd formulated Plan B, which included hiding in the dark at his boss's house.

Plan A started simply. While job hunting, he'd run across a short article referencing a previous story about five diamonds trying to make their way home to the Netherlands. A young man named Van Der Mark now had the diamonds and would presumably return them to his relative overseas. At least that's what Perry gleaned from the blurb.

He decided to steal the diamonds. He wasn't certain if the guy was stupid enough to have them on him, but he figured either way, he could get the guy to turn them over. He spent a couple of hours planning it out, then hunted down Van Der Mark. He broke into his apartment with ease only to find the guy gone and, according to an itinerary on his table, on his way to the Netherlands.

Plan A got a little complicated when the guy's flight was delayed and Perry had to use illegal pass codes he'd acquired over the years to break into the computer and find out when he was actually leaving. The new flight left this morning. He could've just bought a ticket, but he didn't want his name exposed.

Which brought him to Plan B, crouching in the shadows of his boss's house. Former boss, he reminded himself, which was what made Plan B workable and likable.

He was getting cold. He peered up at the kitchen window again. The shadow was still visible.

It did feel strange that at this moment, he wasn't the least bit apprehensive. He was prone to nervousness, which his boss cited several days ago when he was fired. Something about not being able to handle the pressures of the job, among other things.

Yet here he was now, not a nervous bone in his body.

He stood, adjusted his turtleneck, and stepped up to the back door, which was Windexed to the point of near invisibility.

He knocked.

He heard shuffling. A pause.

He knocked again.

"Who is it?"

"Me," Perry replied. "Perry."

The back door swung open, and Perry smiled, not because he was glad to see Miles, but because his boss's hair stuck straight up on one side and his eyes were puffy and bloodshot.

"Perry?" Miles said, holding tight to a piece of toast and wearing a shocked look. "What are you doing at my house this time of night?"

"It's technically morning."

"It's still dark outside! What are you doing here?"

"I wanted to talk to you."

Miles tightened his fancy robe. "Now? Why? What else is there to talk about?"

"Please. Just a little of your time."

"No. You need to leave. Now."

"That's it? You're just going to kick me out to the streets?"

"What about that job with the airline? I gave you a good lead on that."

"I got hired."

"Fine. Great."

"Then I got fired. On the same day."

Miles leaned forward with a disgusted expression. "Then maybe, *Perry,* the problem isn't me, like you keep claiming. *Maybe* the problem is *you.* Maybe it's because, like I stated for three consecutive job reviews, you do everything haphazardly, with no reason or sense behind your decision making. You couldn't carry out a plan if your life depended on it."

"Maybe," Perry said and, with one swift motion, pushed Miles backward into his own home. "Maybe not." He stepped into the kitchen and shut the back door. Miles stumbled into the cabinet behind him, then held up his hands before Perry even reached into his bag to pretend he had a gun.

"What do you want?" Miles cowered on the floor, his hands raised straight above him and his eyes wide.

"Sit down," Perry said and pointed to a kitchen chair.

Miles scrambled over to it. "Look, listen, I can help you. Maybe we could—"

"Shut up." Perry took the phone off the counter. "You're going to leave a message for Maggie that you're sick and you won't be in today and possibly tomorrow."

"Are you going to kill me?"

Perry wanted to laugh. This guy was as pathetic as he'd always suspected. "Maybe. If you don't cooperate."

Miles nodded eagerly. Perry removed a roll of duct tape from the black satchel that hung over his chest and beside his hip. He instructed Miles not to move.

"Now," he said, thumping his hand against the roll of tape, "it's time for Perry to be the boss."

Chapter 4

Every half hour, Danny jolted awake and reached through the dark toward the red glowing numbers on his digital clock. Sleep was something he wasn't taking for granted anymore, but in the last four days it had only come in short spurts. But they were deep short spurts, and he kept wondering if he might oversleep.

Peering through blurry eyes, he focused on the time.

His alarm wasn't set to go off for another fifteen minutes, but he rose anyway and opened the shades, revealing an inky black sky and Mr. Hellman rolling his trash to the curb. Switching on his bedroom light felt like the sun had just parked itself in his reading chair. He closed his eyes and shuffled toward the bathroom where he hoped a splash of cold water would help him make it to his coffeepot.

The mundaneness of his morning ritual soothed him. Since Saturday, all he'd wanted was for life to return to normal. It hadn't, but this was a step in the right direction.

As the cold water hit his face, he remembered the phone ringing at 1:30 a.m. In the fogginess of sleep, and perhaps some desperate hopefulness, he thought it was Maya calling. "Baby," he answered, smiling through his exhaustion. "It's okay. I forgive you. I love you."

"Baby" turned out to be Martha Crowder—surly and not fond of nicknames—from the scheduling office, wondering why he'd forgotten to make his preflight check-in call yesterday.

It was the first time in fifteen years of flying he'd forgotten to make that phone call.

He downed two cups of coffee, managed a piece of toast although he wasn't really a breakfast person, then put on his uniform. He studied his reflection in the long mirror on his closet door. Three stripes, not four. His wings didn't have the star and wreath on top. Not yet, anyway. He'd make captain someday. Every time he put the uniform on, it meant something to him. He held on to that thought. Even if it didn't mean anything to anybody else, it should always mean something to him.

Shoving the shiny black hat under his arm, he grabbed his flight bag and headed to the airport.

A small, internal tingle of excitement surprised him as he got off the shuttle that took him from the parking lot to the doors of the pilots' lounge. He stepped away from the building for a moment. The western runways spread widely across the horizon. A 747, dipping low and elegantly like a dragon, roared by the control tower. It was tradition for a captain to pass low at home port before the final landing.

The ground rumbled. The buildings trembled. Then, like an atmospheric sink hole, the sound was swallowed up and gone.

Danny watched the runway. A plane turned into position, firing its engines, hot and orange against the morning haze. It built speed, then lifted effortlessly into the air, like it balanced on the tip of the finger of God, raised to the heavens in glory.

Another roaring wave enveloped him. Danny smiled.

Yeah, this was his element. *At five hundred miles an hour, you can leave a lot behind.*

After punching in his code, he swiped his card and headed down into the stairwell, emerging into a room barely alive with activity. He put his jacket and heavily decorated flight bag down among the hundreds of others. He'd begun collecting stickers for his bag when he first started flying—any that seemed like they'd make a great tattoo. So far five were inked onto his body: three on his shoulder and two between the shoulder blades. He'd probably add another one soon. Thankfully, he'd had the sense to stick to symbols that had nothing to do with interpersonal relationships. He had Billy Bob and Angelina to thank for that inspiration.

He kept that thought—that he wouldn't have to scrape a tattoo off his arm—in mind as he gathered the information he needed for his flight, logged on to the computer for any alerts, then checked his mailbox, where he found a memo announcing that the crew of Flight 1945 would meet in conference room number eight.

Sometimes there was a meeting beforehand, sometimes not. Usually not, so he wondered why it was needed as he paused in front of the big screen television for some early morning sports highlights. He liked this television. All the Atlantica pilots had pitched in for it. They'd bought the television, fifteen recliners, and two large leather couches. *Sometimes you have to make your own perks.*

He headed to the conference room.

Opening the door, he discovered another first officer standing in the corner, looking down at something. The man whirled around, his eyes wide. Then he slumped in relief, glanced at the doorway, and walked toward Danny. They shook hands. "James Lawrence."

"Danny McSweeney."

With a flick of his other wrist, James shut the door and asked, "Do you know who the captain is?"

"Uh…" Danny had glanced at the crew roster on the memo but couldn't remember the captain's name now.

"C. J. Brewster-Yarley!" James said in a whisper.

Danny nodded, trying to recall why that name sounded familiar. When he flew the regional legs, he knew all the other pilots and flight attendants, but flying international changed all that. Since he was based at the largest hub and busiest airport in the world, with over six thousand international flights leaving every month, it was rare he flew with the same pilots. And if he did, it was long enough ago that he couldn't remember their names. He kind of liked it, though, because each trip meant he'd get to meet a few new interesting people.

"She's the one!"

"The one?" Danny asked.

James looked like an explanation might be too exhausting, but he went ahead with it anyway. "Remember? She crash-landed in the Bermuda Triangle nine years ago. It's the last recorded water landing of a jetliner."

He did remember. Who could forget? Everyone survived.

According to accounts, it happened exactly like it was supposed to. Thanks to the calm voice of the captain directing them, passengers evacuated in a civil manner into lifeboats. It wasn't until after they were rescued that any of the passengers realized they had been sitting right in the middle of the Bermuda Triangle.

It became a sensational story. Every major news magazine covered it, thanks to footage from a helicopter that was giving tours over the islands. Danny remembered that the captain refused to be interviewed, so all accounts were from the rest of the crew or passengers. He'd wondered why she hadn't wanted to tell her story.

"She's a legend," James continued, "and not just because of that crash-landing either."

"What do you mean?"

"I've just heard a few stories, that's all."

"What kinds of stories?"

"You don't know about the *blog*?"

"What blog?"

"The blog started about her. If you fly with her, you add a comment about your experience. It's all anonymous. You should read some of them. They are so hilarious."

The door swung open, and nine flight attendants streamed in, escorted by a woman whose pursed, fire red, and overly lined

lips led the way. Before they even got into the room, the senior
flight attendant made an impression that explained the lips.

"I'm GiGi. Two capital G's." She threw up her arms. "We got
a memo. Why are we having a meeting?"

"It's at the discretion of the captain," Danny said.

"Yes, I'm aware of that. But nothing in the memo indicated
why, and we've got plenty of things we need to be doing other
than waiting around for a meeting."

James leaned in and made a cat noise, but GiGi had cat hear-
ing. Every hair on her body stood on end. Even her eyebrows
looked offended.

"Is there a *problem*?"

"No ma'am," Danny tried.

"Don't you dare call me 'ma'am,'" she snarled. "Why in the
world do you think I went to the trouble of introducing myself as
GiGi?"

"This is going to be a long flight," James whispered.

"Would you shut up?" Danny whispered back, but it was too
late. GiGi circled the table like an animal stalking prey, smacking
her gum loudly. Danny got the feeling gum wasn't the only thing
going to be smacked.

"I'm fifty-five years old," she declared loudly, "and if you think
I'm going to take a first officer's lip for one second, then you'll want
to pack a parachute, because halfway across the Atlantic, you're
going to want to jump out."

Danny glanced at the other flight attendants, two men and

six women. Two looked amused. The other four, their backs against the whiteboard, stood at attention.

James cackled. "Whoa, there, little lady. Let me get a lasso and see if we can't wrestle your hormones to the ground."

Instinctively, Danny stepped away from James as GiGi's aqua-painted eyes widened in preparation for the death rays about to shoot out. But James had moved to the whiteboard. Popping off the lid of a dry-erase marker, he asked, "Do you know what flight number this is?"

"Nineteen forty-five," one of the flight attendants said.

"You are a weird, little man," GiGi growled from the other side of the room.

"Don't you see the connection?" James scribbled the flight number on the board. "This may not mean anything to you all," he said, addressing the crowd, "but I bet it means something to our captain. Flight 19: five Avenger torpedo bombers disappeared off the coast of Florida, inside the Bermuda Triangle, never to be found again. One of two search planes disappeared as well." James paused dramatically. "In 1945. Get it? This is Flight 1945."

"*What* does that have to do with us?" GiGi asked.

"Captain Brewster-Yarley crash-landed *inside* the Bermuda Triangle and lived to tell about it. Except that's the thing—she won't tell about it. And according to the blog, you should never, ever ask her about it."

Then, as if she had materialized right into the room, everyone noticed the captain.

Danny cleared his throat. GiGi turned, regarded the captain with little more than a glance, then stepped aside, her eyes still glued to James. But James's full attention was on Captain Brewster-Yarley.

Her coarse, gray blond hair was cut like Princess Diana's, poofed and frizzed as if it had never seen a hair product. She didn't make eye contact with anybody as she opened a folder she held, scanning it with tired-looking eyes. Her thin, shapeless lips were colorless to the point that her teeth were the only thing setting them apart from her face. A hint of color on her cheeks might've helped her look like she didn't belong in a coffin, but the only color on her was a shiny, gold tie tack.

"Weather could be a problem," she mumbled. "Might hit some turbulence. Could be a storm coming out of Canada, but this comes from people who claimed it would rain this morning." She closed her folder. Still without making eye contact with anyone, and in a voice Danny strained to hear, she asked, "Anyone have any questions?"

Danny wasn't certain James would live long enough to ask any questions if GiGi had anything to do with it.

If James's expression was a one-hundred-watt, long-lasting bulb, and if GiGi's was mood lighting, the captain would be a night-light. Yet even the tiniest movement on her face could be seen by everyone in the room. She looked at the whiteboard.

"I was born in 1945."

Danny wasn't sure if he should nod as if that was an interesting and ironic bit of trivia, or whether in honor of GiGi, he should pretend that birth year was a moot point. He stood motionless, hoping everybody would focus on James, who looked like he wanted more information. He was nodding eagerly, grinning like it was his birthday or like he might be high on dry-erase fumes.

The captain glanced back down at her folder. "We'll have an impaired woman onboard. We'll also have a Dutch prisoner being escorted back to the Netherlands by the FBI." She gave the whiteboard a long glance, then her gaze circled the room and she left.

Danny let out the breath he was holding. James flung his arms wide. "Whoa! *Whoa!*"

GiGi marched across the room, her finger pointed at James. "I don't want any lip from you. Do you understand me? I eat first officers for breakfast."

James smirked. "Obviously you're not missing any meals."

A hot, stinging sensation shot through Danny's chest. He'd never thought one could die from cringing, but for a brief moment he thought he might drop dead.

James winked. "See you onboard, sweetheart."

GiGi spun on her heel, knocked her way through her fellow flight attendants, and marched out of the room. The others, glancing back at James and Danny, followed her out.

Danny turned to James. "What are you doing?"

"They're not called Slam and Clicks for nothing."

"Excuse me?"

"Can you believe it? Brewster-Yarley was born in 1945! That's unbelievable!"

What was unbelievable was that she hadn't been bought out by the airline to take early retirement. She was old by airline standards, especially these days. They walked out of the conference room, and James headed toward the stairwell. Danny hung back, hoping James would just keep walking and talking, but after a moment he turned and waited for him.

"She was born in 1945. This is Flight 1945. It has the number 19 in it. Flight 19 was the most famous Bermuda Triangle disappearance recorded."

"Fascinating. Listen, why are you harassing the flight attendants? We're going to be spending hours and hours with them. The last thing we want is for them to give us a hard time."

"Ignore the Slam and Clicks, Danny. They think they're all that, and they'll raise Cain, you know? Then we land and what do they want? Dinner. On us. Every one of them thinks they're entitled to dinner on the pilots. I've actually seen them eat lobster dinners, wipe their mouths, and then get up and leave."

Danny sighed. It had happened a time or two with him, but not always. Most of the time the group didn't stick together anyway. He was about to question exactly what "Slam and Click" meant when James started talking again.

"I won't lie. This is making me nervous. I mean, I'm not a numbers guy, you know? I watch *Lost* with the rest of the country, and I do find the Hurley's number thing fascinating, but I don't really believe in meaning behind a sequence of numbers."

"Unless of course you're flying, where latitudes and longitudes come in handy."

"Funny." James stopped and turned to him. "It could happen to *us*."

"Murdered by flight attendants? Yeah, I think that's a real possibility."

"*No*. The curse."

"What curse?"

A look of disbelief crossed James's face. "Haven't you heard the stories? About the captain?"

What was this? The grassy knoll of the skies?

James groaned and stared at the ceiling for a moment. Danny moved past him and finished the stairs, emerging into the terminal area where he hoped to disappear into the sea of people. But it was early, and there was no sea. Just a sidewalk puddle's worth of people, hardly enough to get lost in.

"You have got to read the blog. It's legendary! Ever since that Bermuda Triangle landing, at least once a year, something really bizarre happens to her. She's had an eagle hit her windshield. Her landing gear has gotten stuck four times. Remember that London flight where all those people had that strange flulike thing and had to be quarantined on the Tarmac because they thought it was the bird flu? That was her!"

"If we get lucky, maybe Sasquatch will be onboard."

"So you think the Triangle is a crock?"

"I've flown through it hundreds of times. It's a body of water. Just as many accidents happen everywhere else."

"In 1991, a salvage ship found five Avengers in six hundred feet of water off the coast of Florida. But when they went down there, it *wasn't* Flight 19."

Danny had met his fair share of people. He'd learned to get along with a host of different personalities—captains with a lot to prove, first officers who were atheists, flight attendants who were lonely and hoped not to be by the time they touched down. Every once in a while, though, he had the unfortunate luck of flying with someone who caused his nerves to hum the *Close Encounters* theme.

"Huh." Maybe if he sounded like he was buying it, this guy would back off. It seemed to work. With a satisfied smile, James plopped his hat on top of his dome-shaped head.

"I hear she's weird too," James added after they'd walked a bit.

By James's standards, Danny wasn't sure if weird would have a solid definition to stand on.

"I mean, like, really weird."

Well, that cleared things up.

"As long as she can fly an airplane, I don't care if she's Amelia Earhart reincarnated," Danny said.

He wished he'd stuck with "huh," as James launched into a long explanation of why Amelia's plane was never recovered.

Chapter 5

On any ordinary plane trip, Lucy Meredith would not have chosen to wear stilettos. She wasn't great at wearing them anyway, and practicing long strides with any kind of elegance while dragging three suitcases and a Jimmy Choo bag made her calf muscles quiver.

Hoping her off-the-shoulder red polka-dot blouse with matching headband did enough to distract from her imbalance, Lucy struggled to the ticket counter. Parking her sunglasses on the top of her head, she attempted to lift her biggest bag onto the scale.

The agent behind the counter gave a disapproving scowl as he helped her with it. "Well," he said, glancing at the scale, "you're over the weight limit. That will cost an extra seventy-five dollars, unless you want to dump a few things in the garbage can."

The symbolism didn't escape her. She was bringing a lot of baggage on this trip, in more ways than one.

"I'm going on a two-week trip to the Netherlands," Lucy stated. "How do they expect you to pack for two weeks with two tiny bags and a carry-on?"

"Last name?" asked the man, who clearly couldn't care less.

"Meredith."

"I said your last name."

Lucy dug into her purse, found her e-ticket, and handed it over to the agent along with her passport, driver's license, and a suitable pout.

Glancing at the bag on the scale he said, "I'll need a credit card too."

"Fine."

Why not? She had already racked up a ton of money on her credit cards just to go on this trip. Why not pay a little extra to make sure all her baggage came along?

Thankfully, her second bag was underweight by one pound. The agent handed over her boarding pass, and she could finally take advantage of the feeling that she looked like a million bucks. Whisking her hair and purse over her shoulder, she wheeled her carry-on toward security.

With total confidence, she handed the TSA employee her boarding pass, then reached down, pulled her shoes off and flung them over her shoulder, holding them by the straps with a single finger.

"Ma'am," the older woman said, "you don't need to remove your shoes yet. You have a ways to go in the security line."

Lucy only smiled and wiggled her beautifully pedicured toes, painted red with small white polka dots.

It was time to live a little, to let go of convention. Convention said that if you were having a midlife crisis at the age of twenty-six, you should go to Las Vegas or an all-inclusive resort in Mexico. Instead, Lucy decided to go Dutch.

And not without good reason.

Go Dutch—the defining moment when Lucy had realized that not once, but twice now, she had been dumped by a man into whom she'd poured her entire life.

It was a Friday in May when she'd suggested a quaint Italian bistro she'd seen reviewed in a newspaper. Lately, they'd done nothing more than stay in, order pizza, and rent a movie. She'd spent four hours in a department store picking the exact right dress. To her, *bistro* was Italian for "new outfit."

The evening went as planned until the waiter set the bill between them. She watched Jeff's face strain to remain expressionless, and then, like the cork of a wine bottle, out popped the words, "Let's go Dutch."

At first, she thought he was proposing, since he'd always dreamed of taking her to the Netherlands.

Turned out he wanted to split more than the bill.

It made sense to Lucy to travel to the very place that made her realize the man she thought loved her couldn't invest in her dinner, much less her life.

She planned the trip carefully. Though she'd never been in therapy, she imagined a therapist would tell her to face the pain in her life, and what better way to say to yourself you're ready to move on than to take on an entire country?

She'd determined to visit dairy farms, learn to plant tulips, channel Anne Frank, attempt to understand Rembrandt beyond what it did for her teeth, try on at least one pair of clogs, and only read books by dead female authors.

Jeff would never see her in this outfit, and that, she believed, was what was so empowering about it. She wore it for herself, not Jeff. She wore it just for the sheer joy of what a polka dot can do for your mood.

Finally making it to the conveyer belt, she placed her carry-on, purse, shoes, and a quart-sized Ziploc bag in a bucket, then flashed a grin at the man waving a wand. Her fairy-godfather. He didn't smile back, but he was probably trained not to. Very self-disciplined, the man who resists the smile of a woman in polka dots.

She put her stilettos back on and walked toward her gate, breathing deeply and assuring herself that no matter what, she was not going to fall apart over this. For the first time in her life, she was seeing clearly.

Lucy pushed open the door to the bathroom near her gate and hauled her bag across the tile toward the first stall. But when she opened the stall door, she yelped.

So did the man curled up on top of the toilet, clutching his stomach. "What do you want?" he shouted. Thankfully, he was fully clothed.

Lucy stumbled backward, bumping into the stall door behind her. It flung open, and she lost her balance. She sat on the adjacent toilet, grabbing at the toilet paper to keep herself from falling in.

After half of the paper unrolled and the door stopped swinging, Lucy tried to compose herself, which was no small thing considering one stiletto lay a foot away and she was, well, sitting on a toilet.

"Get out," Lucy said.

"Me?" the man said. "You get out!"

"Sir," Lucy said in a firm but kind tone, "you are in the women's bathroom."

The man sat up a little and leaned forward, his hand still on his stomach. "No, you're in the men's bathroom."

"Please!" Lucy reached for her shoe. It was inches from her fingers when she got a clear view of the evidence that immediately proved her wrong. Urinals! She quickly gathered her shoe, her suitcase, her bag, and what was left of her dignity. How could she not have noticed this was the men's bathroom?

"Next time try napping elsewhere!" Lucy snapped. The *men's* bathroom. Men. *Men!*

Don't go there.

As she stepped into the swarming traffic of hurried passengers, she adjusted her clothing and her headband, then took some lip gloss out of her Ziploc bag and applied it. This was not going to be about men. She wasn't going to let him…them…the species…the subspecies…take any more of her time.

And if it took milking a goat and staring at windmills to get her mind where it should be, then so be it.

"I'll do the walkaround," Danny said, referring to the outside inspection that had to be done before takeoff. He was about to descend the Jetway stairs that led out to the Tarmac when one of the ground personnel walked over and waved his hand.

"Captain's already down there."

James and Danny peered out the Plexiglas at the Jetway. "Why is she down there?" Danny asked.

"I told you, she's weird," James said.

"Maybe she's just thorough."

"Thoroughly weird."

Danny followed James onto the craft, where they were abruptly stopped at the cockpit by GiGi. "So we have a prisoner."

Danny thought she might be talking about him. He sort of felt chained to James's mouth.

"Apparently so," Danny said. "We'll board him before the rest of the passengers."

"Of course we'll board him before the rest of the passengers," GiGi snapped. "The question is, where do we put him. The answer is that we'll put him in the very back. Let's just hope that whoever is escorting him had the brains to wear something that doesn't scream federal agency. It is such a pain when passengers get paranoid."

"I've boarded various prisoners," James said, "and there's never been any problem. Most people don't even know they're onboard."

One of the other flight attendants scooted up beside GiGi. Like a wildflower that had snaked itself through a thornbush, the blonde offered a wide smile and a firm handshake. "Kim Gilliam. Nice to meet you."

"I'm Danny."

James stepped forward. "And I'm willing to bet the last time your roots were blond was in seventh grade."

Kim's smile dropped.

"I'm just kidding with you." James snorted. "You look great. And GiGi's hair looks eighty-three-point-two percent natural."

Danny shoved James toward the cockpit as he gave the women an apologetic glance. GiGi's eyes could have melted steel. Kim looked like she would melt with embarrassment.

"Get the checklist ready. I'll be right back," Danny said. He stepped out of the cockpit, closed the door, and cleared his throat.

"That's James. I'll try to keep him out of your hair." Danny swallowed. "I mean, out of your way." He glanced at GiGi, hot and fuming like summer heat on a Tarmac. "Again, I'm sorry." *Thornbush. Wildflower. And now, ladies and gentlemen, a pansy.*

Stepping into the cockpit, Danny sat down and pulled out his maps. "It's going to be a long flight if you keep this up."

"You gotta show them who's in charge. If you don't, they'll start handing down orders."

Danny noticed James's wedding ring. "You're married?"

"Yeah. Fifteen years."

Danny kept his mouth shut, but how a man like that could stay in a relationship for fifteen years made the mysteries of the Bermuda Triangle look like an eight-year-old's magic trick.

"You?"

"Um. No. I was engaged. Didn't work out."

Danny looked up and noticed something strange, and it wasn't James. Bright yellow sticky notes stuck to various spots on the windshield like denim patches on a pair of jeans.

"Are those…?"

"Yeah." James pointed to the one on the far left. "It has our flight number on it."

Danny studied the notes, which had everything from weather forecasts to wind direction written on them, until Kim appeared. "Our prisoner is here."

Danny and James followed Kim out of the cockpit. "Where is he?" James asked.

"Down below. With the captain."

Danny and James walked down the Jetway stairs that led outside, where they found Captain Brewster-Yarley with a petite woman and a handcuffed man. The prisoner's thin, white hair stood up like there was a breeze, except there wasn't. He didn't look dangerous, just old and tired.

James cackled. "What'd he do? Rob a nursing home?"

Danny hoped James would keep his mouth shut about the woman escorting the prisoner. She was around forty, with dishwater blond hair pulled back into a low ponytail. She carried a firearm and looked like she knew some serious self-defense moves for people just like James.

She showed her badge and introduced herself as FBI Agent Dee Tasler. "This is Leendert Rijkaard. He should be on your manifest."

The man took a deep breath of morning air, closing his eyes for a moment. He must've been locked up for a long time if airport air seemed fresh.

"I'm Captain C. J. Brewster-Yarley. This is Bubba and Boy," the captain said, nodding toward Danny, then James. She walked forward to shake the agent's hand. Danny smiled even though he didn't get the joke. James didn't smile. Agent Tasler didn't look like she knew what to say.

"I told you!" James whispered.

"She's kidding," Danny whispered back.

"No, she's not. 'Bubba' and 'Boy' are what they used to call the engineer and navigator back in 1930 or whatever. This is what I'm talking about. It's just going to get worse."

The captain glanced from the agent to the prisoner, inspecting them like they were part of the walkaround.

Agent Tasler put away her badge.

"Um, as is procedure," Danny said, filling the silence, "we'll board Mr. Rij...uh, Rik..."

"Rijkaard," the prisoner said.

"Before the other passengers. We'll seat him in the back of the plane."

"Okay to remove the handcuffs?" Agent Tasler asked.

The captain spoke up. "Where is your other agent?"

Danny looked around. There didn't seem to be anyone else with these two.

"He got sick last night. Food poisoning." Agent Tasler nodded toward Rijkaard. "We both had the beef."

Rijkaard wasn't following the conversation anymore, instead looking up at the windows of the plane. The flight attendants, clustered together, peered out the window. Rijkaard waved and grinned.

"Knock it off, old man," Tasler said.

"I don't like the idea that you're escorting him by yourself," the captain said.

"I don't like the idea either, but this is an extradition, and believe me, it's going to be a lot easier to do it now than refile the paperwork and start this whole process over again. He's harmless."

The captain regarded the prisoner, who seemed to be enjoying the female attention.

"Want to—how do you say it—pat me down?" His English was a little hard to understand, but his intention was clear.

Tasler yanked him closer. "Keep it up, Dutch boy."

"Are you going to be able to keep him under control?" the captain asked.

"I won't make a scene." He grinned. "But I can no promise that my charm won't be distracting."

"Keep the cuffs on him," the captain said sternly, "and hand over your firearm."

"My firearm? I don't see any reason why—"

"It's nonnegotiable. It's my aircraft, and I won't allow a dangerous weapon in the cabin."

Unfortunately, Danny thought, that didn't apply to James.

The agent sighed and handed over her gun.

"Boy, escort them to their seats, please." The captain stared forward, her feet spread and one hand tucked against her lower back.

James returned to the plane, Tasler and Rijkaard in tow, and Danny wasn't sure if he should follow or stay.

"You want me to…" Danny gestured in opposite directions with his thumbs.

"Find out if Rijkaard is married."

Danny's thumbs froze midair.

"I'm joking with you, Bubba. Come on, let's get this plane ready. It's a beautiful day to fly."

Chapter 6

J ake's iPod, normally a nice distraction from the outside world, did little more than keep his paranoid thoughts from escaping out his ears. As he sat and waited to board the plane, he watched the people around him. Everyone looked predictably normal or abnormal, but nobody looked like they wanted anything from him.

His mind waded through the murky waters of regret. He'd always despised people who couldn't be satisfied. In his many years as a musician barely making ends meet, he'd met his fair share of those who couldn't be happy unless they had more. He'd also met cheapskates who wanted the entertainment free. His band played venues that promised one amount but paid another when it was over.

He'd determined long ago not to want more than he had, and everything was going as planned until Idya Van Der Mark offered him more than he had. That's what bothered him. Why hadn't he refused it? What had compelled him to carry five diamonds, not to mention his life, over the Atlantic Ocean for an old woman he'd never met?

Through the course of his hardly remarkable life, he'd wondered what it would have been like to have more family. He was an only child, and his parents had died within two years of each other. But he'd never known anything else, so what was so appealing about a distant grandmother who spoke English only when forced? His parents had once explained to him that she was kind of old school, proud to be Dutch and intolerant of English seeping into their world at every turn. It stung her when they'd decided to move to the United States. She disliked the bigness of America, from the cars to the food to the ego.

He pondered his motivation. It certainly wasn't the thrill or the challenge of it all. He was a musician, so motivation wasn't one of his strengths. He would eat off the dollar menu for the rest of his life if it meant he could sleep until three in the afternoon.

Jake's gaze roamed the crowd, but nobody caught his eye. The only person looking at him was a three-year-old who had his finger plugged up one nostril. Still, Jake's heartbeat had yet to find a comfortable rhythm after being startled awake by a woman dressed from head to toe in polka dots.

He dreaded the long trip, but he knew how to sleep just about anywhere, so he hoped the time would pass with a good, long nap on the plane.

The diamond pouch taped to his belly did nothing for comfort, though. Duct tape could hold miles of pipeline together, so he figured it would hold five small diamonds on a slightly pooched, dollar-menu belly. Ripping it off once he got there—if he got there—would prove painful but profitable. It couldn't be worse than having back hair waxed, which their drummer did three summers ago to impress a woman who didn't even shave her underarms.

He turned up the volume on his iPod and closed his eyes, lacing his fingers together over his stomach and sliding his hips down so that his neck rested against the back of the chair. It was hard not to daydream of how he might spend the money. First, he'd have a six-dollar hamburger with caramelized onions and two sides of onion rings. After that, things weren't as planned out, but he had twelve hours in an airplane to give it more thought.

Then he heard a snort.

It wasn't from an old man with a handkerchief either.

Jake pushed his heels against the carpet and sat up, opening his eyes.

What he saw made him wonder if someone had slipped something into his cinnamon roll. Or maybe paranoia caused people to hallucinate.

Either way, a pig stared back at him.

The captain went to the back of the plane. James followed Danny, his hands clasped behind his back, into the cockpit. "So, am I Bubba, or are you?"

"That's ridiculous. She isn't going to call us that for the entire flight. She probably just has a dry sense of humor." Unlike James, who had a dry sense of obnoxiousness.

"All I know is that we're not supposed to ask her about the Bermuda crash."

"I know. You told me."

"The last guy who did is now flying regional jets across Nevada."

"Then why did you?"

"I didn't. I was making general references about the Bermuda Triangle on a whiteboard."

The captain appeared, taking her seat and pulling out the clipboard.

"I apologize that you had to do the walkaround," Danny said. "I was on my way out there when—"

"I didn't have to do it. I always do it. I'm the captain of the airplane, and it's my responsibility to make sure that everything checks out. I once had a baggage handler ram into the back wheel. He didn't want to get into trouble, so he didn't tell anyone. I caught it only on the second walk-around. I've also caught pins still in because the red flag fell off. You can't just look for the flags. Because sometimes the flags fall off." She lowered her voice, like she might when gossiping about someone in the room, and added, "The moral of the story is that there may be red flags in your life you don't see because the flag fell off."

Danny pressed his lips together. A chuckle fluttered in his belly, but he wasn't sure if he should allow it out or suppress it. Was she joking or giving genuine advice? James just smirked.

GiGi appeared at the door. "We've got a problem."

"With the prisoner?" Danny asked.

"Yeah, he's going to be problem, I can already tell. But no, that's not the problem I'm talking about."

"What is it?"

"The woman, the blind woman, she's got a…a…" GiGi, Danny had noticed, talked with her hands, so since her arms hung by her side, she looked at a loss for words.

James said, "They already alerted us that she'll be boarding with a dog."

GiGi punched a fist onto her hip. "You're sure about that?"

James turned in his seat. "Yes, Double G, I'm sure. I spoke to the gate agent earlier. And just in case nobody's up on proper Seeing Eye dog protocol, you don't pet it or feed it."

"Yeah, well, what do you happen to do if it's a hog?" GiGi's expression showed no signs of a punch line. "It's a hog, not a dog. A hog. A fat, potbelly thing on a leash. It's got a snout and…and hoofs and…" GiGi looked like she could cry.

The captain stood. "Where?"

GiGi pointed out to the Jetway. The captain left the cockpit and Danny and James scrambled behind her.

Sure enough, on the Jetway with the gate agent stood a woman in dark sunglasses, looking slightly off to the left, and a pig. It looked hungry, though Danny imagined he was stereotyping, since there was no evidence the pig was hungry.

James's mouth hung open, GiGi's eyes glowed with terror, and Danny found his quivering belly laugh had fled, but the captain didn't look alarmed.

The gate agent approached Captain Brewster-Yarley.

"Her name?" the captain asked.

"Anna Sue Givens."

"I see."

"And she doesn't, which is why we have the animal." James smiled.

"Shut up," Danny said.

"The animal's name is Chucky," the gate agent added.

"Why not throw in an 'n' and make it Chunky?" James asked.

GiGi stepped backward as the pig's snout hit the carpet and started rooting around. "We can't have a pig on this airplane! Where's it going to sit? How are we going to get it *in* a seat?"

The captain turned to Danny. "Bubba, get Ted on the phone."

He had no idea who Ted was.

"Ted," the captain repeated. "Get him on the phone. Find out what to do."

Danny went back to the Jetway phone. Kim, who'd been hanging out by the door and listening, followed him.

"Who is Ted?" Danny asked her.

"Ted?"

"Captain said to get Ted."

Danny bit his lip. He didn't know who Ted was, and he had no idea who to call to find out, so he did the only thing he knew to do, which was dial the airport operator.

"Yes…um, this is First Officer Danny McSweeney on Atlantica Flight 1945 to Amsterdam. We're at the gate and, um, we've got a pig that needs to board. It's a seeing-eye animal with a, uh, seeing-impaired woman, so…"

A long pause was followed by, "Sir, it's illegal to call airports with pranks—"

"This isn't a prank." Danny looked at Kim, who chewed a fingernail as she listened to the call. "I'm just not sure what department...um...is Ted there?"

"Let me connect you to security."

"Wait, but—"

She put him on hold.

Kim said, "Don't we have a Disabilities Act specialist?"

"We do?"

"I think so."

The phone clicked again. "Security."

"Um...can you transfer me back to the operator?"

"Hold."

"You're sure we have that?" Danny asked Kim.

"I think I read it in a memo or in training or something."

Another click. "Operator."

"I need the Disabilities Act specialist," Danny said.

"Are you the same person that just called about the—"

"Can you just connect me?"

"Hold on." Danny could hear her flipping through what sounded like a phone directory. Then she said, "Huh. Okay. I'll transfer you."

The phone rang a few times, and then voice mail picked up. "Hi, this is Stephanie Rose, Disabilities Act specialist. I'm away from my desk. Please leave a message, and I'll get back to you."

Danny hung up the phone. "She's not there. Her name is Stephanie Rose."

"I'll call dispatch," Kim said. "See if they can track her down."

Danny returned to the Jetway, where everyone stood watching the pig. "I didn't find Ted, but we're tracking down Stephanie Rose—"

"Stephanie. That's what I meant," the captain said.

Stephanie. Ted. Sure. Easily confused.

Chucky sniffed the air, perhaps getting a whiff of cocktail peanuts being boarded by the ground crew.

A long silence, only broken by the air moving in and out of Chucky's nostrils, caused everyone to shift uncomfortably. Everyone except Captain Brewster-Yarley, who stood with her hands clasped behind her back, her feet spread apart, and her gaze fixed on the pig.

Finally, a dark-haired woman in a navy business suit, presumably Stephanie, breezed down the Jetway with long, confident strides. She didn't need to ask about the situation. The pig made it apparent.

She turned to the woman. "Ma'am, in order to bring an animal onboard, you need to have proper accreditation and certification. We have to be assured this is not a pet."

"I do." She pulled out the papers.

Stephanie looked them over, then said, "Ma'am, will you please step over here?" Stephanie guided her a few feet away, then joined the group, refolding the papers. "Captain, she has all the valid papers. However, I thought this was a seeing-eye animal."

"Isn't it?" Danny asked.

"No. It's a companion animal."

"What's that?" James asked.

Stephanie glanced back at Anna Sue. "They can be used for many different purposes, like children with cancer, the elderly, people in hospice, trauma victims and"—she glanced at the piece of paper the woman had handed her—"the emotionally challenged."

It didn't matter that Stephanie's tone suggested nobody should look. Everyone looked at Anna Sue in her dark sunglasses and her pig on a leash.

"She's not blind?" Danny whispered.

"No."

"Then why does she have dark sunglasses on?"

"Probably for the same reason she has the pig," James blurted.

Everyone looked at the captain, one silent question on their lips: what would happen at forty thousand feet if Anna Sue didn't have her pig?

Stephanie filled the silence. "These animals are very well trained, and many are trained to be on public transportation. We are not permitted to ask any more questions about the disability, only verify that the animal is a certified companion."

"Why not get a boyfriend and be done with it?" James asked.

"We don't have a full flight today. GiGi, get Ms. Givens on a row by herself," the captain said.

"What are we going to do if the pig needs to go to the bathroom? What if it belches? Do you understand what this is going to do to the passengers? Do you understand how upset everyone is going to be?" GiGi stomped her airline-issued pump.

The captain turned to Stephanie. "Contact GiGi's supervisor and alert her to how upset GiGi is about this. GiGi, you're welcome to file a complaint when we return."

GiGi spun on the same heel that had impaled the carpet, then walked back to the plane, ranting about what the passengers were going to have to endure.

The captain beckoned Anna Sue over to join the conversation. "Ms. Givens, we'll do everything to accommodate you, but I ask that you would accommodate us. I'd like to board you last. I need to figure out where to put you both, and we may have to put some special procedures in place. All right?"

"I understand," Anna Sue said, removing her glasses. "Thank you."

"If you'll return to the gate, I'll alert the gate agent when I'm ready for you to board. Thank you for flying Atlantica."

Chucky and Anna Sue started down the Jetway.

"Oh, and Ms. Givens," the captain called, "one more thing."

"Yes?"

"My apologies if at any time you were treated disrespectfully." The captain looked at James. Everyone looked at James.

James gave an apologetic smile and said, "With a name like GiGi, you've got to assume she's not into pigs. It's nothing personal."

A small scowl appeared on her face, but Anna Sue still seemed pleased with the captain's remarks. She turned and left without a word. James went to tell GiGi.

The captain turned to Danny. "When the passengers begin boarding, I want you to discreetly ask if anyone has Ambien."

"Ambien?"

"Now, let's get this plane ready to board. We're already running late."

The captain headed for the plane, leaving Danny to wonder if everything his fellow first officer said about this red-flag, yellow-sticky-note woman was true.

James returned, stopping beside him and watching the pig waddle out of sight. "Pork," he said. "That's one way to keep the terrorists off the airplane."

Danny sighed. "Is there anything that will keep you off the airplane?"

Chapter 7

Lucy watched passengers grumbling and checking their watches. She couldn't care less when the plane took off. She had nothing but time to burn. She ignored the fussing crowds and took in the sights from the large window that gave her a great view of the busy runways.

She was having a hard time fighting off the urge to horde Cinnabons while waiting. That's all she needed, not to be able to fit into any of the new outfits she bought for the trip.

While she waited, Lucy allowed herself to think of Jeff. It would not do any good to suppress the feelings. She needed to face it all, let herself grieve that the relationship was over, try to figure out why it failed, and return to America completely healed.

She'd first met Jeff at an engagement party for one of her friends. He was the date of an acquaintance of the engaged, but when Lucy stepped out on the balcony for some air, he seemed to forget he'd come with anybody or why he was there in the first place. For forty-five minutes, Lucy drank champagne but tasted only compliments. Like two magnets snapping together, they were instantly attracted.

He wasn't serious with the woman who'd brought him, he'd said. The next day he called, wanting to see her for lunch.

In retrospect, his character hadn't been foremost on her mind. And she had to admit, it was intoxicating to be the one who stole the guy, since for most of her life guys had been stolen from her.

Still, was it completely unpredictable that he'd gotten restless? He couldn't even commit to a date for one night without flirting with someone else on a balcony.

Emotion swelled in her throat, and she allowed it. She'd fallen hard for him, and denying it would only prolong the pain. Sucking in deep breaths through her nostrils, she closed her eyes and tried to center herself.

Focus on what you want your life to be. See yourself happy, married, wildly in love. Picture it.

A loud and jarring announcement instructed passengers to prepare to board Flight 1945. Lucy gathered her belongings and her emotions, taking a moment to swipe gloss across her lips.

She stood. It felt like a defining moment. Sure, she was only boarding an airplane, but it was more than a plane. It was a destiny.

Yet in every mind-focused moment she'd ever conjured, a pig never appeared.

Several people were pointing and talking about it as Lucy moved into line. The woman stood off to the side, near a column and next to a trash can, clutching its leash. The pig looked barely capable of walking. Its belly, full and round, grazed the carpet as it stood sniffing the side of the trash can. The woman wore dark sunglasses, making the situation seem even stranger.

"What's with the pig?" Lucy asked the stranger in front of her.

The woman, in her early eighties, seemed put off. "It's ridiculous, that's what it is!"

Lucy noticed this woman holding the arm of an even older woman, bent like the cane she used to walk. They shuffled forward, the younger of the two commenting on travel.

"What has it come to? First they practically strip-search you, and now you have to travel with farm animals? Disgusting!" The woman turned to Lucy. "They made my mother take off her shoes. Look at her! Does she look like she's capable of taking off her shoes? Or hurting anybody?"

She didn't look like she was capable of making it onto the airplane.

The woman's tart tone continued. "My mother is one hundred and three years old. This is the first time she's ever flown on an airplane. And she's subjected to *this*!" Her shaking hand directed everyone's attention to the woman in sunglasses. Her voice lowered. "I saw her talking to the gate agent, which means she's going to be on this flight!"

Her mother looked up at her like she'd just noticed she was talking. "What'd you say?"

"Nothing, Mother." She gave Lucy a woeful look. "I can only pray we're not sitting near the pig. If we are, somebody's going to hear about it."

About twenty-five people already had, but Lucy just nodded and tried not to engage. Some people couldn't be flexible. Lucy wondered why the pig was there at all and bet that if George Clooney boarded with his pig, no complaints would arise. Or course, George's pig was dead.

Instead of her usual reading fare of *People* and *Us Weekly,* Lucy had brought something meaningful, something life changing. Patting it with her hand, she moved forward and wondered if she would be sitting next to the pig.

Better it than a man.

"It's hot in here," GiGi said in between, "Welcome aboard," and, "Good morning."

Danny smiled and nodded at the passengers, but couldn't figure out how to slip in, "Do you carry sleeping pills?"

Why did the captain need them? He could just go and ask, he supposed, but something about C. J. Brewster-Yarley made him want another option. So instead, he kept looking for the perfect person, someone with a bright, cheery face and dark circles under their eyes.

"Welcome aboard," Danny said to a woman in polka dots. She looked friendly enough.

"Welcome to my new life," she replied with a smile.

"You don't happen to take sleeping pills, do you?" It sounded as awkward as if he'd just pointed out that her bra strap had slipped down her shoulder. He tried a polite smile, even against GiGi's hard stare.

"Why?" the woman asked, suddenly not as cheery.

"Those bright, sunny polka dots might keep you awake." *Grin. Sell it. Come on. Sell it.*

A small smile returned to her face as she glanced down at herself.

"You look ready for a great trip," Danny said, patting her on the back and helping her along.

"Thanks." She continued on to her seat.

"Welcome aboard," GiGi said, then whispered, "Why are you asking people for sleeping pills?"

"Just roll with it. The captain's orders."

"Ugh. I've flown with some weird people—welcome aboard— but this takes the cake. I'm all for women in aviation, but there are women and there are freaks."

"She's a hero, you know," Danny said. "Welcome aboard."

"So I hear. I'd have settled for a quiet disposition, but that's just me." GiGi stepped aside to help a woman who looked old enough to remember life before airplanes. The woman with her was already complaining about the pig.

Through a tense smile, GiGi assured her the pig wouldn't be a problem.

James came out of the cockpit. "I have to go get the pig lady. Captain wants me to apologize and make her feel comfortable."

"You could start by calling her Anna Sue," Danny said.

"Right. Anna Sue-eee!"

"Welcome aboard. You're not seriously going to keep this up the entire flight."

"Hey, I'm not the one with sticky notes all over the windshield."

"You're not the one in charge, either, so let's make this as easy as possible."

James smirked. "Yeah, right. You've got a long flight ahead of you."

"You're being a little dramatic, aren't you? Welcome aboard."

"No, you're in denial. The plane isn't even off the ground and we've got a prisoner and a pig. Should I say more?"

"No, you shouldn't."

"Don't say I didn't warn you. This is just the tip of the iceberg. I have to go board a woman with a pig now."

"Don't complain. I've got to hunt down sleeping pills from passengers."

"Why?"

"That's what the captain said to do."

"What for?"

"I don't know."

James raised a skeptical eyebrow, then lowered his voice. "I've got a bottle of Ambien."

Danny turned to him. "What?"

"Shhh."

"You have sleeping pills with you?"

"Lower your voice, would you?"

"That's against FAA regulations. You can't take sleeping pills when you're on a trip."

"Did I say I was taking them?" James asked with mock innocence. "I also have low blood sugar, but don't let that get out." He winked.

"You could be suspended for having those." Danny was careful to not even take Benadryl, which could render him unconscious for hours.

"Do you want them or not?"

Danny glanced into the cockpit, then at the passengers. "Fine."

"They're in my bag. Inside pocket."

GiGi returned, fanning herself. Danny wanted to remark that it might be her hot glare causing the cabin temperature to rise, but he didn't need more trouble. He was already about to be in possession of a drug that no pilot should ever have or get from another pilot.

"This is going to be a long flight," she said. "The guy in 20E is already asking for a blanket. We haven't even closed the cabin door yet! And did you see the guy clutching his stomach?"

Danny shook his head.

"I asked him if he got airsick, and he went pale. I mean, this is not good."

"Mix in the pig and we've got a Leslie Nielsen movie." Danny cracked a smile, realized he shouldn't have, and immediately retracted it.

Kim approached. "We've got a couple on their way. Gate agent says they're about five minutes out."

"We're already running late. Why not another five minutes, right?" He asked her to greet the remaining boarding passengers. He found what he hoped was James's carry-on in the closet, dug around in it, and found the pills. Hiding them in his pocket, he went into the cockpit.

"All right. I've got the pills," he told the captain.

"What pills?"

"The sleeping pills you asked for."

"I was joking, Bubba."

Danny blinked.

"Did you think I was going to crush them up and feed it to the pig in applesauce?" she asked.

Unfortunately, yes, that thought had crossed his mind.

"Where did you get sleeping pills?"

"Doesn't matter. I'll just put them—"

They heard shouting. The captain rose from her seat and went to the door. An elderly woman's screechy voice quieted the plane.

"Does it have a ticket?" she yelled. "Is it a Gold Star member?"

GiGi, scraping loose hairs back into her chignon, cast a pleasant look at the other passengers. "Ma'am, the pig isn't going to be anywhere near you."

Which implied it would be near *someone*.

"It's the idea, don't you see? It's the idea that I'm flying with a pig. Don't you remember the days when you stewardesses wore nice clothes? suits? pantyhose? makeup? What has happened to this industry? Is there an all-you-can-eat buffet in the back? Am I supposed to serve myself coffee out of a machine near the bathrooms? This is not what flying is supposed to be!"

The captain turned to Danny. "Get me some applesauce."

Danny smiled.

"Now."

"Seriously?"

"Bubba, do I look like I'm kidding?"

Chapter 8

U nder normal circumstances, the stuffy, diesel-laden air would bring back good memories for Jake. He'd been on his share of tour buses, back when they opened for bigger bands, hoping to hit the big time. He liked the smell. It also reminded him of snow skiing, when you hopped on at the base of the mountain, down where the fumes gathered against the cold ground. It made the ride to the top that much better. If he closed his eyes, he could remember the crisp fresh air of Winter Park.

But he wasn't about to close his eyes. Already, one of the flight attendants seemed suspicious of him, asking him why he was holding his stomach. He'd hoped the pig would be enough of a distraction to keep anyone from noticing him.

He pushed his duffel bag into the overhead compartment, fumbling with it as he tried to keep the bottom of his T-shirt from riding up his belly. The bag fell backward, hit him on the head, then hit a man sitting across the aisle.

"Ow!"

"Sorry," Jake said, scrambling to retrieve the bag. He stepped out of the way to let the other passengers by. A break came in the line, and he had no choice but to call for a flight attendant. The same irritated woman who'd asked about his stomach appeared.

"Sorry. I just have a bad back and can't get my bag up there."

"A bad back and a queasy stomach," she said. "May be a long flight for you."

"I'm sure I'll be fine." He let go of his belly and put his hands elsewhere while he watched a woman half his size struggle to get the bag in place. It was all he could do not to help her, but one wrong move and everyone would catch a glimpse of duct tape on his stomach.

"There," she said, exasperated. "I think I got it." She glanced at him. "You're hot too?"

"Um…I had a girlfriend who thought so. Once."

"I meant you're sweating."

Below each pit, a ring of sweat had formed. No matter how hard he played off his fears, his sweat glands betrayed him.

"Thanks for your help." Jake quickly found his seat, sliding down and wishing he could slide under.

He tried to rationally think through the paranoia, but that was like mixing oil and water. Instead, he pictured Idya Van Der Mark, a woman who lived frugally but kept five diamonds under her mattress. Why? At her age, why not at least sell one and enjoy life a little?

He wondered what they would talk about. Would she have any interest in his almost-but-not-quite-successful band? Would she understand his American lifestyle?

He'd packed lightly, not bothering to bring anything to read.

Now that he was on the airplane, feeling safer, he regretted that he hadn't brought a magazine or something. He pulled out *Sky-Mall* catalog, flipped through it, and laughed at the idea that on the trip home, he could buy anything in there.

He'd rather have a new guitar. Except not really. He loved his guitar. It had a lot of character with its dents and gashes. So what did he want?

Right now, he just wanted to get across the Atlantic.

All right, Lucy reasoned with herself, maybe the polka dots were a little loud. The pilot probably meant it as a compliment, and she was in a heightened state of sensitivity. Possibly elevated to orange.

She hoped she played it off well. Smiles, though hard to come by, covered up what any high-priced concealer couldn't.

Grasping her stub, she looked for her seat, 20D. She spotted it. In between two men.

Before she could manage to roll her eyes, the man in 20E— young, with tanned skin and a hair part that looked like it might fall off the side of his head—locked eyes with her, glanced at her ticket, and quickly unfastened his seat belt. "You're here?" he asked.

Lucy nodded.

He grasped a yellow notepad and a pen and, with a gentle-manly gesture, offered her the aisle seat.

"Oh, you're kind. Thank you. I'm fine where I am, though."

She maneuvered her way into the seat, pushed her Jimmy Choo handbag under the seat in front of her, and adjusted her outfit so it wouldn't wrinkle too badly. On her other side sat a dull-looking man without much interest in anything but his reading, which was fine with her. She planned to do some reading herself.

The blond man on her other side sat back down and fastened his seat belt. He smiled, this time a little nervously, but he looked nice enough. She tried to relax, scanning the heads of people all around her, wondering where they were going and why.

A flight attendant approached and addressed the man in 20E. "Yes?"

"May I have another blanket?"

The flight attendant's eyes widened at the request, but she nodded and left. The man glanced at Lucy. He held the first blanket in his lap. "I get a little cold sometimes."

"Sure."

"And tired."

He spread the blanket over his legs and tapped his pen against the notepad he carried. He jotted something down, turned the notepad over, and then stared forward.

"Where are you headed?" Lucy asked with a grin.

She refused to be a man hater, even though she really wanted to be. Men should have the benefit of the doubt, and she realized she had the power to give it to them, to perhaps see them as they couldn't see themselves. She imagined this man to be kind, caring, and respectful of women. She imagined it over and over in her head as she watched him call for a fluffier pillow.

Danny felt relieved as they made their way through the preflight checks even as he observed a sticky note with all the flight attendants' names on it. Despite her eccentricities, the captain appeared to be a capable woman with no particular agenda except to get everyone over the Atlantic to Amsterdam. He wasn't certain if he'd be called Bubba the entire flight, but watching James being called Boy was fun enough to tolerate his own nickname.

James, the nonflying pilot on this flight, was already complaining that he wouldn't log any flying hours, and even hinted that they should turn on the beacon now. Danny had heard this argument a handful of times from pilots who'd become bitter over the years about pay cuts. Since they were paid by the hour, some cheated and turned on the beacon, which was attached to the computer that logged their hours, before they left the gate.

Danny never worried that much about money, but maybe he should've.

As the captain rattled off the list, Danny checked everything from the fuel gauge to the flight plan loaded into the flight management system. He marveled at her efficiency. Loading the flight plan was cumbersome, but she did it quickly and accurately. Taking her lead, Danny checked the switches as James crushed up four Ambien tablets.

"Are we ready to push back?" Danny asked.

"Not yet," the captain said. "Bubba, you're going to offer our honored guest some applesauce." She handed him a small, plastic container of Mott's. "Dump that Ambien in."

Danny peeled back the foil, and James poured the dusty, white contents in, stirring it with his finger. "Are we breaking the law?" Danny asked.

"No. The animal wouldn't assist the woman off the airplane in an emergency, and if it gets out of control, it could cause serious problems during an evacuation. She should be just fine with the animal sleeping next to her."

"How, exactly, do I do this?"

"Simply tell Anna Sue that in celebration of having our first pig onboard, we'd like to offer him a special meal. We've got to lighten the mood on the craft, make people feel like it's something special to be flying with a pig. This kind of story can be passed down to the grandchildren. How many people get to fly with a pig?"

"You should've seen the time we served Sloppy Joes onboard," James quipped.

Danny stood, carefully cupping the applesauce container. Slipping out the cockpit door, he found GiGi fanning herself and looking flushed.

"Can we get some air going?" she asked.

"It's not hot enough to supplement with the auxiliary power unit," Danny said.

"Look at me! My bangs are sweaty!"

She did look very hot, but she was also dealing with a lot of pressure. A pig. A prisoner. A man who could vomit at any second. With a lot of bodies onboard at 98.6 degrees, the cabin always got a little hot before takeoff.

"You know it uses fuel," Danny said as gently as possible. Fuel, with a capital F, seemed involved in every decision at the airline these days. As soon as the wheels left the ground, so did the pilot's control of the airplane. The company had calculated that pilots who circled the aircraft in order to go the right direction made too wide of a turn, using more fuel than necessary. Since then, the planes made all the fuel-efficient decisions, including turning themselves so precisely that the company saved millions of dollars a year. "Once we get up in the skies, everything will cool off."

"Did you just tell me to *cool off*?"

"No, I said…I didn't say—"

She glared at his applesauce. "You're snacking?"

"This is for the pig. Excuse me."

Danny pushed past Hot and Bothersome, through a quiet and reserved business class, and to the end of the main cabin, where Chucky sat across two seats next to Anna Sue. Squatting next to her, he smiled warmly and held up the applesauce. "Thought we'd offer our guest a treat before takeoff."

Stroking the pig's ears, Anna Sue looked truly touched. "That is so kind of you. Chucky loves applesauce." Chucky's ears perked up, and his nostrils flared. "But I can only feed him a small diet while onboard. He is trained to eat like a Seeing Eye dog. While on duty, he can't have people food or anything that might cause him stomach trouble. I feed him a small snack once an hour."

Danny stretched the smile farther across his face. "Oh. Are you sure—"

Chucky lunged forward, causing a few people to gasp, and seemed to suck the applesauce right through his snout. Danny and Anna Sue leaned in to find the plastic cup empty.

Anna Sue smiled. "He does love applesauce."

"Maybe that wasn't enough to cause any, um, problems," Danny said.

"I'm prepared. I have Depends."

"Okay."

Anna Sue's smile turned shy. "Thank you for your kindness. I know people don't like pigs. If they just knew Chucky, knew how sweet he is—"

Chucky did look sweet. Or maybe sleepy. Danny hoped forty milligrams of Ambien would be enough. "He seems very nice."

"And he's protective too. One time, an animal control officer tried to tranquilize him. He became infuriated. It's like he knew, sensed what was happening to him. Very, very unhappy."

Through the slight glaze that settled into Chucky's eyes, Danny got the strangest feeling he knew something.

"Pigs are very smart," Anna Sue said.

A few whispers circled around them. Danny leaned toward Anna Sue. "Listen, Anna Sue, I'm sure you're accustomed to people feeling a little awkward around Chucky." He chose his words carefully, unsure how an emotionally challenged woman might react to any observation about her pig.

"If they just got to know him," Anna Sue replied, "he's precious."

Danny smiled in the direction of Chucky, whose gaze had become fixed on the ceiling. He'd grown very still.

"I thought I'd try to lighten the atmosphere, maybe tell a few pig jokes or something. You know, just to get people laughing about the situation." He paused, trying to read Anna Sue while keeping his eye on the pig, who seemed to be regretting the applesauce. "I guess what I'm trying to ask is whether or not that would be okay. How would you feel about that?"

Anna Sue patted him on the arm. "You're kind to ask, and pigs are very smart, but I can assure you, he's not going to understand you're talking about him."

Chucky leaned into the seat, his snout relaxing on the armrest. "O…kay. Thanks. We'll see what we can come up with."

Danny rose and returned to the cockpit, wondering how he felt about deceiving such a nice woman and drugging what appeared to be a perfectly reasonable pig.

GiGi stopped him before the cockpit door. "I don't know what you have to do to make it happen, but I need air. Do you understand me? Cold air." She wasn't finished, but somebody pushed the Call button. "If this is the guy in 20E…" She gasped. "It is!"

"What's wrong?"

"We're not even in the air and he's asked for an extra blanket and two different pillows!"

"Just try to accommodate. Remember, we're trying to reinvent ourselves as the airline that takes care of its—"

"Shut up."

Danny sighed and joined James and the captain in the cockpit. He lowered his voice. "Listen, um, GiGi's asking if we could turn on the APU to get more air."

The captain studied one of her sticky notes, then faced him. "You're being awfully diplomatic."

"I am?"

"Shut the door for a moment."

Danny obeyed as the captain pulled something out of her flight bag. It looked like a metal thermostat one might find in a house.

"It is my experience, Bubba and Boy, that we're dealing with hot flashes."

Danny couldn't help it. His eyes widened like those of an eight-year-old who'd just heard something he should've heard from a parent first. The captain listed this off like a fact sheet, as if it didn't occur to her that she was once in this same age bracket. And female. Even James, always poised to be inappropriate, looked speechless.

"So," the captain continued, "what we're going to do is use this. It's a thermostat." She held it up and turned it around. "It has a magnet on the back. We're going to stick it out there on something metal and tell the flight attendants that it controls the air, that we just got it from Boeing." She handed it to Danny. "Be discreet when you put it up. Don't let them see you do it."

Danny raised an eyebrow. "This will really work?"

"Like a charm. If they think they're controlling the air, they're happy."

Danny left the cockpit just as two harried passengers dragged themselves through the door of the craft.

"Thank you for waiting," said the guy, out of breath. "I didn't want to wait until tomorrow."

"Our flight attendant, Kim, will be happy to help you to your seats and find a place for your carry-ons," Danny said.

The woman grinned as she smoothed her hair into place. "Thank you so much."

Danny glanced down the aisle to make sure all the FAs were sufficiently busy, then found a place for the thermostat on the sidewall near the cockpit. It snapped onto the metal with a loud pop, but nobody noticed. He chuckled.

"What are you doing?"

He whirled around to find GiGi, who moments before had been at the other end of the aircraft, right behind him.

"I'm, uh…fiddling with the thermostat." It nearly came off as a question.

"What thermostat?"

"Boeing installed them so the air can be controlled inside the cabin." Danny pitched a thumb over his shoulder. GiGi rose on her toes to look behind him, staring at the thermostat for a long moment.

She nudged him out of the way. "Which means we should be controlling it, not you." She reached for it. "It's set on seventy-eight! No wonder we're hot!"

Afraid he might blow the whole thing with a single word, Danny simply nodded and returned to the cockpit.

"It's working," he whispered excitedly.

The captain hardly acknowledged him and instead focused her attention on the final checklist. As Danny climbed into his seat, he wondered just how weird—and possibly fun—this flight would get.

Chapter 9

I t seemed whatever Lucy hoped for and truly believed with all her heart was coming to pass. The man to her right, with a calm laugh like a bashful ten-year-old, came complete with manners, a slight sense of humor, and a need to encourage. It seemed his only downfall was that he kept making up excuses to hit on the flight attendants, except even then, he didn't so much hit on them as compliment them on their job.

In all her years of experience with men, starting in fifth grade when she decided Frank Graham's freckles were beyond adorable, she'd never met anyone like—

"What's your name?"

"Hank."

"I'm Lucy."

"I like that name."

She'd never met anyone like this guy. Slightly shy, yet in a weird way convincingly confident. A simple gentleness filled his eyes, except when he seemed to look right through her. Judging by the small smile that stayed on his lips, maybe he liked what he saw.

Lucy rested her head against the back of the seat. Only to herself would she admit she doubted the secret in the book she'd been reading—and why it was called *The Secret* when it didn't seem that secretive since landing on the *New York Times* Best Seller list. But something made her want to try. Not a single negative word had left her lips. Well, that wasn't true. She'd slipped a time or two, but for the most part, she'd managed to exert positive energy, refusing to listen to her mother nag or her boss complain. Instead, just like *The Secret* told her, she filled her mind with damage-reversing images. She likened it to brain waves by Enya.

The flight attendant returned with a new set of earphones and a tight smile directed at Hank. "Okay, I checked these out and they seem to be perfectly intact, so you shouldn't have any problem with one side sitting slightly lower than the other. Okay?"

"Thank you so much," Hank said, taking the earphones. "I appreciate that you'd do this for me."

Lucy watched the flight attendant start to say something, then leave with a confused look on her face.

"You're nice," Lucy said, gently nudging his shoulder with hers.

"I am?"

"Yeah. That's why she looks confused. It's rare to find a nice person."

Hank wrote something on his notepad, then turned his attention to her. "You're nice too."

"My thoughts are sending out a magnetic signal that draws the parallel back to me."

He didn't respond, probably because a positive attitude came naturally to Hank, which meant she had the good fortune to sit next to someone with favorable karma. She, unfortunately—no, not unfortunately. She had to rid her vocabulary of that word. She *fortunately* had to work hard to press into existence good things for her life, which meant focusing her energy toward the positive.

"So what takes you to the Netherlands?" Lucy asked.

"Business."

"What kind?"

"Consumer reports. What about you?"

"I got dumped by a jerk of a guy and I'm trying to put my life back to—" Lucy closed her eyes and took a deep breath. "I'm revisiting the idea that I'm a whole and happy human being, independent and without need of an alpha male."

"What's an alpha male?"

Lucy smiled. "I like you even more." These days omega males were becoming attractive. Sizing up Hank, though, he didn't seem on either end of the spectrum. Perhaps a beta, the kind that could overthrow the alpha but was secure enough not to.

Lucy reached into her bag and pulled out her book, brushing her hand over it. "Have you read this?"

Hank leaned over to look at it. "*The Secret?*"

"You'll have to get your hands on a copy. It's really a—"

Then Lucy heard a woman's voice behind her. "Jeff, can you put this up there?"

"Yeah, just a sec."

Lucy whipped around in her seat, clutching the top of the headrest to pull herself up. By the time her eyes cleared the top of the seat, all she could see was the back of a blonde in very tight jeans. She disappeared through the galley.

"What's the matter?" asked Hank. The man on her other side gave her a cordial glance but said nothing.

Lucy turned around, panting as she gave birth to a strong, invisible wall of energy to surround her.

Hank's hand shot up, and he pushed the flight attendant's button.

"No…no, I'm…I'm…" The plane started to spin.

The flight attendant started toward them with a mean look on her face. She punched off Hank's Call light. "What is it? The carpet's the wrong color?"

"Something's wrong with her," Hank said, pointing at Lucy.

The flight attendant's angry gaze shifted to concern as she noticed Lucy. "Are you okay?"

"I'm…" *Breathe. Breathe. Breathe.* "I'm fine. I'm just…I'm warm…"

The flight attendant shook her head. "I knew it. I'll turn down the thermostat and bring you some water."

"Thanks." Lucy smiled and tried to take deep yoga breaths, but it felt like her heart might punch through her breastbone. She covered her chest with her hands.

"Are you feeling ill?"

Ill. No, she wouldn't claim *that* for herself. "No, I'm feeling excitable."

The flight attendant returned with a cup of water. "How are you feeling? Cooler?"

"Yes. And happy."

She closed her eyes and tried to talk herself out of the idea that she had just heard Jeff's voice reply to a blonde with hair like silk. It was a figment of her imagination. A negative energy burst caused by the guy on her left with the permanent frown marks between his eyebrows.

She turned toward Hank and felt a peaceful warmth fill her. "Tell me why you like life."

Jake continued to flip page after page in the *SkyMall* catalog, though he wasn't focusing much on what one could purchase at forty thousand feet. Strangely, he missed his parents. His father was killed in a car accident when he was eighteen, then two years later his mother succumbed to a cancer she'd fought for five years. He'd mourned deeply, then decided to move on. That's what they would have wanted him to do.

But he felt a sense of solitude that made him think about why he'd taken this gig. He had nobody to rely on but himself, no parents to ask for money or wisdom. A sense of self-survival, of desperation came over him as he slumped in his seat, his hands casually entwined over his belly.

The man sitting next to him looked over. He had a round, wide face, and bulging eyes. His hair, oily and scraped to one side,

made him look older than he seemed to be. Jake guessed midforties, but he was never good with ages. When he waited tables and
a group of women came in for cocktails, his worst fear was that
one of them would ask him to guess their ages. He'd purposefully
go low, but he still usually offended someone. Once, to be safe, he
told a lemonade-guzzling woman she didn't look a day over
twenty-seven. Turned out she was nineteen—a nineteen-year-old
who smoked and whose forehead creased like an accordion with
every expression. They'd tipped a measly five percent.

The man next to him said something, not noticing or caring
that he was listening to his iPod. Jake unplugged himself.

"They're late. Again. When are they going to figure this thing
out and get us where we need to be—on time?" said the man. His
voice was too small for his body.

He stared at Jake, waiting for a response. "Yeah."

"It's called professionalism. There's no storm outside. We
waited ten minutes for that chick and her boyfriend to board,
probably because she couldn't find the right color lipstick, you
know? Meanwhile, the rest of us have to wait."

"I'm sure we'll be in the air—"

"I'm a pilot myself."

"No kidding."

"I pilot the Global High Airship."

"Interesting." *Not.*

"Those guys up there," he said, nodding toward the cockpit,
"they're just a bunch of airborne computer operators. My ship, it's
all about skill and talent. You get hit with a burst of wind in a

blimp and it can *kill you.* One hundred and fifty-two feet long, sixty-eight feet high, thirty-seven feet wide. *Seventy thousand* cubic feet of helium, my friend." Helium Head had a flare for drama, since Jake knew nonflammable helium was only dangerous in the hands of boys who wanted to sound like girls or bands who were bored to death on the road. The man droned on. "It's six inches taller than a 747. Anybody can fly a plane, but there's nothing like hovering over a baseball stadium, you know?"

"No, not really."

"Name's Eddie." Eddie waited. "Yours?"

"Jake."

"You gotta have a bladder of steel, man."

"Excuse me?"

"Those guys are up there sipping their coffee, probably reading a book or two when they're in the sky. I can be up in the air for six hours, no bathroom breaks. There's no bathroom in my gondola." Eddie then conceded that the Fuji Blimp, which he made a goal to fly one day, came complete with a bathroom and six passenger seats.

Jake nodded, smiled in a way to convey that he didn't mean it, then began putting the buds back in his ears.

Eddie, though, kept talking. "How many pilots do you think work for this airline alone?"

"Ten billion."

"There are only a hundred and fifty blimp pilots in the world. That's one-five-o. More people have flown the space shuttle."

Jake wondered if they all came with an inferiority complex like this guy. Eddie was the Toyota Yaris of the aviation world. No matter how fuel efficient it was, there was no getting around the fact that it could be crushed like a soda can by a midsized sedan. The vividly colored Yaris, its only impressive attribute in Jake's opinion, had nothing on the colorful personality beside him.

Jake noticed Eddie's sweater. Pinned above his chest were aviation wings—except it was only half a set. No wonder the guy had a complex. One lonely wing: can't go airborne without a lot of hot air.

As Eddie described the time he nearly had to land on Virginia Beach during tourist season, Jake rolled his head toward the aisle. Maybe when the flight took off, he could find an excuse to sit elsewhere. Closer to the bathroom might be a step up.

Then again, he didn't want to draw attention to himself.

Chapter 10

Have you ever pulled a circuit breaker for the beacon light?" James asked. He'd been quiet for a total of one and a half minutes. Danny wished the captain would tell him to shut up, but strangely, she seemed not to notice.

To Danny, James sounded like white noise he couldn't turn off, especially after the five-minute explanation on why Ann Coulter was hot. That opinion confirmed that he would not be going out to dinner with James when they landed in Amsterdam. Usually the pilots, sometimes accompanied by the flight attendants, found a restaurant near the hotel. Danny liked going with the group. Interesting conversations usually emerged. With James, though, it was hard to tell what would emerge.

"You know you can do that, right?" James asked. "It's especially helpful in Amsterdam, where they can fine you a bazillion dollars for turning it on too soon. So you pull the breaker and the beacon light on top doesn't show, but it starts logging flight hours. You know, when you're, like, stuck at the gate forever. Once you push back, you just plug it back in, the light goes on, and all is well."

Danny glanced at the captain. She was busy writing something on a sticky note.

Everyone *knew* this. They normally didn't *talk* about it.

The airline had been having trouble with breaker pulling since the pilots took gigantic pay cuts after 9/11. A memo went around telling everyone to stop turning their beacons on early, so a few pilots figured out the breaker trick.

Admittedly, Danny had been tempted. His pay cut seemed to be at the core of his problems lately. He never actually pulled the breaker himself, but he hadn't objected once when it was done, especially since the captain had done it.

On this flight, though, he didn't think that would go over well. Captain Brewster-Yarley seemed unpredictable when it came to acceptable and not. Danny respected her for making James apologize for the pig comments, as she seemed to have a certain level of morality. But she also drugged the pig without informing Anna Sue.

Now, though, she studied the maps and seemed oblivious to the conversation.

GiGi came to the door. "We're ready."

James grinned. He didn't say anything, but his face did, and Danny prayed it wouldn't come out of his mouth, whatever insult he was about to let fly.

"All right, secure the doors and prepare for takeoff," the captain said.

"Finally," growled GiGi, and she left, slamming the cockpit door.

James laughed as he stood and secured it. "You gotta love the Slam and Clicks."

"You keep saying that," Danny said. "What does that mean?"

"It's the sound they make when they slam the cockpit door and it clicks. The Slam and Clicks."

Danny cut his eyes sideways to his female captain. That sort of line was the kind of insult you lived to regret for a very, very long time.

"Just do me a favor," Danny said. "Don't call her that to her face, okay? Chucky and Old Man Felon are already making this an interesting flight."

James grinned and nodded toward the captain as if to say, *Don't leave her out of the equation.*

Danny sliced his hand across his neck like his mom used to do when he started to say something inappropriate. James put his hands by his face and shook them back and forth, pretending to be scared.

"What's going on?" the captain suddenly asked.

Danny rolled his eyes. Why couldn't James just shut up? "Hey, I didn't say it," Danny said. "I call them flight attendants to their faces and behind their backs. James is the one who's fond of nicknames."

James wasn't pleased, and Danny felt like a fifth-grade tattletale. Then again, he didn't want nine flight attendants mad at him either.

"I'm talking about the cabin door. It just opened again." She pointed to a glowing light on the console that indicated the cabin door was open. "Bubba, go find out what's going on."

Danny climbed out of the cockpit to find Kim about ready to knock.

"We just got orders to unarm the door," she said.

"Orders? We're already behind schedule. Why are we waiting for another passenger? And unarming the door is at the discretion of the captain. "

"I don't know. No explanation was given."

Danny watched the Jetway. Who was it? Some celebrity? That was all he needed.

A man the size of a twelve-year-old, with a thin mustache and strides too long for his legs, walked toward them, carrying a hard briefcase and an even harder expression. A laminated photo ID swung back and forth across his tiny chest.

"Who is that?" Kim whispered.

Danny wasn't certain, but if it was who he thought, the sinking feeling in his stomach was about to last the entire flight.

"…so I was the mime in the family. It was really great. I got to make the kids laugh but never had to speak."

It took every ounce of her energy, but Lucy focused on Hank and not the urge to stand, pretend to need the restroom, and spy on the back half of the cabin to see if that was really Jeff she'd heard.

"I've never met a clown, at least out of makeup. What an interesting job."

"I enjoyed it very much."

"But you don't do it anymore?"

"No. My parents died in an accident, and my brother decided to sell the company so that we could all go to college."

"What did you major in?"

"Indecision. I couldn't figure out what I wanted to do for the rest of my life. I knew I loved cars, so I worked as a mechanic. Then my sister, who is a police officer, let me help her with an auto theft task force. I had to fly out to Las Vegas, and that's when I realized I really liked planes. Now I'm flying on a plane."

Lucy snapped her fingers. "That's right! See it, believe it, receive it. You know, Hank, don't let it stop here. Why not own your own plane? Why not own your own airline?"

"I guess nothing's impossible with God, right?"

"Nothing's impossible, period. So many people are held back by fear. If there's something you want out of life, nothing can stop you."

"Except a plane crash over the Atlantic. Sorry…I've been told I have a dry sense of humor." Hank smiled. "Anyway, you gotta walk—or fly—by faith, not by sight."

"It's the sight part that's crucial, Hank. If you can't see what you want, you'll never get it." She patted her book. "In these pages, Hank, is the power. The power to live a fulfilled and successful life. The power not to worry about who might or might not be on the plane."

"The pig looks pretty nice to me."

"Don't let his good looks fool you." Lucy blinked as she realized he meant the *actual* pig onboard. That made two of them.

Her eyes filled with tears. As her cheeks dampened, Hank noticed.

"Are you okay?"

Lucy waved one hand in front of her face and laid the other on top of her book like she was about to be sworn in. "I'm getting there. My heart believes this, but sometimes my tear ducts don't."

"It's okay to doubt," he said softly.

"No, it's not doubt. It's not. I can see my happiness clearly before me. I see marriage. Three healthy kids. A four-thousand-square-foot home." More tears fell. Her voice a tiny squeak, she whispered, "He's back there."

"Lucy, you and I don't know each other well, but I can guarantee that pig is not going to get you. Pigs are not violent."

"But they can be emotionally detached." Lucy gave Hank a forlorn look. "I'm not talking about the pig that oinks."

"You've lost me if there's a pig that barks."

"A lot of bark but no bite." She laughed and wiped her tears. "I think my ex-boyfriend is onboard."

"Oh."

"I'm not sure, but I thought I heard him. He has this sort of scratchy, annoying voice. He was with a woman."

"Maybe you're imagining it."

"No. My imagination is filled up entirely with positive energy." She stared at the stark, plastic ceiling of the airplane. "But somewhere in the universe, a stream of negativity is pulling at me." That was the only explanation for Jeff's being onboard. That, or the fact that she and Jeff already had this trip planned, so he went ahead with it. As did she. She just didn't think to bring anybody with her.

She took a few deep breaths of the stale plane air, pungent like the smell of a portable toilet. *See it. Believe it. Receive it. See it. Believe it. Receive it.* The problem was that she couldn't see Jeff, but believed he was at the back of the plane, and needed to receive confirmation that he wasn't to keep her tears at bay.

She turned to Hank. "Listen, you can relate, right? I mean, what would you do if an ex you just broke up with came on an airplane with someone else? You'd ask why, right?"

"Personally, I'd ask Z."

Lucy smiled and looked into his ocean blue eyes. "I'm overreacting, aren't I?"

"I think anyone would be curious. It's a natural reaction."

Lucy stared at the seat in front of her, resolve building inside. "It doesn't matter whether or not he's on this plane. Whether or not he's taking another woman on *our* trip. Whether or not she's a fake blonde. Whether or not she's a size eight trying to squeeze into a six. None of that matters to my happiness and the purpose of this trip. He's not in my vision for my future. Not at all." Lucy grinned. "You can feel it, can't you? Neutrons buzzing around the positive energy we're putting off?"

"I don't know. I'm getting a little annoyed that we're still at the gate."

"Don't let yourself go there, Hank. Nothing you can do will get this plane off the ground any faster. Enjoy this moment. Our moment."

Hank flagged down a flight attendant. "Any magazines available?"

"Sir, as soon as we're in the air, I'd be happy to—"

"I might fall asleep, and I'd really like to get some reading done before I snooze."

The flight attendant blinked four times, then left to retrieve a magazine.

"You should," Lucy said.

"Should what?" Hank asked.

"Take full advantage of the service the flight attendants offer. That's what we're paying the big bucks for, right?"

"That and fuel."

The flight attendant returned with *Popular Mechanics*. "Perfect!" Hank said. "Thank you. This is exactly what I love to read. You really know your customers."

The flight attendant smiled politely. "Enjoy."

"You know what?" Lucy said. "I think I'll take a magazine too. Why not, right?"

"Sure," the woman said flatly. Lucy noticed the flight attendants were nicer to men, but she didn't dwell on it.

"You know," Hank said, "it's okay to hurt. It's okay to be angry that someone didn't treat you well. God understands. His Son, Jesus, was rejected and betrayed. Jesus allowed it, but He also prayed. And He forgave them."

"Uh-huh. I'm going to try another route."

Chapter 11

D anny straightened as the man walked toward him. The suit gave him away as a fed. Air marshals used to have the same problem until they allowed their agents to dress casually; otherwise, the suit always gave them away since hardly anyone flew in suits anymore. This guy was no air marshal, but he was definitely with the federal—

"Is he a…?" Kim trailed off as the man approached.

"I was delayed by some very unprofessional security people," the man said. "I'm Miles Smilt, and I'm a federal aircraft inspector. I will be accompanying you on your flight." He spoke with a straight expression and a hint of superiority.

"Right this way," Danny said, gesturing toward the cockpit. He remembered the first time he flew with an aircraft inspector, or ACI, as they were known. The inspector came onboard bound and determined to cause trouble. He sat in one of the two jump seats, his long legs crossed to reveal one gray and one blue sock. It kept distracting Danny. He wondered how a man with mismatched socks could look so smug. The ACI had checked and marked and snarked his way through the eleven-hour flight.

"You're the captain?" Mr. Smilt asked.

"That's what her stripes say," James inserted as they all gathered in the cockpit. Maybe James would be enough of a distraction that Danny wouldn't have to worry about the ACI watching him. Thankfully, Danny was the relief pilot going, so all he had to do was stay in the jump seat and keep his mouth shut.

"C. J. Brewster-Yarley," the captain said, offering a hand.

"I'm Miles Smilt, and I'll be your ACI for this flight."

"Mr. Smilt, take a seat. And next time, make sure you board on time."

Danny sat in the jump seat across from Smilt, who cleared his throat but kept quiet. Danny put on his headset and waited for the captain to contact the ground crew, hoping they didn't miss a procedural step. Without the ACI, it would be just another day in the cockpit. With the ACI, everything came under the microscope. The "sterile cockpit" rule was in order for sure. Most of the time, especially if they sat in a long line waiting for clearance to take off, pilots disregarded the sterile cockpit rule and chatted until takeoff. "By the book" meant absolutely no chatter besides operational until they'd cleared ten thousand feet.

The captain switched on the intercom. "Pilot to ground, anyone there?"

"We got all doors closed, area clear, walkaround complete. Ready when you are."

"Stand by. We'll get clearance."

Danny switched on the radio. "Ramp control, this is Atlantica 1945, ready for pushback, gate thirty-seven."

"Atlantica 1945, cleared to push. Watch out for the aircraft in the alley."

"Roger. Cleared to push."

"Roger that," the captain said. She released the brakes. "Ground, we're ready to go. Brakes off, cleared to push."

"Roger that, starting to push back."

The craft slowly rolled backward. Danny put his full concentration into the task at hand and tried to ignore James, who was humming, albeit softly. Danny recognized an Audioslave song, out of key and never meant to be hummed.

Pretending to fiddle with his headset, Danny glanced at the ACI, wondering if he noticed. He was busy digging through his bag, pulling out folders, clipboards, and some plastic ties for who knew what. Aggravation built in Danny. He cleared his throat a couple of times, but James kept humming like an old man on a stroll.

Anything but Audioslave. That was Maya's favorite band. She had all their records, knew every lyric, the name of every band member, every useless fact about them. She would travel two days to see their concerts, dole out hundreds of dollars for tickets, but couldn't stay with him through a pay cut.

The ground crewman said, "Everything looks good from down here. Have a good flight."

"Thanks. Cleared to disconnect," the captain said.

Disconnect. James hummed, creating the background music for the memory that played through Danny's mind in high definition. She'd actually used that word.

"I feel like we're disconnecting."

"Disconnecting? We spend every hour that I'm home together."

"Maybe what I mean is that I'm disconnecting."

It took three more months for Danny to discover that it wasn't a lack of affection or time or energy or communication, but a lack of resources that caused Maya's disconnect. Namely, membership at the country club, dinners at the fanciest restaurants, and his decision to downsize to a Camry.

"Atlanta ground control, Atlantica 1945. Taxi from gate thirty-seven," James said.

"Atlantica 1945, Atlanta ground. Taxi runway sixteen right via taxiway November Charlie. Give way to American 357 on November Charlie."

"Roger that. Taxi runway sixteen right via taxiway November Charlie, giving way to American 357 on November Charlie."

"All right," the captain said. "I need the taxi checklist."

Danny nodded, pushing the pig, the prisoner, James, and Maya out of his head. Time to do what he'd trained for his whole life, and do it with precision.

"You've confirmed the passengers in the emergency rows are capable?" GiGi asked Kim.

"Two are guys on their way to backpack across Europe." Kim smiled. "Capable *and* cute."

GiGi counted liquor bottles and kept quiet. No amount of lecturing would do her younger counterparts any good. GiGi had been married three times, twice to pilots, once to a passenger she'd met. All ended disastrously.

She'd hoped to find contentment completely alone, but that hadn't worked out well either. Furthermore, she'd never really wanted to be a flight attendant.

Her mother was a flight attendant back when they had to be registered nurses, had to dye their blond hair brown, and were called stewardesses. They wore girdles, gloves, and two-inch heels and padded their backsides if that's what it took to look their personal best. Before 1965 they couldn't even be married, so her mother, along with many FAs, lied about her marital status. She had to quit flying when she became pregnant with GiGi.

When GiGi began working, it was still a glamorous job, and people dressed up to come onboard an airplane. GiGi was named after a passenger who flew once a week on the airline that her mother worked for. Her mother described the passenger as polished, poised, and always dressed to the nines. She said she never could figure out how she flew so much without a single wrinkle appearing on her clothes. She always ordered seltzer water.

GiGi hated seltzer water. She preferred Dr Pepper and, thanks to the preference, would never have to pad her butt.

When she began working international flights, she was one of the youngsters. She'd got on because she could speak Dutch and

German, thanks to her mother, who'd insisted she would get ahead at the airline if she could speak other languages. She had been right.

She remembered watching the older flight attendants, ankles swollen, hair wiry and gray, wondering what it felt like to be at the end of a lifelong career. Now, here she was, at the end of a career she never really wanted, all because Mom thought that's all she could do.

Admittedly, in her younger days, it had been more fun. Men would flirt. She hung out with the girls and stayed out late. When she'd been picked to move to international, it was a highlight of her career.

But as the years went on, it ceased to be as exciting, and now the wear and tear on her body was getting to her. Her ankles swelled. Her lower back ached every time she pushed the cart and stretched to hand over drinks and meals. Patience these days wore thin.

Thin. Once, her navy blazer and midlength skirt hugged her body in perfect proportion. Now, four sizes larger, she left the blazer unbuttoned and wore a slimmer, which started to cut off circulation about midflight. At least nobody could see her cellulite through the polyester blend.

She used to wonder why the older flight attendants couldn't manage more subtle lipstick, but as she aged, she understood now why bright, bloody red was the way to go. It distracted everyone from the gray roots, the varicose veins, and the blouses that tugged open at the buttonholes.

Kim returned from attending to the Call button. "It's the same guy."

"What guy?"

"He keeps asking for blankets, magazines, pillows."

"I know who you mean—Milk and Cookies. He's becoming a nuisance. I'll go talk to him."

"No, that's okay. At least he's nice about it. I'll tell him we're preparing for takeoff and that we're not a cruise line." She smiled. "Although I do know how to make napkins look like bunnies."

GiGi could read the signs. Kim figured GiGi wouldn't handle it with the smile on her face they were paid to wear. And that was probably true. GiGi wasn't in the mood for irritating passengers.

These days, GiGi wasn't in the mood for much of anything. So why not take it out on the one guy who didn't want to be here? GiGi headed to the back of the plane to check on the prisoner.

Agent Tasler sat erect but didn't seem overly alert as GiGi approached. The row in front of them was empty. "Everything okay back here?" GiGi asked the agent.

The agent nodded, but GiGi couldn't help, just out of curiosity, looking at Leendert. A strange sensation swept over her. With his hands neatly in his lap, held close by shiny silver handcuffs barely visible underneath the jacket laid across his legs, Leendert seemed captivated by her question. Awestruck.

GiGi cleared her throat and looked away. Perhaps he looked awestruck because he knew she knew where the coffeepot was. And how desperate could she get? An old Dutch con man in handcuffs?

Still, he looked harmless enough, except for those blue eyes, swimming like watercolor on a canvas.

What was wrong with her? A burst of self-consciousness warmed her skin, so she occupied herself by opening the overhead bin. She shut it and caught Leendert still studying her, like one might study a rose. Now she was thinking like a Harlequin novel.

She could live with that. She gave him a short, cautious smile.

"I miss those day when the stewardesses give the safety demonstration," he said. His English was off, but there was no misreading his body language.

"Knock it off," the agent said to him.

Leendert shrugged. "It was just more—how do you say—personal back then." He looked at the safety demo video playing overhead.

"I'll be back to check on you," GiGi said, looking at the agent. She headed for the galley, remembering a passenger long ago who, after she had given the seat belt demonstration, quipped, "Baby, you can release my seat belt anytime."

He became her second husband. Not her finest moment. Neither was this.

She pushed everything out of her head as she approached Kim. "How are we coming along?"

"We're fine on meal count."

"We got the ACI onboard, so make certain when you deliver the food to the cockpit, you rotate the meal and put fifteen minutes in between. Also, don't forget to serve the ACI."

Kim grinned. "Danny's cute."

GiGi took the coffee urn out of her hand and set it on the counter. "Kim, I know we don't know each other and you have no reason to trust me, but you may need to grab an oxygen mask because your sensibilities are clearly deprived. Don't fall for a pilot. It's like a nurse falling for a doctor. It's cliché and it rarely works. It seems like the perfect match, but with two different schedules and their egos, it's very difficult to manage."

Kim filled the ice box. "That's what struck me about Danny, though. He doesn't seem to have a big ego."

"Maybe James gobbled it up."

Kim cracked a smile. "Have you talked to the prisoner? That guy has some serious charm."

"Maybe you should transfer to 'Con Air.'"

"Honestly, he doesn't look like he could harm a fly."

"Kim, how long have you been flying internationally?"

"Just six months."

"I see. Well, you're still young, obviously talented, but striking me as a little naive."

"Probably. But I want to see the world. Figured this is a great way to do it."

"It is. I've been on every continent. Just don't be another casualty of the industry, you know? Keep it impersonal with those guys in the cockpit. And when you land and everyone goes to dinner, make sure you let them pick up the tab. It helps them feel important."

The PA system crackled to life.

"Good evening, ladies and gentlemen. Welcome aboard Atlantica Flight 1945, service to Amsterdam. I'm First Officer Daniel McSweeney. Your captain today is C. J. Brewster-Yarley, and we also have First Officer James Lawrence. We are currently taxiing into position and will be ready for takeoff in a few minutes. There's a bit of a line, but we'll do our best to get you in the air as soon as possible. Weather in Amsterdam is currently pleasant, about seventy-two degrees Fahrenheit, twenty-two degrees Celsius, with rain expected later. Our flight over the Atlantic looks smooth, and we don't anticipate any major weather problems."

GiGi scowled. "See? As if they're God and can predict the weather."

"On behalf of this Atlanta-based crew, welcome aboard."

Chapter 12

The sterile cockpit light glowed, and Danny tried to stare at it and not the ACI, who was once again fumbling through his briefcase and looking very disorganized. The air rumbled with planes taking off and landing, but the only sound Danny could focus on was hiccups.

"I'm sorry," Smilt said, glancing around. "It's a hereditary, chronic condition. I have no control over it. It hits during allergy season."

The sterile cockpit rule had just been broken by the man supposed to be enforcing it, but everyone kept quiet. Danny tried a polite smile, but Smilt didn't notice. Instead, he searched for a pen while fighting off the badge that kept hitting him in the chin. His hair stuck together in a point on his forehead.

He looked at Danny, who tried to avert his eyes. It was too late.

"Nice day to fly," Smilt said, seeming more together. He straightened, clicked his pen, and turned a few pages over. "So. Here we are."

Danny looked at the captain, who turned around in her seat.

"Why are you talking?" she asked Smilt, pointing to the light.

Danny bit his lip. He'd never heard a captain speak to an ACI like that before. Of course, he'd never seen an ACI speak during the sterile cockpit.

Smilt cleared his throat, swiping his hair off his forehead. "I'm, um, I'm sorry." Hiccup. "I'm a little disorganized today." Hiccup.

The captain turned around and concentrated on the task at hand. Danny studied Smilt for any signs of offense, but he mostly looked embarrassed and wired. Maybe he was new.

Whatever the case, they needed to find a way to get rid of those hiccups. Like a dripping faucet, they came every five seconds, right on cue.

And something told him James would have a heyday with it.

"Atlantica Flight 1945, you're cleared for takeoff."

"Roger that. Cleared for takeoff."

Danny lived for this moment, above all else. It was by far the most dangerous and exhilarating part. The captain would take off from the States, and then Danny would fly home. James wouldn't fly at all, which was a bummer for the "nonflying pilot." They did the time but didn't get to fly. It was part of the job, and all the FOs had to do it, but nobody liked it.

The captain lined the plane up on the runway. It was time to soar and leave a lot behind. Except the guy with the hiccups.

Lucy stared at the Fasten Seat Belt sign. Of course, there was no chance it would go off now that they were about to take off. She tried to think clearly, tried to reason with herself that if Jeff was onboard, it wouldn't be the end of the world.

So why did it feel like it?

She turned to Hank, who was trying to see out a window from their center row, a large smile spread across his face.

"This is the part that just blew me away last time I flew," he said. "We started rolling down the runway, and then it got faster and faster but never seemed fast enough to just lift into the air. But we did, like we weighed no more than a feather! I love how it pulls you back into your seat."

Lucy tried to let it captivate her. She'd flown a lot, mostly visiting long-distance boyfriends, and she didn't pay attention anymore to how it felt to fly. Maybe that's what was wrong with the world. Nobody got excited about seeing a huge hunk of metal gliding through the air.

She grabbed Hank's hand. It startled him, and he turned to her, looking first at their hands, then at her. "Are you afraid?"

Not of flying, but of what was at the back of the plane. She nodded anyway.

"We'll be fine. I prayed before we left that God's angels would guard us."

Lucy tried not to think about Jeff. She pictured meadows filled with tulips, windmills hundreds of years old, cafés with umbrellas and strong coffee.

The intercom crackled. "Flight attendants, we've been cleared for takeoff."

The plane rolled forward, then with a powerful thrust gained speed, pushing Lucy back into her seat. She watched Hank gaze out the window across the aisle like a child. He even let out a laugh.

Lucy smiled. That's what she needed, to be awed again by the ordinary things in life. She closed her eyes, the blast of the engines causing the seat underneath her to vibrate and her bones to tremble. She listened to every piece of metal on the plane shudder. She felt every bump on the runway.

Then they lifted.

Hank laughed again and turned to her, his eyes wild with excitement. "Unbelievable!" he whispered.

The plane turned, and Lucy caught a glimpse of the ground—gigantic planes, hangars, even the airport shrinking by the second. There was a certain majestic power to this she'd never observed before.

They watched out the window together for a moment, then Hank turned to her. "You okay?"

"I'm fine."

He noticed her fiddling with her rubber, aquamarine bracelet. He peered down at it. "WWOD?" He looked up at her. "What does that stand for?"

"You don't know?"

"I've only seen WWJD."

She smiled. "It stands for What Would Oprah Do." And, to her delight, Oprah would do just this very thing…enjoy the moment.

Then Hank hit his Call button for the flight attendant.

"This turn we're making," Eddie the blimp pilot said, "it's all done by the computer."

The fact that he couldn't turn on any sort of electronic device yet was the only thing standing between Jake and peace and quiet. The plane climbed, and hopefully they'd reach their altitude soon so he could turn his iPod back on. Underneath him, he could hear the landing gears fold into the airplane.

Eddie leaned in. "A little known fact: they only give the plane enough fuel to get to its destination. If they fill her up, it makes the plane heavier, and it burns more fuel. So they calculate the exact amount of fuel needed to get to the destination. That's why, if you're circling above your airport for storms or whatever, chances are you'll have to land elsewhere because you won't have enough fuel to circle for any length of time."

Jake wished Eddie would land elsewhere. At least the conversation with Eddie kept his mind off the fact that the diamonds taped to his belly were worth more than anything else on this airplane, including the fuel.

Jake pointed to the pin Eddie wore on his sweater. "Half a wing?"

"It was my grandfather's. Few people know the important role blimp pilots played in World War II. Bet you didn't even know they were used."

Jake hated to admit it, but there wasn't a whole lot he did know about World War II. He had a feeling that was about to change.

"The United States used them for photographic reconnaissance and antisubmarine patrols. From the air, they could see a submarine rise to the surface and radio in its position. During the war, of the more than eighty thousand ships escorted by airships, not one was lost to enemy action." He fingered the half wing and the anchor attached to it. "My grandfather was a hero. Of course, in the eighties, the military cut off funding for the use of airships. Leave it to the government to get rid of something that saved millions of lives." Eddie leaned into his seat and got comfortable. "My opinion? Airships were like diamonds in the rough, you know?"

"Again?" Kim asked, looking up at the light indicating a passenger needed them.

"This guy needs to get a grip," GiGi said. "We've not even cleared ten thousand feet!"

"At least the pig's asleep."

"True."

GiGi normally served on the A-Line team, caring for the front of the aircraft and the business-class passengers, but with the pig and the prisoner, she had a feeling she'd better hang back with the B-Line and make sure nothing catastrophic happened. She'd been A-Line for so long, she'd nearly forgotten what it was like to stare at the long stretch of rows and realize how fast they had to get the food out to make sure it was still hot.

Kim flipped through a fashion magazine. "I am freezing! I've got to tell them to turn the air down."

"I'll take care of it," GiGi lied. Why share the new thermostat? One of these days these young ones would be begging for this kind of air.

GiGi eyed the hot-looking woman on the front cover of the magazine, drenched like it was some sort of personal goal to shine with one's own oil. Of course, puffy lips can sell about anything, she supposed. She also bet there were eight different ads for antiperspirant in the first twenty pages, because at the end of the day, in the real world, not even fat-lipped women can make sweat sexy.

Her mind wandered to Leendert and that small, admiring smile she'd sensed as she talked to the agent. She pushed away the thought of how desperate she must be for affection and decided to treat it like a perk. He did have gorgeous eyes.

"What are you thinking about?"

GiGi cut her eyes sideways at Kim, and now Sandy, who were both looking at her. She realized she was smiling. "Just enjoying how much the pilots must be sweating right now."

Sandy said, "I was on a domestic, and one of the FOs had a total nervous breakdown about the ACI. He had, like, a panic attack or something!"

"Glad nobody's watching us like that." Kim flipped a page.

"Keeps them humble," GiGi said. "And when there's no ACI onboard, sometimes you gotta do it yourself. Lean in, listen, and learn, ladies."

Kim closed her magazine, and Sandy winked.

"This is better than anything you'll find in there," GiGi said, nodding at the magazine. "Okay, this was a while back, when I flew domestics to the East Coast. Every so often, I'd end up with Captain Jerry Boderry. I swear that was his real name." Sandy and Kim cracked up. "Let me sum up Jerry with this illustration. At the hotel, Jerry wore a Speedo to the pool."

The girls grimaced.

"Married, five kids."

"Oh, that's disgusting," Kim said.

"We flew to three major cities. In every one he had a girlfriend to hook up with when we were there, and without ever specifically mentioning them, he did plenty of alluding, like they were some sort of prize. I confronted him about it one time, and he told me if I was lucky, I might become number four."

Kim's jaw dropped. "He did not! What a creep!"

"So, during flight, I snuck his bag out of the closet, opened it, and pulled out his shirt from the day before. I took it to the bathroom, applied a fresh coat of fire red lipstick, and planted a nice kiss right on the collar. Then I folded it, stuck it back in the bag, and, well, the rest you can guess."

Sandy and Kim glanced at each other.

"Ladies, they're all the same. I know you want to think the egos are few and far between, but you give a guy this much power, fuel, and fire, and they can't help themselves."

"I've met some nice pilots," Kim said.

"Yeah. And you're single, right, Kim? You better start putting two and two together."

Kim pressed her lips together, like she was holding in a barrage of disagreement.

"Honey," GiGi said. "Trust me on this. I've been flying a long time. They don't respect us. We're just entertainment for a night."

"What happened to Jerry Boderry?" Sandy asked.

"Well, rumor has it he pays three thousand dollars a month in child support and gained too much weight for a Speedo."

The captain signaled they'd cleared ten thousand feet. GiGi unfastened her seat belt. "All right, ladies. Let's get these people fed and put to bed. And Kim, go tell the freak in 20E that we have two hundred and three other passengers onboard, okay?"

"I think I should punch it again," Hank said, staring up at the light. "Maybe it didn't work."

"They can't get up now," Lucy said, eying him. "They have to wait until it's safe. What did you need?"

"There's not a barf bag in my pocket."

Lucy leaned away. "Are you going to barf?"

"No. But every passenger should have one."

"You can have mine."

"That's okay. I want my own."

"I fly a lot, and flight attendants, they don't really like high-maintenance passengers."

"I think this airline is different. Didn't you hear them before we took off? 'If there's anything we can do to make your flight more comfortable, please let us know. We look forward to serving you.'" Hank smiled. "I like that motto. If everyone could just treat one another like that, you know?"

Lucy studied him. He was dead serious. "Hank, they don't really mean that."

"What are you talking about?"

"They just say that to sound pleasant."

Hank smiled. "Well, I'm going to give them the benefit of the doubt."

"Hank, you're really one of a kind."

"Why?"

"Today there's so much doubt and too little benefit. I mean, there's, like, no negative energy around you."

"Not true. I've got static electricity making my slacks cling."

"I'm serious. How do you do that?"

"God."

"I'm tracking with everything you're saying," Lucy smiled. She was, until he mentioned God. She could trust the universe, which held everything in a delicate balance. Somehow, someway, there was something good for her in this life, something blessed waiting for her. Mother Nature had been giving her signs for weeks.

"God has good things for you, Lucy, if you trust Him."

"I don't believe in God. I'm an atheist."

The first distressed look she'd seen on Hank popped onto his face.

"But I do believe there is an energy we all share that flows throughout the earth, connecting us as human beings. It's powerful. I think it's the force that keeps the good in us, helps us find happiness."

Hank looked down at his hands. "Oh."

"What?"

"It's just, I don't believe in atheists."

"You don't believe in atheists?"

"God says that everyone is given a measure of faith."

"Sir?"

They both looked up to find one of the flight attendants standing above them.

"I think you accidentally pushed your flight attendant Call button. Right? So let's turn this off, and we'll be by with drinks momentarily."

"Actually," Hank said as she turned to walk away, "I need a bag."

"A bag?"

"The blue one. I don't have one." He pointed to the pocket, then smiled. "I would hate to not be prepared."

"Yes. We would hate that too." She turned, and Hank jotted down a note.

"What are you writing over there?" Lucy asked.

"Top-secret stuff." He smiled, turning his pad over.

"So," Lucy said, crossing her arms, "I suppose you want to talk about God, convince me He's real?"

"Not really. I want to talk about why you keep looking over your shoulder to the back of the plane."

GiGi flew down the aisle toward the Call button light. She did not have time for this. Well, that wasn't exactly true. She didn't have the patience for it. She glanced at Leendert, who grinned at her. She didn't return the favor.

"Oh no," she sighed. The light belonged to the guy who couldn't stop clutching his stomach. This was not a good sign. "Sir, are you okay?"

His eyes widened. "Why?"

"Your Call button."

"I know, but why do you assume I'm not okay?"

"You're sweating. Is your stomach still bothering you?"

The guy next to him said, "I have EMT training."

"I was hoping I could change seats. Just something with a little more room."

"I've adjusted the temperature. You should feel it soon. I already feel better myself. As far as seats, there are a couple near the back."

"Great."

The man followed GiGi to the back, passing the cranky old bat who kept complaining about the pig, not that GiGi was fond of the hoofed animal. The woman's ancient mother slept soundly next to her, so GiGi hoped the woman would stay quiet.

"Is this okay?" GiGi asked, pointing to the very last seat on the aisle.

"Perfect."

"Just let me know if you need anything, especially if it gets too hot for you."

"Really, I'm fine. I'm not hot, and I'm not sick."

"Uh-huh. Look, don't play the tough guy, okay? I once flew with a planeload of firefighters coming back from a convention. We hit some turbulence, and well, let's just say those boys were no match for a pocket of air. I'm feeling hot again, so I'll go check the temp, okay?"

The man nodded, and GiGi went up front to turn down the thermostat and check on the A-Line.

"Everything's nice and quiet," Gloria said. "I can't believe you're working B-Line."

"Me either, but I'll survive. I gotta check on our emotionally disturbed pax." GiGi glanced toward the family with small kids and the man who kept insisting his briefcase might be stolen from the overhead bin, then went to see the pig lady.

"How are you two doing?" GiGi couldn't quite muster up the right expression—it hung somewhere between a courtesy smile and complete disgust as she eyed the pig, fast asleep but huffing and puffing like it'd just come off a treadmill. The woman stroked the pig like it had fur, but it didn't—just random, wiry white hairs sticking up like her uncle Ned's. Its pink skin resembled what her legs might look like if she didn't moisturize with pharmaceutical-grade lotion she'd blackmailed out of her dermatologist.

The woman looked at her pig. "He's napping pretty hard. Usually he closes his eyes but doesn't really sleep. He's out cold, though." She sounded slightly nervous. "Are we going to hit turbulence?"

GiGi tried her calm voice, the one she used with FAs who had a hard time getting a grip for one reason or another. "Ma'am, you are perfectly safe. The airplane has been checked out by top mechanics, the pilots have years of experience, and thousands of people travel across the Atlantic every day. I promise, we'll get you there safely."

"But what about the turbulence?"

"Ma'am, turbulence is just part of flying. It's nothing to be alarmed about."

"I'm not alarmed," Pig Lady said, stroking Chucky a little faster, "but I would like to be prepared."

Nothing could prepare anyone for turbulence, which was why most airline injuries were a result of turbulence. The pilots always said it looked like a smooth ride ahead, but in actuality, it was like guessing where an age spot might pop up.

She supposed it was as unpredictable as life itself.

But that wouldn't help Ms. Piggy. "We have very sophisticated computers that predict this sort of thing. Just pay attention to the seat-belt light and you'll be fine."

"Um, okay. Maybe I could get some water?"

"Sure. Just a second."

GiGi made her way to the back to the galley where Kim was ready with the drink cart. "I need a water."

"Everything okay?" she asked as she poured.

GiGi took the cup and gulped it. "As long as that pig and that old lady stay asleep, I think we'll be fine. Is it hot in here?"

"I'm freezing, actually."

GiGi rolled her eyes and vowed to keep the thermostat a carefully guarded secret.

Kim said, "Did you know that Boeing just installed a cabin-controlled thermostat?"

Chapter 13

D anny opened one eye and checked his watch. He'd barely slept, but that wasn't unusual for the first break. The great thing about being the relief pilot was actually flying the airplane on the way home. That meant, however, that he had to take the first break on the way there, which was the hardest to sleep during. Dinner service, alive and active, meant lots of noise and activity, with people getting up and down for bathroom breaks, reading, and laughing at the inflight movies. The other drag was that by the time he returned to the cockpit at the end of his break, the meal they'd saved for him would be just warm enough to tease him into thinking it might taste good.

He still had a few minutes, so he kept his eyes closed and tried to relax. He chuckled as he listened to the A-Line discuss the thermostat. One of the ladies said, "Finally, the temperature feels normal. Don't let GiGi near that thing, and if she turns it down, turn it back."

He had to admit that was a genius move by the captain. Cabin temperature on internationals always became a battle, which was half the reason he carried a sweater with him and pulled it over his uniform when he went on break.

The other half of the reason was to blend in. Most of the time, the business-class passengers had no interest in striking up conversations with anyone, but occasionally, there would be one person who'd wanted to be a pilot his entire life and decided Danny's break was a good time to ask a few questions.

Thankfully, nobody bothered him, but he still only managed a light catnap. He wondered what was going on in the cockpit— whether James had made a fool of himself, whether the ACI had gotten rid of his hiccups, and what, exactly, was the captain doing? She was a curious soul.

He rose and took a bathroom break, pulled off his sweater, then decided to check on Anna Sue and Chucky.

"How are you two doing?" Danny said, squatting by her seat. He looked at Chucky. "He seems perfectly comfortable."

Anna Sue nodded, a faint smile indicating more worry than anything. "He normally doesn't sleep this much."

"Well, flying can do that to people and, um, pigs. Are you...doing okay?" He wasn't sure if this was a safe or even legal question for an "emotionally challenged" woman.

A grin broke through her anxious expression. "Yes, I really am. I have to remind myself sometimes, you know? Everything is fine, I'm feeling fine, so no need to worry, right?" She stroked Chucky.

Danny patted her arm. "Right. Let us know if we can do anything for you, okay?"

"I will. Thank you so much. You've been so kind." She lowered her voice. "And I think the rest of the passengers have accepted Chucky. I haven't heard anybody complain."

Danny nodded, rose, and found GiGi in the back of the airplane. "Why are you back here?"

"Well, Danny, we have a pig, a prisoner, a woman who hates pigs, a passenger who has requested a barf bag, and another one who probably needs one but won't admit it. I thought it better that I station myself here, just in case, you know, something gets weird." She looked at him like it was all his fault.

"Well, it is a full moon."

"Don't remind me."

"Everything okay? Is the prisoner minding his manners?"

"Not as much as the pig. But we'll handle him."

"What about the passenger who wanted the barf bag?"

"He's fine. He's just high maintenance."

"All right. Well, hang in there. Only eight more hours to go."

That, finally, drew a smile from GiGi. "So what's going on in the cocky-pit? Nothing fun with an ACI, I'm sure."

"An ACI with hiccups."

"I guess you have your hands full too." She leaned in. "And Captain Brewster-Yarley? What a wack job, huh?"

"Well, she's easier to handle than James."

GiGi indicated she couldn't agree more.

"Okay, I better get up there. Let me know if people start howling and growing fangs."

GiGi laughed and Danny smiled as he walked to the front of the aircraft. A little kindness went a long way, except in a long-term engagement, in which case it obviously meant nothing.

Gloria moved the drink cart to block someone storming into the cockpit as Danny gave the secret knock.

"Welcome back, Bubba," the captain said.

"Um, thanks. How's it going up here?"

"Great," James said flatly.

Danny buckled into the jump seat across from Smilt and tried a friendly smile. Smilt nodded as he tapped his pencil against his clipboard, his gaze wandering around the cockpit like he hadn't been sitting there for two hours.

The captain sighed, loudly. It was almost a moan, enough to make everyone turn, but not quite enough to assure one that inquiry was needed.

"I remember the old days, you know," she said, staring out at the clouds as they passed through the top of a thunderhead. "They used to let kids come up here, sit in our laps, and look out the front. You know they used to serve sodas up here in *glasses*? Real glass, like the windshield. Nothing but a thin sheet of glass separating us and a five-hundred-mile-per-hour wind. Still gives me shivers when I think about it. Anyway, I miss that kind of service. Of course, we have it better than those before us. It wasn't so long ago that the pilots got the leftovers, if there were any. Times have changed." She sighed again.

Danny glanced at James, whose expression screamed, *Bermuda Triangle! Please!* If what James said was true, he'd be an idiot to bring it up. But then, James was an idiot, so one could only wait and see.

"I'm really going to miss this windshield." The captain reached out and touched it.

Danny cleared his throat. "Ma'am? Miss it?"

"This is my last flight."

"You're…"

"Retiring?" James finished.

"Only because I have to."

A twinge of panic shot through Danny. Where were the balloons and the cake? When a pilot retired, it was a huge deal, especially for their last flight. The retiring pilot got to choose the trip and the crew. And the pilot's spouse and family could come along in first class, reserved seats. There was some sort of big dessert onboard. Signs, posters, banners. At the overnight hotel there would be champagne and more cake. And weather permitting, at home port the pilot would make a low pass before landing.

But there had been no fanfare at the airport, nothing indicating a celebration was planned. Nobody mentioned any of the captain's family or relatives being onboard.

Danny glanced at the ACI for his reaction. Smilt stared at his pencil like it might jump into the conversation at any moment.

"We, uh, didn't know," Danny said, more meekly than intended.

The captain's fingers left the windshield. She glanced at one of her sticky notes and said, "So, Bubba, what's your story?"

"My story?"

"He's disengaged," James said with a wry smile. He laughed. "That's funny. 'Disengaged.' Maybe there's a double meaning there, huh, Danny? Engagement didn't work out because you were disengaged? I'm only kidding. Don't freak out."

Danny clenched his jaw. "I'm not freaking out."

"You look like you're about to, man. Sorry. Maybe I'm reading body language wrong, but your knuckles are white and your jaw muscles are protruding."

Danny bit his lip and tried not to glare.

"I'm sorry to hear it didn't work out," the captain said.

This was getting awkward. Danny didn't want pity, but he didn't want an obnoxious disregard for his pain either. He felt a warm blush crawl up his neck, and when the long silence kicked in, he did what he knew he shouldn't. "Her name was Maya. We dated for six years, three of those engaged."

"I guess her name still is Maya, isn't it? She's gone but not dead, Danny. Although, if it's easier to think of her as dead, maybe that's the route you should take to get over her," James said. "Corpses are definitely less hot."

"I'm over her," Danny hustled into the conversation. Nobody had to know they'd just broken up—if he could keep his stupid mouth shut. "She wasn't the right one. I mean, *isn't* the right one."

"It took six years to figure that out?" James groaned and patted his belly like he'd just eaten a twenty-ounce steak. "You're more of a man than I am, Danny. I couldn't wait that long, you know what I mean? A man has needs." James's eyes widened as he turned to face Danny. "Unless, of course, you broke the sixth commandment."

"Boy," the captain said. "The sixth commandment is thou shall not kill."

"I didn't break, I mean…look, it's none of your business—"

"Don't go all sixth commandment on the messenger," James said, holding up his hands. "I'm not the one who etched it into a stone tablet." James jabbed a thumb toward the sky. "The Big Man upstairs is the one who said no funny business before marriage. Let me put it in a way you can understand, okay? Song of Solomon, right? The book's all about sex. Those two were clearly hitched. It says his dove was all locked up before he got there."

"I have no idea what a dove has to do with this, but I loved Maya and—"

"Let me make it simple. You're the apple tree, Danny, and you need to keep your apples to yourself, okay? Clear enough? You disregard His rules, but then you want His blessings? God's not some pie-in-the-sky, cosmic vending machine of blessings, Danny. He doesn't hand out free quarters to sinners"—James grinned—"but the good news is that you have a long life in front of you. You've got plenty of time to make it up to God."

That didn't sound like good news. It sounded like failure waiting to happen.

Danny stared at the ACI. He could almost read his thoughts. *Come on. Get aggressive. Would love to write you up for a temper problem.* Maybe God was thinking the same thing.

Any defense he made would sound pathetic. How do you explain that a six-year relationship went up in smoke over the lack of a six-figure income? And how could he admit to anyone that he'd suspected all along that Maya was more in love with the idea of marrying a pilot than the pilot himself?

They'd met not long after 9/11. Things looked unstable for the entire aviation industry, which in a life filled with an abundance of bad timing, meant that he was, of course, going to meet the most beautiful woman he'd ever seen.

About three years after 9/11, things stabilized, but would never be the same. He was making half of what he would have had 9/11 never happened, but he had to either accept it or find a new occupation. Even with Maya's income, they were barely able to afford their condo. Living apart seemed impractical and even more costly.

Every conversation they had seemed to revolve around money. One night he said to her, "Maya, who cares where we live? Who cares if we don't have the fancy house and the expensive cars? We've got each other. That's all that matters."

She got up and left, slamming the door behind her.

That was the first in a very long line of red flags.

"If you get lucky," James said, "maybe God'll give you a second chance."

The ACI stared. Danny gripped the bottom of his seat to keep from trembling. He didn't want to talk about Maya or his sin or anything else about himself. He wanted to crawl over the back of James's seat and knock him unconscious. But what ended up coming out of his mouth was more mortifying than either of those things.

"Captain, what about your crash into the Bermuda?"

Lucy groaned, leaning forward and resting her forehead on the back of the seat in front of her. "What would you do if it were you, Hank? What if you thought you had an ex-girlfriend onboard?"

"I've never, um, dated anyone."

"You haven't?"

"I'm kind of shy."

"You don't seem shy to me."

"You're easy to talk to."

Lucy felt the tension melt off her body. "That is very sweet of you to say." She leaned toward him. "You know what? I don't have to know, do I?"

"You don't?"

"No. Who cares if he's on this airplane? I'm a complete person without him. I'm happy without him." She grabbed a *Sky-Mall* catalog and began flipping through it. "They have the coolest things in here."

"I can go back and check if you want."

Lucy slapped the magazine closed. "Would you?"

"Sure. I think you'll feel much better knowing either way."

"It's ridiculous for me to think he's onboard. I'm certain it's a figment of my imagination. Besides, even if he is onboard, I'm completely over him."

"What does he look like?"

"I've got a picture of him right here," Lucy said, reaching into her wallet. She pulled it out and handed it over without looking at it. It was a photo taken at a party they'd attended a few months back. Jeff slouched on a couch, a cheesy party grin on his face, while Lucy hugged his neck, their cheeks pressed together. It was one of her favorite photos.

Hank studied the picture. "What's his name?"

"Jeff."

"All right. Let me go see if Jeff is onboard."

"Not that it matters," she said as Hank unbuckled his seat belt.

"Are you certain you're going to be all right if he is?"

"Absolutely." *Unless he's with a blonde.*

"Okay. I'll be right back."

Hank turned and walked toward the back of the airplane. The man to Lucy's left seemed to be trying not to eavesdrop. Closing her eyes, Lucy focused and centered herself. She allowed only positive thoughts into her head, which at the moment were hard to come by, so she focused on Hank, a kind stranger she was fortunate enough to sit next to on a long airplane ride.

She tried not to count the seconds, but it seemed he was taking a long time, which was probably a good sign. Most likely, he hadn't spotted Jeff and was looking one more time.

And then, from the back of the plane, came a bloodcurdling scream.

Chapter 14

G iGi whipped around, nearly dropping the coffee urn. "Did someone just scream?"

Kim nodded, and they filed out of the galley and into the main cabin. It wasn't hard to spot the commotion. The elderly woman who'd made such a stink about the pig was standing and waving her hands. A few other people stood around her.

"What is it now? The pig's making a pass at her?" GiGi stormed down the aisle, glancing toward Miss Piggy, but no unusual activity came from that portion of the plane.

Call buttons started going off just as GiGi reached the huddle of people. "Sit down. Please, everyone, sit down." The passengers complied, except the elderly woman who stepped right in front of GiGi.

"It's my mother!" she gasped. "My mother!"

GiGi looked down at the elder of the two women.

"I can't wake her up!"

GiGi turned to Kim. "Make an announcement asking if there is a doctor onboard. Then alert the cockpit." She focused on the old woman, who at first glance looked asleep. Or dead. An icy chill raced up GiGi's spine.

"Attention, if there is a doctor or nurse onboard, please push your Call button. Thank you."

GiGi knelt beside the unconscious woman, taking her hand and patting it lightly while discreetly placing two fingers under her wrist and checking for a pulse. "Ma'am? Ma'am?"

"She's not responding!" cried the old woman.

"I don't think we have a doctor onboard. The captain's coming," Kim whispered to GiGi.

"Ma'am? Can you hear me?" GiGi moved her fingers a few centimeters, still trying to find a pulse.

Kim tried to calm the unconscious woman's daughter, but she yanked her arm away. GiGi knew her next move would cause a lot of distress, but she had no choice but to confirm her suspicions by attempting to find a pulse in the woman's neck. Sandy brought the paddles.

Someone tapped on her shoulder.

"I can help," the man said. She recognized him as the passenger seated next to the stomach-clenching kid.

"Are you a doctor?"

"No. I'm an airship pilot. But before that I was a lifeguard. I have EMT training. I can do CPR."

"A lifeguard." GiGi found it hard to imagine, but maybe he meant in his younger years.

"Step aside, people. Give her room to breathe," said the man.

GiGi and Kim exchanged glances. That was probably not necessary.

He squatted, his backside bumping into the seat across the aisle, and pushed up the sleeves of his sweater. He took the probably-dead woman's hand. "Ma'am?"

"We already tried that," GiGi said.

He checked her pulse, put his head to her chest, and did a few odd things with her elbow before he finally stood and pronounced, "I'm going to start CPR."

"You can't," said her daughter. She wiped her eyes. "She has these." She pulled folded papers from her purse. "Do Not Resuscitate papers. She's wanted to die since she turned eighty-eight. She specifically states in these to not revive her by any means."

"She's definitely dead," said the lifeguard guy. "In these cases, we just do CPR to make everyone feel better."

GiGi glared at the man, wondering why he hadn't been more tactful. They were never supposed to pronounce anyone officially dead while onboard. It meant a lot of hassle, often even taking the plane out of service.

"What's going on?" The captain stood behind GiGi.

"What's going on," the old woman screeched, "is that my mother is dead, and it's because of that pig!"

In a low voice, GiGi said, "We can't find a pulse."

The captain, along with everyone else, looked down at the woman, who still, despite the lack of pulse or color in her cheeks, looked peaceful. Peacefully dead. The captain put her fingers on the woman's neck, checking both sides, and then the wrist. She turned to the daughter. "How long has she been like this?"

The elderly woman wailed, covering her mouth and shaking her head. GiGi slipped the captain the papers, knowing she'd ask in order to determine whether or not they had any reason to attempt resuscitation.

"I thought she was asleep," the daughter said. "Maybe…a couple of…hours."

"Cause of death unknown," said the lifeguard guy.

"Would you shut up?" GiGi whispered. "It's rather obvious why she died."

The captain asked the passenger across the aisle to temporarily move to an empty seat and then helped the woman sit down. "Let's get her some water."

GiGi nodded at Kim, who rushed away.

"I just can't believe this," the woman said. "I can't believe she's gone."

"Ma'am," GiGi said, "obviously your mother had a very long life. I know this is sad, but perhaps not unexpected?"

"To let that *beast* onboard! This is an elderly woman. How is she supposed to react to conditions like that!"

As far as GiGi could tell, the woman was so old it was possible she wasn't even aware she was on an airplane, much less an airplane with a pig.

"I am going to sue!"

"All right, ma'am," the captain said, "you need to calm down and take a few deep breaths. We're here to help you."

The in-another-life guard said, "Captain, from one pilot to another, my suggestion would be to—"

"Return to your seat."

With an audible huff, the man stomped away.

Another tirade was about to burst from the red-faced daughter when a man approached from the other direction, kneeling beside her and taking her hand. She almost ripped her hand away, but then she looked at the young man's face. They all did. Plump tears balanced on the rims of his eyes.

"I lost my mom too."

The elderly woman glanced around, but seemed drawn back to him as he handed her a handkerchief.

"What was your mom's name?" the blond man asked.

The woman hesitated, looked across the aisle at her mother, and said, "Henrietta. Everyone called her Hetty. She hated to be called Mrs. anything."

"Hetty." The man smiled, and GiGi recognized him as the guy keeping the flight attendants busy with his requests. Her first impulse was to order him back to his seat, but the old lady was responding to him, so she took a "wait and see" attitude.

"I'm Hank. What's your name?"

She raised an eyebrow at him and said, "Well, to you, young man, I am Mrs. Kilpatrick."

Hank smiled and put his other hand on top of hers. "Mrs.

Kilpatrick, I can't imagine what you're going through right now, but I do know what it's like to lose a parent unexpectedly."

Mrs. Kilpatrick's gaze drifted to her mother again. "The doctor said she was in good health. I was taking her back to her birthplace. My father is buried there. He died thirty years ago. She was longing to see her homeland again. I tried to talk her out of it, but she insisted."

"Mrs. Kilpatrick, if it wouldn't embarrass you too much, I'd like to pray for you right now."

Her gloomy eyes brightened. "Are you a pastor?"

"No." He smiled. "Just your run-of-the-mill Christian."

"Then *why* in the world would I want you to pray for me!" her voice boomed. "Get out of my face. All of you. Let me alone." She slumped in the seat across the aisle from her mother and wept.

The man looked shocked but not angry. "Of course." He backed away, and GiGi felt a twinge of sadness for him. But if he asked for softer tissues, she'd smack him.

"Mrs. Kilpatrick, I'm going to have Kim stay with you for a moment while I confer with my pilots," the captain said.

"While you're up there, get in touch with your airline's attorney," Mrs. Kilpatrick said.

The captain nodded. "GiGi, accompany me?"

GiGi followed the captain up the aisle and past grumbling and worried passengers, all trying to get a glimpse of the tragedy.

What she wouldn't give for your run-of-the-mill, sick, cranky passenger right now.

Jake settled into his seat. A scream and some commotion caught his attention before he sat down, but a flight attendant instructed everyone to stay in their seats. Thankfully, he'd relocated away from Eddie before that announcement.

However, he couldn't help feeling a sting of paranoia. It wasn't often one heard a scream on an airplane, and he'd assumed if he did hear one, it would be his own. It was silly, he knew. Also silly was taking the inflight movie *The Italian Job* as a secret sign that his life was going to end in a dramatically bloody, Hollywood sort of way.

He'd chosen the very last seat, the one nobody wanted by the restrooms and the galley, where the pungent smell of filtered sewage water created discomfort matched only by the frightening sound of a sucking toilet. If you ever fell in while flushing, you'd probably lose a limb.

A variety of passengers shared the back of the airplane with him, including a man with dreadlocks who nodded off every few seconds and a teenager reading *Playboy* like he was the only one on the aircraft. On his other side sat a stern-looking woman next to an older man. Jake wondered if they were together, as they spoke to each other once in a while. Maybe father and daughter, except one sounded Dutch.

Dutch. As frightening as this all was, meeting his Dutch grandmother seemed equally as terrifying as losing his life by diamond couriering or a limb by airplane lavatory. He knew what she looked like, which was half the problem. In every picture he'd ever seen of her, she stared at the camera like it had personally insulted her.

And then *he* had personally insulted her by not being Dutch enough. Dutch enough? Not Dutch at all. The only hint was Van and Der. He was American, and sometimes an insult to that country too. But he loved his country and all the opportunity it offered him, though much to his parents' dismay, he rarely took it.

They'd come to America hoping he'd be a doctor or lawyer or *something*. They never understood how hard he worked at his music, and they died long before his band started to do more than practice in garages.

Closing his eyes, Jake slid his hands over his belly again, but this time for a nap. He let his iPod blare and decided to talk himself out of his paranoia.

He was on a plane thousands of feet in the sky over the Atlantic. He was perfectly safe.

Now, if he could just tune out that toilet.

The cockpit was hot, and Perry wanted to loosen his collar, but he didn't dare. He didn't move a muscle, except for his arm, which inched slowly toward a storage bin to the left of his jump seat. The conversation continued.

"Look, I didn't mean to offend you."

"Let's just drop it. I'm more concerned about what's going on in the cabin," Danny replied.

"The captain will let us know when she can."

"I realize that."

"Had I known you'd slip up on the Bermuda thing, I'd have saved my speech for later."

"Why not save it, period? Thanks."

"Speaking of saved, you're not and I think you should be."

"Let's just concentrate on the—"

The knock startled them all.

"Mr. Smilt, would you mind?" Danny asked.

Retracting his hand, Perry rose and unlocked the door.

"All right," the captain said as she entered, "I've asked GiGi to join us. We have some things to discuss. An elderly woman has died. We've already passed Gander. We could make an emergency landing in Iceland, but we'd have reroute and turn back to get there."

GiGi spoke up. "Let me remind everyone that we have an emotionally challenged woman onboard, and I'm not talking about the dead lady's daughter."

"We'll refer to her as Hetty, not 'dead lady,'" the captain said.

"GiGi brings up a good point," Danny said.

"The pig lady could be unpredictable," James said.

"Her name is Anna Sue," Danny added.

The captain continued. "Landing in Iceland will cause a huge inconvenience for everyone, and I'm not certain it would solve the problem. Frankly, the problem is unsolvable, as the woman is dead. However, continuing on to the Netherlands will cause other problems. Either way, I believe we're going to have distressed passengers. So a decision will be made, we'll make the best of it, and we'll show a united front. Mr. Smilt, what do you think?"

"I, uh…of what?"

"Should we make an emergency landing in Iceland or proceed to the Netherlands?"

"We land in the Netherlands," Perry said. "There's no question about it."

"Mr. Smilt, there's always a question about it, and ultimately it's my call," the captain said. "However, I happen to agree with your assessment of the situation."

"What?" GiGi yelped. "You're telling me that we're going to have a dead woman on our flight *along* with her daughter, who wants to murder all of us and serve up the pig for breakfast?"

"We're not going to let the passengers know there is any other option," the captain replied. "We will take extra care and assist our passengers in coping with this. We are all going to remain calm. Understood?"

Everyone nodded, so Perry did too.

"Bubba, I want you to go into the cabin, talk to Mrs. Kilpatrick."

"Me? Why?"

"Because you're naturally likable."

"What…what does that have to do with, um, dead people?" Danny asked.

"We need someone with the ability to calm her down. You have that effect on people."

"No, I don't."

"You do, Bubba."

"No, I really don't. I wouldn't even know what to say."

"You explain to her that we're going to clear a row at the back of the airplane. We're going to lay her mother across the center row and cover her with a blanket. Mrs. Kilpatrick is welcome to sit wherever she wants."

"But...but..."

"GiGi, you and the rest of the flight attendants are going to move everyone forward as far as you can."

"Who's moving the body?" GiGi asked.

"Bubba, there was a man onboard who offered to pray for Mrs. Kilpatrick. GiGi can find him. He'll help you."

"Why can't I move the body?" James asked.

"Boy, quiet. After you get Mrs. Kilpatrick and Hetty settled, Bubba, I'd like you to check on Anna Sue."

The flight attendant groaned. "I am telling you, she is going to flip out, if she hasn't already. We are talking about an emotionally challenged woman. She was already about to chew a hole through her lip at the possibility of turbulence. What is she going to do now? A woman is dead and her daughter thinks it's because of the pig! I mean, I'm not emotionally challenged, and I feel like *I* need to assume the fetal position."

"Bubba can handle her. All right, let's begin. I'll make an announcement from here."

The cockpit door opened. Danny and GiGi left. The pilots resumed their positions in their seats.

"Mr. Smilt, I suppose you've never had this much excitement on a flight," the captain said.

Perry tried a polite smile. "Yes, well, as they said, you've crash-landed in the Bermuda Triangle. This is a piece of cake."

Her smile faded, and she turned so he could only see the back of her head, which was fine with him. He had what he needed for Plan C.

And Miles thought he had poor planning skills. Please! He had a sack full of diamonds within reach and now possessed a gun he'd happened upon while pretending to inspect storage bins in the cockpit. Unlike Miles, Perry could be flexible, and this kind of flexibility and attention to detail—like the gun he'd stolen from the storage compartment—gave him an even bigger edge.

The gun comforted him. He'd sensed the captain's suspicions from the beginning. Or maybe he was just nervous. Whatever the case, a dead body, as long as it wasn't his, could only work in his favor at this point. It already had, in fact. It had distracted an entire cockpit full of people enough for Perry to slip the gun from the storage compartment into his briefcase.

He didn't know if he could endure much more of this "Bubba" and "Boy" talk, especially about girlfriends and God. He wanted to scream *shut up,* but he knew he must remain quiet, calm, and under the radar.

Now he just had to find Jaap Van Der Mark. And if another dead body came out of it, so be it. At least he'd be rich.

Chapter 15

W hat's going on back there?"

"A woman died."

Lucy covered her mouth. "Oh, that's terrible." Hank seemed shaken. "Are you okay?"

"I'm fine. I just feel bad for her daughter. It doesn't matter how old or young you are, losing a parent isn't easy. If you'll excuse me, I'm going to take a moment to pray for her."

Lucy retracted her hand. "Now?"

"To myself."

"I'll do the same."

"You don't believe in God."

"I'm praying to the universe." Lucy closed her eyes, centered herself, produced thoughts of life rather than death, and pictured bright lights. But no matter how hard she concentrated, she couldn't stop wondering whether or not Hank had seen Jeff back there.

She opened her eyes, and waited for Hank to open his. Several minutes passed and Lucy grew impatient. Finally, though, he finished. He looked sad.

"Are you okay? Are you thinking about your parents?"

"No." His voice was distant. "I just...I'm worried about that woman."

"She's in a better place. I don't know where that is or what it's like, but I believe with all my heart that good people find peace after death."

"I'm talking about her daughter. She's very angry, and I don't think it has anything to do with her mom's passing away."

"How do you know she's angry?"

"She yelled at me when I asked if she would like me to pray for her."

Lucy gasped. "She did? What a jerk! People are so pathetic. I mean, Hank, you're a kind, decent person. That's obvious before you even say anything! She's probably just a horrible, bitter person."

Hank turned to her and frowned. "Lucy, how can you say that? You don't even know her."

Lucy blinked. Okay, that was true, but in the order of the universe, people bond over other people's weaknesses. It's a fight-or-flight sort of thing. And they were on a flight that almost erupted into a fight, so...

"You're right, Hank. Absolutely. I didn't stop to think about that." She realized it was going to take some finesse to get details out of him about whether or not he'd spotted Jeff while being lambasted by a passenger. To ask now seemed cold. She wasn't cold, just focused. "Maybe I've been overly harsh with Jeff too," she tried. "He is, after all, human." *Subhuman, but human nevertheless.*

Hank didn't take the bait.

"It's just that when someone hurts you, your first instinct is to hurt them back. Of course, that's wrong." She tried to say it with conviction.

He smiled at her with a warmness she wasn't expecting. "It's natural to feel that way. It's human nature."

Lucy's head spun. If it was human nature, why didn't it seem to faze him that a woman came unglued on him? Hank seemed a little unnatural.

"Once," he began, "this guy was giving my sister a hard time. She's a police officer, and he thought she didn't fit in as an undercover cop, so he kept trying to make her feel bad about herself."

"What'd she do?"

"Ultimately she proved him wrong by being great at what she does, but it wasn't easy. I wanted to put him in his place."

Lucy smiled. *Exactly.* Except she had a sneaking suspicion he didn't.

"But I didn't."

"Of course. Because that would be wrong." Lucy thought she might be getting the hang of this.

"Perhaps, but the real reason I never did was because my sister is really good at that in her own right. I mean, she has this amazing ability to just throw people to the ground with her tongue. She got in trouble for it all the time when we were kids. She also has a terrible temper. I thought if I tried it, I'd just look stupid."

Lucy's mouth hung open because the universe wasn't feeding her a response.

"And then I wondered why I cared. I did some deep soul searching with the help of the Holy Spirit, and it turns out I was dealing with some insecurities about myself. I never felt like I measured up to the rest of my siblings because I can be shy, so God is helping me realize He made me like this and that I have my own strengths."

Lucy stared forward, trying to find her centeredness, trying to capture any negativity that might be causing her own self-doubt.

Self-doubt. That was it. That was the negative energy burst that continued to blind her points of light. Even as she thought it, a dark shadow crawled across her tray table and over the seatback of the passenger in front of her. Lucy shuddered, but then realized it was the shadow of the flight attendant who stood over them.

With a particularly sour expression, she fixed her gaze on Hank. "I realize you're probably due for a pillow fluffing, but the captain would like your assistance moving the body to the back of the airplane."

"Of course." Hank rose and trailed after the flight attendant, disappearing down the aisle.

Lucy closed her eyes and tried to control her mind, but it kept wandering to one thing in particular. It kept her attention like a giant, colorful monarch or Brad Pitt.

And all the brain power in the world couldn't keep her from reaching for it.

Danny marched aft, denying eye contact to passengers while wondering which regional jet he would be banned to for the rest of his flying career. He couldn't believe he'd asked the captain about Bermuda, but he did have a long and painful history of saying inappropriate things under duress, particularly during childhood. James's face had said it all. He'd just made the Sasquatch equivalent of all verbal blunders. He'd rather have made a huge flight mistake and gone back to sim training than face whatever he'd face from the captain. Strangely, he respected her. Or maybe he just respected the idea that she didn't want to talk about the crash, that she never sensationalized it.

His mind entertained this unpleasant topic in order to avoid thinking about another unpleasant topic: moving a dead body. He'd never seen a dead body outside a casket, which in his opinion was the only place one should be.

Was she stiff? Were her eyes open? If he thought Chucky might help, he wasn't above petting a pig at this point. He decided to check on Anna Sue first, since the dead woman was far less likely to burst into hysterics and Mrs. Kilpatrick already had.

He found her concentrating on Chucky, a frown on her face.

"Anna Sue, how are you doing?"

She looked distracted and didn't acknowledge him.

"Anna Sue?"

She tore her gaze away from the pig. "What's wrong? I'm seeing some commotion."

"We've had a medical emergency. The captain will explain in a moment. How are you two doing?" he asked.

Chucky stayed asleep, though his ears twitched occasionally.

"I've never seen Chucky sleep this much."

"If only everyone could sleep like that on a plane, right?"

Anna Sue nodded. "I wish I could. Are you certain we're not going through turbulence?"

"Turbulence? No ma'am. If we go through turbulence, the captain will turn on the seat-belt sign."

Her eyes darted above her, and she let out a long sigh, like she'd been holding her breath. "Okay."

Danny patted her arm. "Okay. So you're feeling okay?"

She nodded. "Yes, I am. Thank you for asking."

"I'll come check on you later, okay?"

"Okay."

Danny walked toward the back of the plane and was met in the middle galley by GiGi and a thin, squeaky-clean young man who didn't look like the type who could handle seeing a dead body. As Danny approached, the man combed his fingers through his neatly parted hair.

"This is the guy the captain wanted," GiGi said with an exaggerated gesture that indicated she was baffled by the choice.

The young man stuck out his hand. "Hank."

"Officer Danny McSweeney. You're certain you can handle this?"

"Yes."

"And we all have to handle Mrs. Kilpatrick," GiGi said.

"I can't imagine how upsetting this is to her," Hank said.

GiGi rolled her eyes. "The dead woman was older than dirt. You can't tell me her daughter didn't consider her mother's time might be upon her. She's just using the pig as an excuse to sue."

"I disagree," said Hank. "I think she's genuinely upset. Something else is probably going on, you know? She's using the pig as an excuse for something deeper."

"Are you a psychologist?" Danny asked.

"No. Just something my dad taught me." Hank looked at Danny. "The deceased's name is Hetty."

"I seriously doubt we'll be paging her, but thanks anyway," GiGi said.

"It's nice to put a name with a face," Danny tried. "Or, um, a body."

"Let's just get this done," GiGi said.

They made their way toward Mrs. Kilpatrick and Hetty. A small group stood clustered around them, while other passengers stared wide eyed at Danny as he passed.

"Folks, move aside. Return to your seats," he called.

The crowd cleared. Mrs. Kilpatrick sat hunched with one hand covering her face.

"Mrs. Kilpatrick?"

She looked up. "What?"

Danny squatted next to her and lowered his voice. He wasn't sure what approach to take, but decided on a factual but compassionate angle that left no room for her opinion. "We're going to move your mother to a back row and move the passengers forward. We'll alert the authorities in the Netherlands, who will arrange transportation for you and her to wherever you would like."

Mrs. Kilpatrick's chin quivered. "To the funeral home. My mother's wish was to be buried next to my father."

The intercom crackled, and Danny knew the captain was about to make the announcement.

"Ladies and gentlemen, this is your captain speaking. A woman onboard has passed away. While it is very unfortunate and we offer our condolences to her loved ones, she passed of natural causes." A rush of whispering filled the cabin. "I need everyone to listen very carefully to my instructions. If you are seated in the back of the cabin, we are going to move you forward to a new seat assignment. We do not have a completely full flight, but this will mean that most of our rows will now be full. We are going to move the woman and her family to the back of the plane. We will not make an emergency landing as we are over the Atlantic Ocean right now, so we will continue to our destination of Amsterdam. I ask for your full cooperation in this matter. Everyone should remain calm, composed, and cooperative. We will arrive in Amsterdam in approximately five and a half hours. If you would, please keep this woman's family in your prayers. Thank you."

"All right, Mrs. Kilpatrick," Danny said, "we're going to go ahead and move your mother. Would you like to remain here or move to the back of the airplane with her?"

Mrs. Kilpatrick stared at her mother for a moment, and through the cloud of bitterness that hung over her, Danny could almost see a stream of memories flowing between them. But then she said, "What are you waiting for? She's not going to get up and walk back there by herself."

"We're waiting for the flight attendants to get the passengers situated."

"Well, I hope the pig is comfortable."

"Sir, we need you to move forward."

Jake had just settled into a comfortable position, listening to music, his thoughts syncing with the heavy rhythm of the bass guitar. Since he'd moved to the very back of the plane, his back against the wall of the toilet, he'd felt better. He could watch every movement on the airplane now and not wonder what was going on behind him.

Maybe this was what it felt like to be in the mob.

He'd watched the flight attendants move passengers forward one by one and knew his time was coming. Soon enough, the flight attendant with an aversion to warm temperatures stood over him.

"The woman—how did she die?" It was a stupid question, but he needed to hear that she didn't die because she was carrying something very valuable and someone murdered her.

"She was very old. *Very* old."

"Can I stay back here?"

"I'm afraid not. We're moving the body back here."

Jake considered his options. On one hand, he didn't want to be near a dead body, but on the other hand, he'd felt much less afraid since relocating, and a dead body couldn't kill him. Haunt him, yes. Kill him, no.

"I'd rather stay back here."

"That's not an option, sir. Please, I need to move you forward."

Jake looked at the old man and young woman on the opposite side of the airplane, the couple he'd studied earlier. "They're not moving."

The flight attendant followed his gaze. "That's a special circumstance."

"Look, I'd feel better if I could stay here. I don't care about being near a dead body." He did, but he tried not to show it. He caught her looking at his hands gripping his stomach.

"Are you still feeling sick?"

Roll with it. "Yeah. Maybe an ulcer." He remembered this flight attendant seemed sensitive to temperature. "Plus, it feels cooler back here."

She straightened. "You're right. It does feel cool back here, doesn't it?"

"Much cooler." He moved his hands around on his stomach for effect. "I'm afraid being with the other passengers might feel stuffy. Then I might get clammy, then sweaty..."

She started fanning herself. "Okay, you can stay back here. But I'll warn you that the daughter of the woman who died is very upset. It may not be a pretty scene."

"I'll keep a low profile."

"I'll take her under the arms," Hank said, "if you'll get her feet."

"Let's be careful and go slowly," Danny said, trying to distract himself from Hetty's large bunion and two large corns bulging from underneath knee-highs that had fallen way short of the knee. She wore turquoise sandals like his grandmother used to, which did nothing to hide her overgrown toenails, a quarter of an inch thick. Danny squatted and reached underneath her knees. Normally, something like this would require pausing and deep breathing to prepare, but people were staring and the guy named Hank didn't hesitate for a second. Danny'd prepared for a lot of things in his training, from engine failure to loss of cabin pressure, but not once did they simulate how to move a dead body.

He'd read somewhere that Dutch women were the tallest in the world, and though Hetty's back was curved, she still held on to that height, making her heavier than Danny expected. His neck veins bulged.

As they lifted, Hetty's head rolled and one arm flopped to the side. Someone gasped. Danny hoped it wasn't him. He didn't know what to look at. Her knee-length skirt? Her feet? The way her mouth opened like she was about to moan? Hank?

Hank. He locked eyes with Danny and gave him a reassuring nod. Danny nodded back. He wasn't sure what they'd confirmed—maybe that they were both wigging out but didn't have the luxury of showing it.

Suddenly Hank spoke. "Come on, Hetty. We're moving you to some comfortable seats. We'll take good care of you and get you back home where you belong."

A sense of peace rushed over Danny, like when he landed an airplane safely. He smiled at Hank, then looked at Hetty. What a life. A hundred and three years. The stories she could have told. Who had she loved? Who had she lost? He found himself holding her with as much care as he would anything of great value.

"Right here?" Hank asked.

"Yes."

It was an awkward angle, but Hank managed to squeeze between the seats and carry her through, one knee on the seat while the other leg hopped backward. They gently laid her across the seats. Hank folded her arms across her chest, gently brushed her hair out of her eyes, and then handed Danny a blanket. Together, they draped it over her. The only thing it didn't cover were the tips of her sandals and those old toes. Danny marveled at where those feet could have traveled in a hundred and three years.

"Can you reach a seat belt? We need to belt her in."

Hank looked confused.

"Everyone has to belted in," Danny explained. The last thing they needed was to hit turbulence and have her unexpectedly fly through the air. Hank snapped a belt loosely around her waist.

"Thank you." Danny shook Hank's hand.

Mrs. Kilpatrick blotted her eyes. "Thank you," she whispered, and sat in the seat across the aisle. Hank, hands clasped in front of him, started to return to his seat.

"Young man," Mrs. Kilpatrick said.

Hank turned. "Yes?"

"My mother would have approved of you." Her tone was not light or friendly, but in her eyes Danny sensed an earnestness. "She was very religious. I suppose that's why she lived so long." Her gaze fell to her mother's covered body, then wound its way up to the small crowd that had gathered to watch. Then it moved to the man sitting in the very last row by the toilet. "Who is he?"

Danny turned. He hadn't even noticed him. The passenger's head barely showed above the seats. Instead of looking at them, he watched the television screen on the seatback in front of him.

GiGi spoke up. "He's the one not feeling well. It's cooler back here, so I told him he could stay. The last thing we need is for a passenger to get sick on us."

That was true. Danny turned to Mrs. Kilpatrick, who held her face in her hands. "Okay. Mrs. Kilpatrick, let us know if there is anything we can do for you."

"Just get me on the ground."

"That we can do."

Danny looked at Hank. "Thanks again for your help."

"You're welcome."

Danny gestured for GiGi to follow him. When they were out of earshot of Mrs. Kilpatrick, he said, "Okay. I want you to record everything on a piece of paper exactly how it happened. I'll do the same. Hopefully her emotions will settle down and she'll concen-trate on getting her mother buried rather than suing us. But just in case."

"Danny, she's going to sue. Bank on it."

Danny shook his head. Frankly, Mrs. Kilpatrick was the least of his problems. Now he had to return to the cockpit.

Chapter 16

Ms. Meredith, is there anything else we can help you with?"
"Definitely. I cannot live without the Successories Attitude poster. That's pretty much my life's guiding light, you know? Attitude can make all the difference in the world."

"Yes ma'am. And would you like that framed?"

"Yes. Framed."

"All right. I have the Successories Attitude poster, the Pop-Up Hot Dog Cooker, the Upside Down Tomato Garden, the Aerating Lawn Sandals, and the iSqueez Foot and Calf Massager. Is there anything else I can do for you?"

"Ohhhh, I'm really eying *The Lost Art of Towel Origami* book."

"That's a popular one."

"And it's got step-by-step instructions?"

"Along with detailed, full-color pictures."

"Wow. Nice."

"Shall I add it?"

"Sure."

"All right, ma'am. Your total is—"

"Hold on." Lucy turned to the man sitting on her left, who was directing a full-blown stare her direction. "Can I help you?"

"Can I help *you*?" he retorted.

"With what?"

"Never mind."

"No, what?"

He shook his head. "It's just that I've never seen anyone actually, um…"

"What?"

"Shop. On an airplane. With that magazine." He pointed to the *SkyMall* catalog laid open on her drink tray. "And I fly nearly once a week."

"They happen to have very cool things in here."

"I've also never seen anyone use the airplane phone."

"Okay, look, I think you need to just"—suddenly Hank returned; Lucy reeled the words back in and tried a calmer voice— "look at it from a different perspective."

"Oh, I am." The man grinned. "Right now I'm thanking God for my wife. I thought her shopping trips to Target were bad, but she's got nothing on you."

"Ma'am?"

Lucy's attention was drawn back to the friendly voice on the other end of the phone. "Yes, um, just charge it to my card. Thanks." She hung up the phone.

Hank's eyes widened. "I didn't even know they had phones on airplanes!"

"Yeah. See? Right here on the other side of the remote control for the television."

"It's like being at home." He smiled.

"Yes," said the man to her left, "except it'll cost you your year's bonus to make a phone call, and you've only got six channels to choose from on this television."

"That's one more than I have at home."

The man raised an eyebrow at Hank's comment, then went back to reading his newspaper.

"So, what did you do back there?" Lucy asked Hank.

"I had to help move the woman who died."

"Ick!"

"It wasn't that bad."

"How's her daughter?"

"Sad." Hank noticed the magazine. "So what are you doing?"

"Shopping." She pointed to the page. "Look at this. I didn't buy it, but it's cool. It can water fourteen plants while you're away. And this lantern stays lit for ten days."

"Do you camp?"

"No."

"Why do you need a lantern?"

"You know, um, in case Armageddon happens."

He laughed. "Sure."

The man next to her leaned in. "I suppose the calf and foot massager will come in handy during Armageddon too? And I don't know about you, but in my book, everybody experiencing the end of days needs to know how to fold a towel so it looks like a rooster."

Lucy swallowed, trying to hold back a surge of emotion. She didn't need this guy's lip. He made her feel insecure. Sure, she liked to shop, and her shopping habit increased during emotional duress. She supposed it was the equivalent of a smoking habit, but to be fair, it wouldn't cause cancer.

Hank turned to the man, smiled, and said, "And I guess that Rolex tells time in some extraordinary way?"

The smug look slid right off his face, and he brushed his hands against his silk shirt. He tapped at his shiny watch. "It takes a year to build these."

"Hmm. Good use of time," Hank said.

The man snapped open his newspaper and went back to reading. Lucy turned to Hank, wide eyed and giggling. "That was funny. But unexpected. I didn't think you would say...I mean, that you would, you know..."

"Stand up for a newfound friend?"

"Thanks."

"You remind me a lot of my sister Cassie."

"Oh?"

"She likes to shop. My father always told her she was trying to fill a void in her life."

Lucy looked away. That thought had crossed her mind as well.

Hank laughed. "I think she just likes clothes."

Lucy laughed too. "Well, I don't suppose I really needed all that stuff. I don't even eat hot dogs. Real hot dogs, anyway. I eat tofu hot dogs. But I do like to make creations out of towels. I went on a cruise once, and every day the cleaning lady made a different animal for me. It was terrific."

Lucy realized that, for just a moment, she'd completely forgotten about whether or not Jeff was onboard. It felt good. The more she'd tried not to think about him, the more she did. It was a relief to forget about it.

The quiet of the cabin settled her. Conversations lulled. Reading lights went off. A couple people snored. She was beginning to feel tired herself. She'd vowed to get some sleep on the plane so she wouldn't be too exhausted for her trip.

But first, she needed a bathroom break. She rose and Hank stood, letting her through like the gentleman he was. She noticed new passengers had filled in the gaps where no one had been sitting before the woman died. The cabin looked crowded. She set her sights on the bathrooms located in the middle of the plane and started toward them.

Then something caught her eye.

Through the darkened cabin, she immediately spotted him. His platinum, spiky hair glowed, looking almost green. He didn't notice her, though, being to busy gazing into the overly made-up eyes of the woman she'd seen when they boarded the flight.

In what could only be described as a knee-jerk reaction, Lucy's feet left the carpet and she dove headfirst over Hank's lap and back into her seat, crawling over him like an unruly toddler, careful to keep her head below the seats.

As she knocked into her other row-mate, he rolled his eyes. "What is it now? The duty-free cart is coming by?"

"Bathrooms are full," Lucy panted. "Not supposed to form a line. Don't you listen to the flight attendants' instructions?"

He went back to reading.

"I would've moved," Hank said as she maneuvered herself into a sitting position.

"He's back there!" Lucy said in the whispering equivalent of a yell. She sounded like milk being steamed at Starbucks.

"Who?"

"Jeff." She clutched Hank's arm, no longer able to feel any positive energy around her. "I guess he got moved forward with the rest of the passengers in the back." She covered her mouth. "I can't believe it. I can't believe he is on *this* flight with another woman!"

"Okay, okay," Hank said, holding her arm. "It's okay. You're going to be fine."

"I don't know." She sucked in a deep breath that pulled her nostrils closed. "He will not enter my aura. He is barred from my—"

"Lucy," Hank said, "you're hyperventilating."

"No, no. I'm deep breathing. I'm restoring the natural balance of oxygen to my…" She did feel a little lightheaded. Before she knew it, Hank had punched the Call button. "Oh, Hank, no, that's not necessary, I'm just…" The cabin spun. Thankfully she wore her seat belt.

A flight attendant appeared, the friendlier one.

"My friend here is feeling a little lightheaded," Hank said. "Nothing bad, but I think she could use a wet washrag, maybe some water?"

"I can wet some paper towels."

"That's fine. Whatever you have."

"All right. I'll be back."

Lucy's hands trembled, and her body shook. She had not expected this reaction. Anger, yes. Complete meltdown, not out of the question. Passing out? That meant some sort of ion was out of balance.

It baffled her. She'd maintained a very healthy perspective on it all for at least three weeks.

"You're going to be fine," Hank said.

"I just need a little water, that's all."

"No, I mean in life. You're going to be fine. You're going to get through this."

Lucy looked at him, tears coming to her eyes. "You think so?"

"You're a strong person. I can tell."

Lucy laid her hand on his forearm. "Thank you."

The flight attendant returned, handing over sopping paper towels and a small glass of water. "This is stressful on everybody. Don't feel bad," she said.

"I'm already feeling better," Lucy replied, glad to have the excuse of a dead body onboard.

"My name is Kim if you need anything else. I'll come check on you in a few minutes, okay?"

"Okay, thank you. I really am feeling much better." She sipped the water and blotted her forehead. She focused. Recentered. Drew from within herself everything she needed.

"Are you feeling better?" Hank asked.

"Yes. I need you to pose as my boyfriend."

The first sign that Danny might be murdered in the cockpit occurred when the captain asked James to take his break. It wasn't time or his turn and, with the ACI onboard, was certainly against protocol.

Since returning to the cockpit, it had been mostly quiet, thanks to James's leaving, except for a few comments made by the ACI, most of them pertaining to how bored one must get staring at clouds and dark sky for twelve hours. Danny guessed he was trying to set them up, get them to confess to reading a book or magazine in the cockpit. He was an odd duck for sure, but nothing compared to the woman sitting next to Danny.

The silence was undone by a strange noise behind them. They turned to find the ACI fast asleep, his head fallen backward, his mouth wide open. With each breath, his snoring gained momentum.

"He's asleep!" Danny whispered. "Wow. With that kind of snoring, maybe he's got sleep apnea or something. That's a little scary. I'd hate to see him behind a wheel in five-o'clock traffic."

That didn't stimulate any conversation or even cause a chuckle. Several agonizing minutes later, though, the captain began to speak.

"You know, Bubba, sometimes life is like a good tailwind. It can get you there fast, but at the end of the day, you still must land the plane, and if your landing gear gets stuck, you're probably going to crash anyway."

Danny nodded to be polite, because he had no idea what she was talking about, though he suspected it wasn't the actual plane. He wondered if this was code for "I'm going to have you flying pond hoppers for NAIA college basketball teams for the rest of your life."

He couldn't hold it in any longer or he might explode. He turned to her. "Captain, I'm so sorry. I didn't mean to mention your Bermuda incident. It just sort of came out. I didn't want to talk about Maya, and I just…I'm sorry. I don't want to lose this job. I love flying. I've invested a lot of years." Was he talking about Maya or his job now? Maybe both. Though the apology didn't seem close to enough, he was certain he wore the most desperate expression capable of a human.

The captain did not so much as glance in his direction. Her countenance did not change. Instead, she continued in a calm, nearly inaudible voice. "I thought you wanted to hear about Bermuda."

She *was* talking about Bermuda? Or was this another discombobulated metaphor?

Danny figured he had no choice but to lay his cards on his table. What did he have to lose, really?

Well, his job. But he'd already broached the subject with her, and contrary to James's claims, smoke did not shoot out of her ears.

"Ma'am, I'd heard you don't like to talk about that."

"Where'd you hear that?" She paused. "The blog?"

"Yes. I mean, no. No! I don't read that. I don't even know about it. I mean, I didn't, until today when James told me." Danny bit his lip, trying to get all his words lined up in proper order so he didn't sound like a raging liar. "You know about it?"

"Well, it is on the World Wide Web."

"Look, that's just an awful thing to do. People like that, who don't have anything better to do with their time, they're just stupid. Don't pay attention to them."

"Hmm."

Hmm? Danny wanted to say more, but what more was there? The captain's body language was like a broken traffic signal with all three lights glowing at once. He didn't know whether to go, stop, or slow down.

"It was a typical day. Bright, blue skies. A moderate pax load. Nothing seemed out of the ordinary, not that it should. It was just an ordinary day. But that's how all days start out. Something makes them extraordinary, but an event has to happen, you understand? Without the event, it will always be ordinary."

"Right." *Just roll with it, Danny.*

"We lost power in both engines and started dropping. I

managed to regain partial power in one engine, but it wouldn't get us back to land. I knew I would have to land in the ocean, so I landed in the ocean, just like we're trained to do."

Danny wanted to ask more. How could she sum up an event like that with a few sentences? Wasn't there more to tell? How did it feel? What went through her mind? Did people remember to use their seats as flotation devices?

"Nobody died. That's amazing."

"It's because I was flying the MD-80. The engines are on top of the wing. If I'd been flying this 767, it might've been a different story. We came in hard, and had those engines been on the bottom of the wing, it could've ripped the entire plane apart."

"Why didn't you talk about it? I mean, I completely respect that decision, but most people would want to talk about it, share their experience, give the details."

"I called every passenger aboard the plane that day and apologized."

"But it wasn't your fault."

"I'm the captain. I'm responsible for them." For the first time, Danny noticed her demeanor change. She turned to face him. "What I'm trying to say is that James is partly right. You're responsible for Maya."

Maya? Now they were on Maya?

"You were responsible for her emotional well-being, for keeping her pure until you could commit to be with her for the rest of your life. Instead, you took her out for a test drive. But you forgot you were on a test drive and decided you wanted to keep the car."

"But she left me."

"At the end of the day, you're the captain. God put you in charge of caring for her. It doesn't matter whose fault it was."

Danny looked away. That was the most ridiculous thing he'd ever heard. And how'd they get from the Bermuda Triangle to Maya and now to God? The captain didn't strike him as particularly religious.

"Bubba, James has the wrong idea about God."

James had the wrong idea about everything, but that was another topic. Apparently Danny had the wrong idea about the captain.

"You would've done anything to get Maya back?"

Danny was having a hard time following the conversation, but his career probably depended on it, so he decided to take it one sentence at a time. "Yes. Of course."

"God feels the same way about you."

Danny folded his arms. What next? A speech on how big a sinner he was?

She continued. "You're right. It was someone else's fault that the plane went down. An engineer. A mechanic. A designer. A good person to be sure, but someone made a mistake."

Back to the airplane.

"And it doesn't matter that for twelve, fifteen, twenty years they never made a mistake," she said. "This one mistake, it would've cost them everything."

"Would've?" Danny unfolded his arms. "Had you not taken

the blame." A long pause stretched between them. "It cost you a lot." Ridicule. Speculation. A blog full of gossip about her.

"It cost God a lot more to repair the damage done by our mistakes." She smiled, causing Danny to smile back, but it was more like following the lead of a dance partner than being overtaken by happiness. It was the first smile he'd seen on her. "So I get blogged about. I think it's funny, to tell you the truth. I mean, the things they come up with."

"So they're not true? That something bad happens to you once a year?"

"I guess it depends on your definition of 'bad.'"

"Um…what's your definition of 'bad'?"

"A crash water landing. After that, everything's a piece of cake."

Danny smiled. "I see what you mean."

"Every time I hear the wheels touch down on the runway… when I hear that skidding sound they make, I thank God. Danny, Maya's a skid mark. Not big, ugly, and tar black. Probably really pretty. But either way, one indicating you were coming in too fast in the first place. Just thank God your wheels are touching the runway."

He wanted to remind her that he didn't leave Maya, she left him, and it wasn't about commitment but money, but though nothing she said really made sense, it had meaning in a way he couldn't explain. In a way that made him feel he didn't need to defend himself. And that maybe God handed out second chances like free quarters to a vending machine.

"Ahhh!"

Danny jolted nearly out of his seat. The captain flinched. They turned to find the ACI's arms flailing and his eyes darting wildly around the cockpit. Then, like he'd just been caught naked, he froze, laughed sheepishly, and slowly released the briefcase he was clutching. "Sorry. I suffer from night terrors."

"If you're tired," the captain said, "you're welcome to rest in the cabin."

"No, I'm fine. It was just a moment of, uh…hiccups are exhausting. I'm fine." He rearranged the papers on his clipboard.

A knock rattled the door. The ACI got up, peered out, and opened the door for James, who popped in with a wide grin. "I feel like a million bucks. I swear, I slept as hard as the dead woman in the back of the plane."

Danny sighed. If Maya was a skid mark, James was that horrible burnt-rubber smell that came with it.

Chapter 17

After an attempt at a short nap, GiGi decided to start preparing breakfast. She had nothing else to do, and this way she wouldn't have to rush. She poured herself a cup of coffee and got busy.

Strangely, she wondered why the guy in seat 20E hadn't rung his Call button. She'd waited for him to. *Wanted* him to. Before he was nothing more than an exaggerated annoyance she'd nicknamed Milk and Cookies. She'd met her share of challenging passengers before, but none quite as high maintenance as this man.

Yet after watching him with Hetty, she found herself drawn to him, and not because he was young and polite, parted his hair like her grandfather, and had perfectly dreamy blue eyes. Three times she'd been tricked into thinking beautiful eyes translated into a decent heart. Three divorces later, eyes rarely fooled her anymore.

So what, exactly, drew her to him? Sure, he was polite and pleasant, even when asking for his third glass of ice-cold water in an hour, but there was something more. Something about how he treated the dead woman.

Maybe he knew how he treated the dead was going to affect all those still alive.

It had. His words had a calming effect on GiGi, like rocky road ice cream or a bad highlighting job on a prettier woman.

She decided to check on him. Why not? Maybe he was suffering silently, traumatized by the events. She made her way up the aisle, pretending to check on all the passengers. Most were beginning to wake to the early morning sounds in the cabin.

Finally, she came to 20E. He was writing something on a notepad. When he noticed her, he smiled.

She hadn't been nice to him. Why was he smiling at her?

"Hi, GiGi."

And calling her by name?

Her smile came easy. "Hey. I just wanted to check on you, see how you're doing."

"Oh, I'm fine. Thank you."

Perplexing. He needed everything under the sun until it was offered. She tried not to dwell on it.

"You're sure? Can I get you anything?"

"No, thank you."

"We're fine." The woman sitting next to Hank leaned into the conversation, placed her hand on his knee, and spoke in a voice loud enough for a crowded subway station.

"You two are traveling together?" GiGi asked.

"I'm sorry," said the woman, glancing behind her, "could you repeat the question, a little louder?"

GiGi cleared her throat and focused back on Hank, who for the first time looked uncomfortable. "I just wanted to thank you for your help earlier."

"It's no problem."

She knelt next to him. "I also wanted to apologize. I was rude to you, and it was uncalled for. It's just been a long life—flight, I mean. A long flight. I did London and Scotland last week, and I'm exhausted. But I shouldn't have taken out my frustrations on you."

"It's okay. I realize it's been a difficult flight."

Emotionally challenged woman. Pig. Prisoner. Bleeding ulcer. Irate woman with dead mother. If they only knew.

"How is Mrs. Kilpatrick doing?" Hank asked.

"She's calm. So is the pig. That's all I can ask for at this point. I think the rest of the flight is going to be pretty uneventful."

"Please tell the captain I think you're all doing a terrific job handling these situations."

"I will. Thank you." GiGi rose just as Kim approached.

"I need you," Kim whispered.

GiGi turned to follow her. "What's going on?"

"Leendert is upset."

"About what?"

"I don't know. The agent is trying to handle it, but I thought I'd better alert you."

"All right. Finish getting breakfast ready." Kim went to the galley, and GiGi approached Agent Tasler and Leendert. "Everything okay?"

Agent Tasler's hot glare sliced into GiGi. "I'm fine. We're fine."

Leendert didn't look fine, though. Beads of sweat lined his brows; his ruddy complexion had turned pasty. His winsome eyes appeared unfocused, agitated. He clawed the side of his face with trembling fingers.

"Are you sure?"

"We're fine, *aren't we*, Leendert?"

Leendert nodded slightly, then his eyes grew round and he shook his head, almost in spite of himself.

"What is wrong with him?" GiGi whispered, though there was nobody nearby except Hetty, Mrs. Kilpatrick, and on the other side of the plane, the guy with the stomach condition.

"He's being a weenie." Agent Tasler sighed. "Apparently he has a thing with dead bodies."

"Her toes." Leendert shuddered.

"Or the toes attached to the dead body." Agent Tasler cast a forlorn look in Leendert's direction.

GiGi glanced behind her. The blanket was nearly long enough, but it didn't quite cover her toes. She'd checked. There weren't any other blankets left.

"He doesn't like dead bodies. So we can rest assured he's not a mass murderer?" GiGi smiled.

Agent Tasler smirked. "Exactly. And he can rest assured that if he doesn't get it together, he's going to be dealing with me in a far less generous mood."

"Can not you move me?" Leendert asked, gasping for his breath in short spurts.

"He does look a little…"

"A little nothing. He's perfectly fine," said the agent. "We're not going anywhere."

He didn't seem to be faking it.

"Breakfast will be served soon," GiGi said to Leendert. "Maybe that will make you feel better? Toast does wonders."

"Toes? Did she just say toes?" Leendert's voice quavered.

"Toast. *Toast*," the agent stressed in a firm voice. She sighed and looked up at GiGi. "All this for Amsterdam."

"Pardon me?"

"I took this assignment because I thought it would be fun to see Amsterdam. Agents like to volunteer for these kinds of transports when they're going somewhere cool. My buddy had to transfer a guy back to Hawaii." She sighed. "I'm not certain this will be worth it."

"Amsterdam is really interesting. The canals are amazing. Don't miss Anne Frank and Van Gogh."

The agent smiled. "Thanks for the encouragement."

"Sure." GiGi turned, deciding she better check on Ulcer, who ironically seemed the least likely to give her one.

Sleep deprivation was doing a number on him, but no matter how hard he tried, he couldn't fall asleep. Instead, Jake closed his eyes for short, intermittent periods and tried to decide whether he was a schmuck or a good person.

A schmuck would've taken all the diamonds, changed his name, and fled the country, leaving his elderly grandmother—whom he'd never met and didn't really want to—high and dry.

He wasn't a schmuck, because by definition he'd actually have to carry out those plans instead of just think about them.

He wasn't a good person either, though, because a good person would insist on returning all of the diamonds and not taking any for himself. He would stand by his convictions that he didn't need more than he had.

So he was somewhere between a schmuck and good person. A schmerson. He could live with that.

That took a total of ten minutes to ponder. He needed something else to fill his mind.

He stared at the dead body for a while. Well, the toes of the dead body. It didn't repulse him. It didn't even make him glad he was alive. It made him hope he never lived to be old enough not to care about footwear.

Another ten minutes.

He needed something to dwell on, not just think about. Dwell. Dwell. Dwell.

Okay, Idya. Why not?

The truth was, if he could admit it to himself, he wanted to meet her. She seemed gruff, but maybe that was because she had a deep voice and spoke in a guttural language. He got defensive at the thought of going by "Jaap," but what twenty-something guy wouldn't? "Jaap" sounded like a pure-bred, long-haired miniature dog that liked to bite. Maybe he could win her over to the name Jake. Maybe once they met, she'd see him as Jake.

He wanted to know more about her. She'd told him she acquired the diamonds after her husband, Jake's grandfather, died, and it had something to do with World War II, but that's all he knew. He wanted to understand the dynamic between his parents and Idya…what kind of misunderstanding kept them an ocean apart? He wanted to know more about his grandfather too, who died when his father was little.

All of this, of course, would be far less complicated if he could be assured he'd arrive at her doorstep alive.

"You doing okay?"

Jake's eyes flew open, and he sat up straight. "Me?"

"Are you feeling okay?" The flight attendant stood above him again.

"Oh, uh, yeah. Better."

Her nose lifted into the air. "It feels warm back here."

"Um…I don't know. I mean, it feels fine to me."

"You're not sweaty?"

Well, he couldn't say that. "Now that you mention it, it does feel stuffy."

"I'll be back." She stormed up the aisle.

Jake settled back into his seat. Thanks to the flight delay, his iPod battery died a few hours back, and he'd already watched *The Italian Job* twice. He tuned in to the cartoon channel and clipped the earphones on.

As he glanced across the aisle beyond the dead woman, he noticed the old guy looking at him. Staring at him. A full-blown stare, the kind that normally caused Jake to ask, "What are you looking at?" Or, if it happened to be a woman, break into a wide, charming, borderline goofy grin. At least that's how his friends described it. Jake stared back for a moment, hoping to make the old guy look away, but he didn't. Jake balked.

Forget about it, he told himself. He was just an old guy, probably senile or nearsighted or something.

Jake slid down in his seat, only to have to slide back up as the flight attendant returned.

"Somebody turned the thermostat back up to sixty-eight!" She flung her hands toward the ceiling. "Why warm the breakfasts? We might as well be in a microwave oven! It'll cool down in a moment, okay?"

Sure. Whatever, lady. Just beat it.

Jake sighed. He really missed hanging out with his band.

Lucy sat still, enduring the small lecture on self-esteem from Hank. She fought back tears while simultaneously fighting off an enormous influx of negative energy. The cabin doors were sealed, so whatever negative energy happened to be floating inside the airplane had nothing to do but roam around like a bloodsucking tick, looking for someone to attach itself to.

Well, it wasn't going to be her.

But as Hank continued to talk about who she was created to be, irony chased every thought. She'd not only been rejected by her boyfriend, but rejected by a guy she asked to simply *pose* as her boyfriend. There were no commitment issues, nothing more to do than continue what he was doing, with perhaps a quick hand-hold if Jeff stood up and glanced over, or maybe a walk together back to the bathroom.

Instead he'd said, "Lucy, my faking it as your boyfriend isn't going to make you feel any better."

Sure it would. It definitely couldn't make her feel worse. She was almost certain it would make her feel really great.

"Lucy," he continued, and she tried to pay more attention to him, "you're a beautiful, intelligent, warm, and interesting woman." *But.* "You don't need me to pose as your boyfriend. Let's leave that kind of role-playing to the undercover police." *Huh?* "Jeff brought along this woman so soon after his breakup because of his insecurities. He feels like he needs someone to make him a complete person. But you know that's not true."

The Secret was not holding up its end of the bargain. She'd envisioned—with complete clarity and resolve—Hank's changing his mind, but so far he hadn't. Instead, he picked up the Airfone.

"You're calling someone?"

"I'm going to call Cassie." He took out his credit card and swiped it.

"Who?"

"My sister. She knows stuff."

"Like what?"

"Your predicament. Out of all of us Hazards, Cassie knows about things like this the best." He concentrated on dialing the number.

Lucy wanted to point out that it wouldn't be nearly as difficult a predicament if he would just pose as her boyfriend for the rest of the flight.

"Cassie, hi! It's Hank! You won't believe where I am. An airplane... I know... Yeah, for that job I got... No, I still don't have a cell phone. It's this phone they have on the airplane. You put your credit card in, and you can make a phone call while you're over the ocean!... I know, isn't that cool?" Hank glanced at Lucy and smiled.

She tried to smile back, but the dude to her left was distracting her by spying on them while pretending to read.

"Well, listen, I've got a question for you. I've got a friend here named Lucy and she's in a predicament."

With a capital P, Lucy added silently.

"She and her boyfriend broke up... Um, I don't know, hold on." Hank looked at Lucy. "How long ago?"

"Six weeks," Lucy whispered. It was really three, but she didn't want to sound pathetic. "Can you keep your voice down?"

Hank nodded. "Six weeks ago... Yeah, she's holding up fine. I mean, looking at her, you'd never know her heart was broken."

"It's not broken," Lucy said. "It's intact, but slightly...vulnerable. In a good way vulnerable. The kind of vulnerable that allows you to grow and—"

"But here's the hard part. Her ex-boyfriend is on this flight with a new girlfriend, taking a vacation that he and Lucy were supposed to go on together."

"Can you keep your voice down?"

"Sorry," Hank whispered.

"You bet he's sorry!" Lucy heard the female's voice rage over the phone.

"Cassie, calm down."

Lucy couldn't hear everything Cassie said, but it definitely qualified as a rant.

"Yes, she's sitting right beside me," Hank said. "Why?"

Lucy held her breath.

"Well, yeah, she asked. But Cassie, we both know that..." Hank sighed and glanced at Lucy with a small smile. "I know, but... I don't think she... Okay, hold on." Hank held out the phone. "Cassie wants to talk to you."

"Me?"

"Yes."

"Why?"

Hank didn't answer, just pushed the phone closer to her and shrugged like there was nothing more he could do. Lucy tentatively reached for it and put it against her ear.

"Hello?" she whispered.

"Hi," came the voice on the other end of the phone. Peppy. Friendly. Definitely some positive energy flowing. Lucy relaxed.

"Hello."

"I'm Cassie, Hank's sister."

"Yes."

"So, I can't believe you're in this situation. Unbelievable. The *nerve* of that guy!"

Lucy smiled. She liked this vibe.

"Have you prayed for him?" Cassie asked.

Lucy stopped smiling. "Um, I don't believe in Go—"

"He doesn't deserve it, but you should. The last thing you want is to have him chained to your conscience for the rest of your life because of bitterness. You have to forgive him or he'll be like a brick wall stopping you from ever finding true happiness."

That was true enough. Maybe that's why she felt so much negative energy around her. That and the guy to her left.

"Uh-huh," she said.

"Okay, so first things first, Lucy. We're going to pray."

"But I'm not a—"

"Believe me, neither am I. Out of my entire family, I'm the least spiritual. I was born with a love for mascara that to this day cannot be explained. But God doesn't care how eloquent we are. He's listening and ready and willing to help us, okay? So, let's just go before our Father now, and, God, we ask that You help Lucy. She's in a horrible spot right now. She loved this man, and to see him with another woman is breaking her heart, Lord. I pray in the name of Jesus that this man would suffer for the way he's made Lucy feel. I pray that he would be humiliated. Embarrassed. Realize what a horrible mistake he's made by letting this precious woman go."

There was a long silence. Lucy leaned forward, gripping the

phone, straining to hear what would happen to Jeff next. Then a sigh blasted Lucy's ear.

"I'm sorry, Father. Obviously, we need to forgive him. I know that. I am sorry. That is no way to start out forgiving someone. Lucy, I'm sorry. Like I said, I'm not great at this sometimes. I pray, Lord, that You would help Lucy forgive him from the bottom of her heart. I pray that she would know that even though this man hurt her, You never will. Help her cling to Your love, Lord, and allow You to mend what has been broken. You love Lucy with all Your heart. May she feel that love every day. In Jesus's name, Amen."

Lucy held her breath.

"In the meantime," Cassie continued, "I don't see why we can't make this putz believe you're with Hank."

Lucy let out a nervous laugh.

"Look, you're trapped on an airplane with your ex and his new girlfriend. Sometimes you have to go into survival mode. Don't do it out of anger. It's not vengeful. It's just practical, until you can get your feet on the ground and get to a safe place."

Lucy smiled. She liked this woman. "That's a great idea, but I don't think your brother's going to go for it."

"He's shy. I've been trying for years to get him to come out of his shell. Women like him, but he doesn't see himself as the dating type."

"Well, he thought I shouldn't try to fill a void by pretending we're together."

"Oh, brother. Let me talk to him."

"Okay." Lucy handed Hank the phone.

Hank concentrated hard. "Uh-huh… Uh-huh… Yeah… Oh, I see your point… True… Well, see, that's why I called you. You're an expert… Okay, I'll tell her… No, I promise, I won't forget… Okay, thanks, Cassie. I'll call you when I return… Okay, bye."

"What'd she say?" Lucy asked.

"We met at church, both love traveling, have been seeing each other for two weeks, and will be staying in separate hotel rooms."

"Oh…um, anything else?"

"That you should get yourself to the bathroom pronto, gloss your lips, and put on two coats of mascara. Don't forget the bottom lid."

Chapter 18

E veryone's doing fine," Danny announced, settling into the jump seat opposite the ACI.

When James returned, the captain had sent Danny to check on the passengers. Anna Sue thought she felt the wings tip, but he reassured her. Chucky still slept peacefully with his head on her lap. According to GiGi, their prisoner was freaked out by dead bodies, but awed by the breakfast served and happily engaged in his breakfast burrito and toast. Mrs. Kilpatrick had finally fallen asleep. Danny paused, making certain she really slept. Her chest rose and lowered slowly but steadily. The man with the stomach problem appeared to be feeling better as he wolfed down a fruit cup.

It would be time for the captain's break soon. Danny wondered if she'd discussed Bermuda with James. He wasn't about to inquire. As far as he was concerned, if nobody spoke for the rest of the flight, he'd be perfectly happ—

"I'd like to see the manifest."

Danny looked at the ACI. "The manifest?"

"Yes. Thank you."

Danny glanced at James, the captain, and then back to Mr. Smilt. "Why?"

"Protocol."

"Protocol?"

"I don't know," Smilt mumbled. "Something in a memo. Hand it over, please."

"But…"

"Look, I don't want excuses, okay? There's a lot of weird stuff happening on this flight. You're flying on thin ice as it is."

"Or skating on thin air," James smiled.

"What do you need the manifest for?" the captain asked.

"It's protocol."

"As you well know, the pilots don't keep the manifest. The flight attendants do, if there's one at all."

The ACI appeared frazzled as he waved his pen. "I know. I know that. I meant that. I'm just…" He looked around the cockpit. "I've been off the job awhile. I went to the Mayo Clinic, you know, for the hiccups. So this is my first day back, and I just need some time to get adjusted." He stood, making Danny flinch for some reason. "I'm going to inspect the rest of the plane."

Another round of glances.

"Why would an ACI inspect the cabin?" James asked.

Smilt clutched his clipboard and swiped his hand over his forehead. "I just need some fresh air. And to use the bathroom. Stretch my legs."

The captain turned around in her seat. "Of course, Mr. Smilt. Please don't hesitate. Take all the time you need."

The edge to his expression softened, and he adjusted his tie. "Thank you. I'll return."

He left the cockpit.

"I think the man is in the middle of falling off the wagon," James said.

"Something's off with him," Danny agreed.

"He's probably sneaking into the bathroom for a drink of the devil's draft. If he comes back chewing gum and smothered in cologne, I think it's safe to assume we're dealing with some heavy sin," James said.

"Otherwise known as an addiction," Danny said with a hard glare.

"If you need to confess that, feel free," James said. "An addiction is an addiction."

"And to what, exactly, am I addicted?"

"Women."

Don't engage. Don't engage. Don't eng— "Because I lived with one, you've concluded I'm addicted?"

"One. Fifty. It's all the same in God's eyes. Why, after six years, did you not marry her?"

"I don't think that's any of your business."

"Fair enough. When I travel overseas, my wife's never worried I'm going to be with someone else. That's what it takes to remain pure. And I've had plenty of opportunities. You know how it is. Women see these stripes on your shoulder and turn into complete Delilahs. But if you don't have enough self-control not to have sex with a woman before you marry her, then how can you expect to have self-control at a bar? Or…perhaps in a casino?"

Danny ground his teeth together. "Maybe I don't have enough self-control to keep from punching you in the face."

"You're totally proving my point. Be my guest. I'm sure the ACI would love something to write up."

"You two, knock it off," the captain said. "We've got a problem."

"GiGi, we need you at the front. Um, now." Sandy's voice crackled through the phone.

Touching each seat as she passed by, GiGi swiftly made her way to the front galley. "Sandy, what's wrong?"

"It's the ACI. He's walking around the cabin."

"So?"

"Checking things."

"Checking things?"

Sandy nodded, leaning backward to get a glimpse down the aisle. "He was in here checking the drawers, the door, the coat closet. I mean…?" Sandy's baffled expression picked up where her voice trailed off.

"What did he say?" GiGi asked.

"Well, first he used the bathroom. Then he came out and stared at me. Like, *stared.* Then he asked me some stupid question about the coffee maker and how many degrees Fahrenheit it boiled the coffee to. I explained the coffee isn't boiled, just heated, and he asked if the overhead bins were up to federal standards. I don't even know what he's talking about."

"Where is he?"

Sandy leaned backward for another look. "He's checking the bathroom doors in the midcabin to…see if they open? What the heck is he doing?"

"I'll handle it. What's his name?"

"He introduced himself as Mr. Smilt, like that should mean something to me."

GiGi hit the aisle and stomped aft. This was the last thing she needed today. She found the ACI also walking toward the back of the airplane and tapped him on the shoulder. "May I see you for a moment?"

A hint of surprise passed over his face, but then he recovered and nodded like he was doing her a favor. She gestured for him to continue to the back of the plane and followed him.

"May I ask what this is about?" GiGi put her hands on her hips and leaned forward, indicating he should also keep his voice down.

"Protocol."

"For what?"

"For…for what I do. I'm the inspector." GiGi blinked. "With the federal government." GiGi blinked again. "To inspect the plane."

She glanced down at his badge. "Aren't you inspecting the pilots?"

"Of course I am."

"Then why are you back here?"

"I'm inspecting everything."

GiGi had to take a deep breath in order to finish this conversation. "Why?"

"What do you mean why?" His voice rose. "I'm a federal inspector. I can inspect whatever I want whenever I want."

"But you're the ACI for the pilots. We have our own inspector."

He paused, his eyelids fluttering. "Yes, well." He looked at her gold-plated nametag. "GiGi. Like everything else in this industry, we've had to make changes. Cuts. Downsizes. So now I get to do two jobs for the price of one." He looked at his clipboard, then hugged it against his chest. "I assume your safety demonstration went well? Everyone knows how to release their seat belts? All done with smiles on your faces even though nobody is paying attention to you?"

GiGi folded her arms. What was that, some comment on the fuzzy video they played? It wasn't her fault the equipment didn't work well. If it was up to her, they'd still do live safety demonstrations. Every once in a while, back in her younger days, she liked to mess with the passengers' heads and finish by telling them there would be a pop quiz. People actually went pale. It was a lot of fun.

This, however, was not fun, and she didn't appreciate his tone. One red mark and she'd have to do additional training on a computer, but maybe it'd be worth it to wipe that smug look off his face.

"As far as I can tell," he said, "you're doing everything to the high standard we expect. I'm impressed."

"Great. Impress yourself back to the cockpit where people are impressed with impressiveness." GiGi dialed back her tone a little. She didn't need trouble. "Look, it's been a complicated flight, as I'm sure you're well aware."

"I've taken that into consideration. You've handled yourself properly from everything I've observed. The cabin is orderly and quiet."

When he'd observed all this was a mystery, since he'd been in the cockpit, but she kept her mouth shut.

"Now," he continued, "I will need to see the manifest."

"Why?"

"It should be onboard at all times. I just have to check it off my list."

"I'll see if I can locate it, but as you know, it only has business class, flying-club members, and passengers in need of assistance on it."

"That's it? Not the entire list of people?"

Kim appeared and pulled GiGi into the aisle. "Leendert is freaking out."

"About the toes?"

"He thinks somebody is going to kill him."

"For heaven's sake. Is he on medication?"

"The agent doesn't know what's wrong with him."

GiGi slipped back into the galley to explain to the ACI that she needed to attend to a passenger, but he was gone. She glanced up the opposite aisle and saw him walking back toward the cockpit, inspecting whether or not people had their seat belts on.

GiGi hurried to the agent and Leendert. The agent stood, looking like she wanted to punch something. GiGi felt the same way.

"Now what?" GiGi snapped.

The agent pulled her a few steps away. "This is just a play for attention. Don't fall for it."

GiGi looked at Leendert. He was breathing hard and staring to his left, toward the aisle.

"Are you sure?"

"He's a womanizer. He's been trying to get one of you flight attendants to pay attention to him this entire flight. Of course, since his English stinks, he's crashing and burning."

"Does he have a mental illness?"

"Nothing of the sort."

GiGi glanced at him. "What's he looking at?"

"Don't worry about it. I'll handle it."

"He's going to kill me!" Leendert yelped. Both women whirled around.

"Leendert, shut up," the agent said.

The only people in the back few rows of the airplane were Leendert, Agent Tasler, GiGi, Sandy, the dead woman and her daughter, and Ulcer Guy. The only "him" was Ulcer on the far side of the plane, intently watching his television.

"Who?"

The agent stepped between GiGi and Leendert. "I'll handle

this. Don't engage him. That's only going to make things worse because it's what he wants."

"I'm not comfortable with this. What if he turns violent?"

"He's handcuffed. And he's not violent. He took off with some diamonds from an old lady."

A diamond thief with heartbreaking eyes? GiGi's knees felt weaker than usual.

"Is he going to make some kind of scene?" she asked. "Because we have a federal inspector onboard looking to find any kind of problem."

Leendert jolted forward, engaging GiGi. "Please. I want to move. Please, I bet of you. To the front."

"It's *beg* and you're not going anywhere," Agent Tasler said, pushing him back into his seat. She turned to GiGi. "Okay, maybe if you could cover up her toes?"

"We're out of blankets."

"Here, take my blazer."

"Okay, sure. I'll see what I can do."

GiGi took the blazer and draped it over Hetty's toes. Ulcer Guy looked up and took off his earphones.

"Everything's fine, sir," she told him. "The man across the aisle just requested she be fully covered."

The flight attendant bell rang. GiGi sighed and walked up the aisle. No surprise, it was Hank.

"What can I get for you?"

He pointed to his breakfast tray. "It's just a little cold. May I have it warmed up?"

Milk and Cookies was back. "Can I ask you something?"

He gave her his full attention. "Of course."

"Were you raised with a nanny?"

"A nanny?"

"Or rich? Are you one of those rich people who flies in coach and dresses like you're not rich even though you are?"

Hank laughed. "I'm not rich. I was raised in a large family, have six brothers and sisters. We worked in the family business."

"Catering?"

"Clowning. I was the mime."

Maybe he was making up for lost time. She took his tray. "I'll get you a new breakfast."

"You are so kind. Thank you."

She turned, then stopped. Maybe Hank could calm Leendert down. Do one of those prayer things, smile and tell him it's going to be okay. But nobody knew they had a prisoner onboard, and they should probably keep it that way.

If things got out of control, she could give Milk and Cookies a try. For now, though, things seemed to be somewhat quiet, if Leendert could get his paranoia under control.

Then a noise so peculiar it caused a loud, collective gasp blasted through the entire cabin like a rush of wind.

GiGi covered her mouth, trying to hold in a scream.

Chapter 19

D anny scribbled another bullet point in the notebook he held.

"Can we think of anything else?" he asked. "We've got to be thorough." He'd pointed out the need to write down every behavior they'd witnessed from the ACI so far. If this man was under the influence of alcohol or some other substance, he was far more likely to write up a bad report, or at least an inconsistent one. That could put all of their jobs in jeopardy.

Danny gripped the pen. "Come on, let's think. Anything else? Nobody smelled anything on him? noticed him pouring anything into a beverage?"

"Let's not rush to judgment," James said.

Danny glared at him. "I don't know, James. That seems to be your specialty."

"Don't get defensive," James said, holding his hands up. "You're the one who confessed to living with your girlfriend. This guy hasn't confessed to anything."

"Actions say a lot about a person," the captain said in her quiet voice. "Actions speak louder than verbs."

A few choice nouns plus a couple of inappropriate adjectives clung to the tip of Danny's tongue. He didn't know what verbs had to do with it, but he was horrible at English, so whatever the captain was trying to say was going right over his head. As usual.

Suddenly, over the intercom the flight attendants used to contact the cockpit, they heard screams. Danny lunged out of the jump seat, dropping his notebook. He leaned toward the speaker with the captain and James.

"Was that screaming?" he asked.

Again they heard it, patchy and intermittent.

"It sounds like screaming!" James said.

"Captain!" A woman's voice crackled through the radio. "Captain! It's…it's…"

"Hello?" The captain listened hard. "Over? Over?"

"This is Sandy. Captain!" She sounded out of breath, panicked.

"What's going on back there?"

Danny rushed to the peephole. He could see people moving around, but couldn't identify the problem.

"Please, stay in your seats!" they heard the flight attendant say. "Everyone, stay in your seats!"

The captain switched on the Fasten Seat Belt sign. "Sandy? Can you hear me?"

"Yes, yes, I can hear you."

"What's happening?"

"It's the…the…" More screams in the background.

"What?"

"The pig. It's awake. And...um..."

"Yes? What?"

"Hungry."

GiGi gestured forcefully, abrasively, and with no room for misunderstanding. But she kept her voice calm as she stood in front of Anna Sue, whose wide eyes were shiny with tears.

"I don't know what has gotten into him. I've never seen him act this way." Anna Sue's knuckles were bloodless white as she gripped the headrest of her seat. A passenger nearby started to stand.

"Sir, sit down. *Sit.* Thank you." GiGi refocused on Anna Sue and tried to ignore the horrific grunting and squealing sounds carrying through the cabin. She couldn't see Chucky anymore. He'd disappeared into a galley. She heard a crashing noise, more snorting, and then a bloodcurdling squeal, enough to make any vegetarian go weak in the knees. "What is wrong with him?"

"I don't know. Usually he wakes up in a good mood." Anna Sue put her hands to her cheeks, glancing back and forth, up and down the aisle. "If he's hungry, he usually just nuzzles me with his...his...his snout. He usually eats once an hour, but he slept so long. He's just... He's... He hasn't eaten in...hours."

GiGi tried to determine which would be the bigger problem: a pig on the loose or a hysterical woman. An irritated pig roaming up and down the aisles was going to bring some lawsuits, but she wouldn't personally be sued. However, there was no telling what a hysterical, emotionally challenged woman might do.

Kim hurried toward them, half her ponytail falling down and her lipstick smudged up the side of her cheek. "I don't know… Should we… Does it bite? I'm wondering if we should—"

GiGi made herself sound calm, the way her third therapist used to talk. "Has Sandy contacted the cockpit?" The word *cockpit* hit a high octave, but overall she thought her words were measured and pacifying.

"Yes. She told them. I don't know what they're… Maybe they're contacting the company. I don't know. Maybe we should—"

"Kim, look at me. Keep the passengers calm. Let's not worry about what to do about the pig right this moment. We need to make sure the pig is calm. Can you get Milk and Cookies?"

"He does like chocolate chip," Anna Sue said.

GiGi tried a smile. "Why don't you sit here while we figure out what to do?"

"I've just never seen him so mad."

"Do you have any medication you might want to take, something you carry for emergencies?"

"No. Nothing works on me. The doctors have tried everything, which is why I have Chucky." Tears dripped down her cheeks just as GiGi started to ask if she had any medication for the pig. "I've *got* to have him before we land. I *have* to! Are we landing? I feel the airplane moving."

Yes, the airplane's moving, lady. At five hundred miles an hour.

Hank appeared by GiGi's side. "How can I help?"

A sharp-as-a-knife but familiar shriek pierced the already-noisy cabin.

"Mrs. Kilpatrick," Hank said with a longsuffering expression.

"See what you can do with her. Do that calm thing. That look."

"What look?"

"You know, the thing you did earlier. That thing you did with your eyes."

"I don't know what you're talking about."

GiGi gently shoved him on. "Just go. Do your thing."

She looked toward the front of the plane where the pig roamed. She heard screams and noticed people throwing their breakfast food into the aisles. "Okay...okay, this is good. People are offering up their breakfasts. Maybe that will slow Chucky down."

Anna Sue leaned into the aisle to see better. "Oh, um...he doesn't like tortillas."

"What?"

"I've tried corn tortillas too. He won't eat them."

"He's a pig. Shouldn't he just scarf down the entire thing, wrapper and all?"

"I might've, you know, spoiled him over the years."

"So you're telling me he's not going to eat what everyone is throwing into the aisle?"

"Oh, no. No. He loves eggs. They just can't be touching the tortilla or be served with, um, bacon."

GiGi pinched the bridge of her nose.

Sandy rushed toward her. "I've contacted the captain."

"What'd she say?"

"They're discussing it."

"Did you explain the pig is actually *roaming* around the cabin? *Rooting?* Did you use the word 'rooting'?"

"I explained it the best I could. They're trying to come up with a—"

"Forget it. I'll handle it." GiGi returned to the back of the plane and grabbed the intercom. "All right, everyone. We need your full attention. Please, stay calm and listen to my instructions."

She noticed Hank near Mrs. Kilpatrick. He gave her a reassuring nod. But more than that, he gave her a good idea: call the pig by name. It had worked with a dead woman. Maybe it'd work with a pig. It would've helped if the pig didn't share a name with a mass-murdering doll, but she had to work with it.

The pig squealed, causing another round of screams. Hank fanned Mrs. Kilpatrick. Ulcer apparently had the volume turned up on his earphones, because he was completely engaged in whatever show he was watching and had no idea what was going on.

"Hey."

GiGi turned.

Agent Tasler stood with her feet spread and her hands clasped behind her back. "Can I assist you?"

"I don't know. Do you have special training in pig wrangling?"

"No need to be sarcastic."

"I'm not being sarcastic. In case you haven't noticed, we have an actual *porcinus brutus* onboard, and it needs to be wrangled back into its seat. If you come up with any ideas, let me know. In the meantime, go ahead and take your seat." GiGi turned on the intercom. "Ladies and gentlemen, I need your complete and full attention. Obviously, we have a very strange situation onboard. I can assure you that nobody is in danger. The pig is a service animal and is highly trained." "Highly" was a bit of a stretch. "His name is Chucky, and he likes chocolate-chip cookies."

She paused, hoping to hear a few chuckles. Nothing came her way.

"He also likes scrambled eggs, but isn't fond of tortillas. All of you with toddlers can relate, right? So, here's what we're going to do. For those of you who've so generously offered the pig your breakfast by placing it in the aisle, if you'll please pick that up, unwrap it, and then put the *eggs only* in the aisle, that would really help. In the meantime, we know you're hungry, so Sandy, Kim, and the rest of the crew will hand out all-you-can-eat cocktail peanuts." She took a deep breath and hoped this would work. "Thank you for your cooperation in this matter, and thank you for flying Atlantica."

Then she heard, "Leendert! Leendert?"

Shiny lip gloss and four coats of mascara later, Lucy sat ready to prove she'd also superficially moved on. Except now the man supposed to be helping her prove this was being called away yet again.

Not only that, she was certain Jeff hadn't spotted her yet. He was too busy tending to his girlfriend. Lucy checked herself in her compact mirror one more time. She looked too tired. Why hadn't she brought her skin brightening cream onboard? Oh yeah. It was over three ounces. Traveling with it never occurred to her when she bought the twenty-ounce tub.

The pig raced by again. She'd thrown her breakfast burrito into the aisle, but there was no way she was going to unwrap it for a pig. Sighing, she decided to add some blush. She wanted to glow like she'd found happiness.

She'd tried four dozen blushes through the years, but she'd never managed to find that color that made her look like she glowed from within. She had to settle for looking like life was a vacation. Or at least like she'd just come from a vacation.

"He could be a while."

Lucy glanced at the man next to her. He smiled.

"He'll be back," she said.

"Maybe."

"Why do you care?"

He shrugged. "You just look anxious. And not about the pig."

"I've been sitting here trying to capture some positive energy, but all I feel is disappointment, fear, and bitterness."

"Welcome to life."

"You know what? Why don't you just go back to whatever it was you were doing?"

"I was listening to your boyfriend talk to his girlfriend."

Lucy peeked over the back of her seat. "They're five rows back. How can you hear them?"

"Your boyfriend has a loud voice."

That was true. Jeff didn't have volume control. At a party, restaurant, bowling alley, or airport, his voice beat out everything.

"He was talking about you."

Lucy scoffed. "How do you know?"

"In the last five minutes, he's said the word 'ex' eight times."

Lucy wrapped her arms around herself. Her stomach roiled with a sick feeling of inadequacy. She was just an ex? No name?

The man leaned toward her. "Look, I'm a lawyer. I've got a Rolex and seven-hundred-dollar shoes. I can make a very good impression when I want to."

"What are you suggesting?"

"I help you out, and you go to dinner with me in Amsterdam."

Lucy swallowed. He had to be in his midforties. Not bad-looking—red hair, tan skin, and an Ed Harris smile. And he did dress nicely. Was that a silk shirt? But hadn't he mentioned a wife?

Lucy traced the edge of her hairline with one finger. What was she doing? Trading one man who was supposed to pose as her boyfriend with another man offering to do the same? Was that cheating?

She mentally paged through *The Secret*, trying to remember anything that addressed this situation.

"You could stand up, pretend to need something out of the overhead. I could help you," he said.

"We're supposed to stay seated."

"Then we'll wait until the time is right." He grinned like he wanted something.

"Maybe I'll just wait for Hank."

The man laughed. "You think that guy's going to impress your ex? I mean, no offense, he's nice enough, but he's small, skinny, and in case you haven't noticed, a little geeky."

"Fresh faced."

"Okay. Whatever. It's your life." He went back to reading his newspaper. "I'm just saying, that chick your ex is with is hot, and he's not going to care or notice unless you one-up him. It's how life works, which is why I wear a Rolex."

"But don't fly first class?"

"They were booked for this flight."

"What did he say about me? You said you could hear him."

The man tucked his chin, chuckled a little, and said nothing.

"What?"

He glanced at her. "You are desperate, aren't you?"

"I don't need his approval."

"Right."

"You're a jerk."

"No. He's a jerk for leaving a beautiful woman like you."

Lucy paused, waiting for that weak moment of being swayed by flattery to wash over and leave. "I thought you said that chick was hot."

"But not classy like you are." He looked her up and down. "Not everyone can pull off polka dots."

Lucy stared forward. It was now or never. She couldn't let four coats of mascara go to waste.

Danny could not endure this any longer. "The ACI's out there. There's no telling what he's writing down."

"I need more time to think," said the captain.

She'd been thinking for five minutes. At the same time, James gabbed about how he used to rope calves and ride bulls on his grandfather's farm when he was ten years old and felt sure he could get the pig too.

"Ma'am, with all due respect, I think we need to take some kind of action now. This situation is getting out of control and quickly."

"Bubba, people make most of their mistakes in life because they open their flaps too soon. They want to jump and act on instinct. Instinct is critical, there's no doubt about that, but often-times, if we stop and think about what we're doing, we'll understand better how to handle a situation."

Danny didn't say it, but he was pretty certain this was one of those moments when you wanted to go with your gut and then tell stories about it later. He tapped his feet against the carpet and watched the captain, who sat in her seat, clasped her hands together, and thought.

Twice Danny interrupted her, volunteering to go out and at least be a presence in the cabin. Twice she put a stern finger up, indicating she was not finished thinking.

Then, finally, she said, "I'm going out there."

"I'm telling you, I can lasso that pig," James said.

"I'm not worried about the pig right now."

"You're not?" Danny asked.

"Something is not right with that ACI. I'm going to go find him." She unbuckled her seat belt.

"What about the pig?"

She paused at the cockpit door. "Under no circumstance are you to leave the cockpit."

Danny nodded. They were never to have two pilots out of the cockpit at once, except on the rare occasion that one pilot was on break and another needed to use the restroom. Then a flight attendant had to stand in the cockpit and the flying pilot had to put on an oxygen mask.

"Unless…" She looked out the peephole.

"Unless what?"

She left.

"Unless what?" Danny asked James.

"I guess unless things get really out of control."

"I don't know." Danny sighed, scrubbing his face with his hands. "Half the time I don't even know what she's talking about." His head was starting to pound. "Okay, let's come up with some ideas on how to catch this pig, just in case we can't find a lasso. I thought maybe we could block one of the aisles with a couple of beverage carts, maybe have two big guys sit with their backs against them so the pig can't push them over, and then—"

"I think we should get some of those tiny vodka bottles. Get him drunk."

"That's your solution? How are we supposed to make a pig binge drink?"

Suddenly, someone pounded at the door. James looked through the peephole. "It's GiGi."

"Make certain she's alone."

"She is. She's got a cart blocking the aisle."

"She must be terrified."

"Um…she looks mad."

"Let me in!" GiGi hollered through the door.

"Let her in."

James opened the door, and GiGi shoved him aside. She slammed the cockpit door, and it clicked as she turned around. "What is going on? The captain is out there!"

"Yeah. We kinda figured that out," James said.

"She's doing nothing about the pig! She's looking for the stupid ACI."

Danny tried a calm voice. "She sort of thinks he's a, uh…"

"The *pig* is terrifying people!"

"Personally," James said, "I'm never eating bacon again."

"Look, GiGi, I appreciate your take on this, but what do you want us to do? We can't leave the cockpit."

"The captain said, 'unless things got out of control,'" James added.

Danny shot him a look. "She didn't say that. She just said, 'unless.'"

"With the captain, you have to read between the lines, Danny."

GiGi's nostrils flared like a raging bull's. "*What* do you call this? I'd call it out of control!"

"The pig isn't hurting anyone," Danny tried.

"Look, Danny," James said, "GiGi's right. If this doesn't qualify for out of control, what does?"

Danny held his head in his hands.

"Danny had the idea of using a couple of the carts to barricade the pig," James offered.

"That's a start," GiGi grumbled.

"We're not supposed to leave the cockpit," Danny protested.

"We're also not supposed to have a wild animal on the plane. I've got a bunch of people in hysterics, six of my flight attendants crying, and a pig who isn't fond of tortillas. I need your help."

Danny tried to listen to his gut.

James said, "Leave GiGi here, as is protocol, and try to get the pig under control. What can the ACI say? We did nothing? How is that going to reflect on us? It'll be fine. I've got the plane. It's all under control in here."

Danny took a deep breath. GiGi, normally overbearing, looked desperate.

He stood. "All right. I'll go. But James, whatever you do, do not leave this cockpit."

"I know, Danny. Just go."

Chapter 20

J ake had been dreaming the equivalent of a running-through-a-daisy-field dream. It was a ridiculous dream and he knew it even while he enjoyed every moment of it. He wanted to stop, but it was like skipping. Once you get into a groove, it could carry you a long way. So he skipped along like a little kid, enjoying every fabricated moment his mind created.

He saw his grandmother taking him on a long walk by the North Sea. Sharing albums full of memories. Giving him wisdom he was too young to understand but that would transform his life someday. Fixing him enormous scrambled-egg breakfasts, which was strange because he hated eggs and had no idea why he would dream about them.

He knew it was silly. He'd never met his grandmother as a child or otherwise, and was now an adult with a job he was certain met nobody's standard as a job. And by the few conversations they'd had on the phone, he knew this wasn't a woman who would have warm cookies waiting for him.

But he was asleep, comfortable, and happy, so he kept dreaming and tried to ignore the strange screams that filtered in every once in a while. He figured it was his conscience bending his dream in an Andy Warhol sort of way, trying to save him from believing it.

"It's him!"

That shout came in a weird moment, right as his grandmother handed him a lavishly wrapped gift box. He continued sleeping, though, until something knocked him in the shoulder, forcing him to open his eyes.

The screams were real. He stood up, slamming his head into the plastic ceiling above him. "Ow!"

"Sir, sit down!" A flight attendant rushed by, grabbing Jake's shoulder and throwing him back into his seat.

A set of unfamiliar eyes focused on him. A blond dude knelt next to the old lady whose mom died, fanning her with a magazine. "You okay?" he asked.

Jake rubbed the top of his head. "What's going on?"

"The pig is loose." He mouthed it, holding his hand up to block his words from the old lady.

Jake looked around, noticing immediately that the old guy and his younger woman had disappeared. "Where'd they go?"

"Who?"

"That couple on the other side of the plane, sitting in the back row like me."

"I don't know. I think the guy freaked out about the pig or something. He ran that way."

Jake noticed the dead woman's toes were now covered.

"Stop fanning me!" the old lady barked. "All the air in the world isn't going to make any difference!"

"How about a cup of water?" the blond guy asked her.

"Fine. Just stop hovering over me."

The man climbed out of his seat, looked around in the galley for a moment, then sat across the aisle from Jake. "I guess I should wait until a flight attendant comes back."

Jake tried not to engage, as the whole idea of sitting back here was to avoid everyone else, but his curiosity got the better of him. "Why are there eggs spilled all over the floor?"

"The pig is hungry, but he doesn't like his eggs wrapped in a tortilla, so they've asked everyone to get the tortilla out of the way." He thrust his arm across the aisle. "Hank."

"Hi."

"Man, this has been some flight. This is only my second trip flying."

"Oh. Wow."

"Yeah. I guess they're not usually like this."

Jake smiled. "Never flown with a pig or a dead person before."

"Don't you think the flight attendants are doing a good job?"

Jake nodded. Besides being obsessed about whether he was the right temperature, he supposed they were decent. At least they let him sleep instead of waking him up for breakfast.

Hank sighed. "I guess I should go back to my seat, but I don't really want to. It's peaceful back here."

Jake nodded, which was why he'd love it if this guy would return to wherever he came from. "They'll catch the pig eventually."

"Oh, it's not really the pig. It's a woman."

"Snoring?"

Hank laughed. "No."

"Talking your ear off?"

"Sort of. But in a good way. She's really sweet. She's had the terrible luck of finding her ex-boyfriend onboard with another woman."

Jake winced. "Ooh. Ouch."

"Yeah." Hank rested his head against the back of his seat. "She wanted me to pose as her boyfriend, make him jealous."

"That's a good idea."

"Except she's a perfectly wonderful person without him. I told her she doesn't need a guy to make herself feel worthy."

"Are you a psychologist or something?"

Hank laughed. "No."

"Huh. So you're not going to go along with her plan?"

"Well," he said, a smile slipping onto his lips, "after considering it and getting some advice from my sister, I think I will. My sister Cassie always says I'm not bold enough, you know? She says if I want to date, I need to put myself out there and take the risk. So I'm thinking, why not? Why not risk it for a girl in polka dots?"

The girl in polka dots who had nearly attacked him in the men's bathroom? Aside from that, she was good looking.

"Well, good luck." Jake hoped that would end their talk. It amazed him the kinds of conversations that took place on an airplane. He'd once heard a woman confess an affair to a total stranger sitting next to her. For two and a half hours she went on about every detail of her life. Maybe it was easier to talk to a stranger.

"What's taking you to Amsterdam?" Hank asked.

"My grandmother."

"Oh, how nice."

"I've never met her."

"Wow. That sounds interesting."

"We'll see." Jake cleared his throat. "I've always wanted a grandma, you know?"

"Doesn't everyone?" Hank smiled.

"Yeah."

"Family is important. They mean everything to me. I don't know what I would do without them. It's worth it, even if it takes going halfway around the world to get to them."

Jake nodded. It affirmed something inside of him, something he hadn't been able to explain.

They heard the pig squeal again.

"You should go," Jake said. "There's nothing more romantic than saving a woman from a pig. You'll be her hero forever."

"Good point. Thanks."

The man rose and hurried up the aisle. Nice guy. Jake wished him the best. Polka-dot girl was hot.

Score one for the team, dude.

Danny found GiGi holding on to a wall and picking egg off the bottom of her shoe.

"GiGi! Why aren't you in the cockpit?"

"Don't have a cow. I came out to help with the pig. Gloria's there for now."

Danny wanted to argue that she'd completely disobeyed his order, but he had more pressing issues at the moment.

"Okay, listen," he said, "I need vodka, or whatever you have. As much of it as you have."

She looked like she might take off her shoe and impale him with it. "This is no time for a joke. We could all use the alcohol, so don't tempt me."

"It's not for *me*. It's for the pig."

GiGi folded her arms. "And how, exactly, are you going to do that? Every time anyone comes near him, he charges or squeals or blows fire from his nostrils."

"I haven't quite figured out how, but we have got to sedate him again."

"Again?"

Danny whirled around to find Anna Sue behind them.

"What do you mean 'again'?" she asked.

Any explanation froze on his tongue. How was he supposed to handle this? Admit to drugging the animal and risk causing Anna Sue to flip out? Or lie his way out of it?

"Ma'am, you need to go back to your seat right now," GiGi said.

"But I want to know how Chucky is doing. Is he okay?"

GiGi leaned backward for a glance down the aisle. "For the moment, yes. He's eating eggs. So let's just let him eat and go from there."

Anna Sue's soft, saucerlike eyes turned harder. "What are you planning to do to him?"

Danny filled his cheeks with air and blew. "Anna Sue, honestly, I don't know. I mean, I know how to land a plane in the dark and bring a 767 out of a roll, but I have to be honest with you, I don't know how to get a pig back in its seat."

Anna Sue shook her head. "I don't know what's the matter with him. He's a trained animal. He should not be acting this way. The biggest problem I have with him at home is that he likes to chew plastic. I've gotten him a few plastic toys, you know? Sometimes he's naughty and chews other plastic things, but that's it."

Danny realized that despite everything going on, Anna Sue was holding up better than she realized. If ever there was a time for an emotionally challenged woman to come unraveled, this would be it.

"Anna Sue," he said, "you're doing remarkably well. Maybe you don't need the pig with you. At least not right now."

She pondered this. "For a little bit, with all the excitement, I almost forgot I was on an airplane."

"Stay with us, Anna Sue. You're doing fine. Don't go to that place. Just know that we're going to handle it."

She drew in a deep breath. "Just promise me you won't hurt him."

"GiGi!" Kim shouted. They all turned. Kim had her arms raised in a giant "what are you doing?" gesture.

"I know, I know," GiGi said. "I'm getting to that. Hold your horses."

"Getting to what?" Danny asked. He nodded reassuringly to Anna Sue, and she made her way back to her seat.

GiGi rolled her eyes. "Come with me."

Danny followed, still trying to figure out how to entice Chucky to drink hard liquor. Maybe a margarita?

They arrived at the middle of the plane to find the FBI agent in a tizzy, reminding him of a flight attendant. This didn't immediately alarm him, because he was well aware that any woman, law enforcement or not, could become tizzy-fied at a moment's notice.

Along with Agent Tasler, several flight attendants were clustered around the four central bathrooms.

"I stood up for one second!" the agent said.

"Everyone, keep your voices down!" Danny whispered. "Why are we all standing by the bathrooms?"

"One, you can step aside when the pig comes through," GiGi said mildly. "Two, Leendert has locked himself in the bathroom."

"Locked himself in the bathroom? Is he trying to escape?"

"He thinks someone is trying to kill him."

"He's old, he's apparently not fond of dead bodies, and I think he just went over the edge." The agent knocked on the door. "Get yourself out here this instant!"

GiGi glared at Danny. "Maybe Leendert could use some vodka too."

"I can bust this door down," the agent said. "One side kick and I've got him."

"That won't be necessary," Danny said. "We can open it using a Bic pen. The question is, what is he going to do when we open the door?"

"The question is, what am *I* going to do?" the agent said, loud enough for Leendert to hear.

"I'm telling you, he's going to kill me!" Leendert shouted through the door.

Danny shook his head. "Who does he think is going to kill him?"

"Some guy in the back of the airplane. It's ridiculous. He's being paranoid. Really paranoid for a man who steals from old ladies."

"So, what do you want to do?" GiGi asked.

"Does Leendert still have cuffs on?" Danny asked.

"Yes."

"Okay, I do not want to draw attention to the fact that we have a distraught prisoner onboard too. The passengers are already stressed as it is. We've got to find a way to get Leendert back to his seat in a calm, peaceful, incognito way. Got it? For now, let's just leave him in the bathroom until he settles down. I've got to figure out how to catch that pig."

Kim said, "He's slowing down a little. He doesn't seem as agitated, but he flips out every time someone tries to reach for him."

Danny leaned against the door of the opposite bathroom, his fingers tearing through his hair. *Think. Think. Think. Not about Maya.* Why was he thinking of Maya at a time like this, with a prisoner locked in a bathroom and a pig roaming the aircraft?

Perhaps it was because Maya represented betrayal. He'd invested six years of his life, and in one day she was gone.

What about the twenty years he'd invested in his career? Would it just as easily slip away? He couldn't let that happen.

With both hands, he pushed himself away from the bathroom door.

Then he got a brilliant idea.

Chapter 21

It was everything she'd dreamed it would be. She stood, pretending to stretch. She turned, waiting for the passenger next to her, who'd finally introduced himself by name—Neil—to stand and embrace her from behind. She had to be at the right angle to see Jeff but not look directly at him.

Lucy knew from the audible gasp that he noticed her a few seconds after she stood up. He started to say something, though Lucy couldn't tell what or to whom he spoke. Then Neil did it up right. Cool as a cucumber, he made sure his Rolex was visible as he nuzzled her neck, then brushed her hair out of her eyes.

In her peripheral vision, she saw Jeff's jaw drop open. She grinned at Neil, turned, and sat back down in her seat.

The positive energy returned like a force field around her. Nothing would bring her down now, not even Neil and his hot-and-heavy breath, anxious to invade her space. He wanted to know, "What restaurant? When? How long will you be in the Netherlands?"

She turned to him. "Let me savor this moment, okay? Just for a second?"

"He looked shocked. I could see him."

"What did the woman do?"

"She was kind of oblivious, from what I could tell."

"I wonder if he'll tell her."

"I wouldn't. I don't want the lady I'm with distracted by anything."

Lucy frowned. She didn't like that.

"Trust me," Neil said. "He's shocked. Don't overplay this thing. Now, about dinner."

Hank returned to his seat, sliding in so gently she hardly realized he was there until he said, "Hey."

"Hi."

"I haven't told you this yet, because we're virtually strangers, but you look really good in polka dots."

"Hank, that is so nice."

"I'll do it."

"Do what?"

He turned to her with an enthusiasm she hadn't seen in him before. Compared to her gale-force winds, he was usually like a still, calm pond with hardly a ripple in sight. Excitability widened his eyes. He took her hand very gently, as though if he touched her all the bones might break. "I'll pose as your boyfriend."

"But—"

"I know I was against it, even after Cassie suggested it, and I still think that you're a wonderful lady with no need for a man's affirmation, but I like you, Lucy. I like you a lot, to tell you the truth. And if I can do you this favor, then I'll do it. I mean, why not? We could walk to the bathroom holding hands or something? Something like that? Was that what you were thinking? Maybe that's too much. Maybe I could just follow you to the bathroom and if he looks up I could comment on how nice you look in polka dots. Yeah, that's better. That's not too much. I don't want to make you feel uncomfortable…" Hank's words trailed off as he studied her face. She was not one for mastering expressions, and whatever expression she wore, it caused his energetic grin to fade. "What's the matter?"

"Oh, Hank…um, it's just…"

He hung his head. "I'm being too forward, aren't I? Cassie says I need to be more forward, but I don't know if that's the best approach. I mean, sometimes things should happen naturally. Like I should pose as your boyfriend only if it fits in naturally, right?"

Lucy pressed the palms of her hands together and put the tips of her fingers to her mouth. How was she going to break this to him? The victory of one-upping Jeff dwindled at the sight of Hank's bumbling attempt not to look embarrassed.

Neil leaned forward. "It's over. We already did it, while you were back there doing whatever it is you do back there. She stood, I stood, I caressed her shoulders and gave her a little nibble on the neck." He paused to wink at Lucy. "The guy's face was priceless. We're going to celebrate over dinner. I know this great restaurant on the canals."

Lucy quickly looked at Hank.

"Oh, sure," he said. "I know I was back there a long time."

"No, Hank. Please, don't think that I... I mean, I knew you weren't comfortable with it, and Neil..."

Neil shot his hand out, smiling in a self-satisfied manner. "Nice to meet you."

Hank shook his hand politely. "Listen, I better go check on Mrs. Kilpatrick again."

Lucy grabbed his arm. "Hank, it's nothing personal at all. You are the sweetest guy."

"Yeah. In a Timex sort of way."

On his hands and knees, Danny used his fingers like claws, scraping every ounce of egg he could off the airplane carpet.

"Man, the service people are going to love this mess," Kim said, head to head with him as she scraped eggs into her own pile.

"I think this is going to work," Danny said. "If he's still hungry enough, this will work."

"What is he going to do when he realizes we've picked up all his eggs?"

"Hurry. Faster. I don't know. Hopefully be mad enough to hunt them down."

Kim smiled. "I think this is a great plan. We're really going to have a story to tell when we get on the ground."

"Are you getting the little pieces? We need everything."

"Danny, slow down. It's okay."

"No, it's not. It's really not."

"Bubba."

Danny fell back onto his heels and looked up. The captain stood above him.

"What are you doing?" she asked.

"I have a plan."

"Why are you out of the cockpit?"

"Unless." What else could he say? That word left a lot of room for interpretation.

He prepared for a barrage of questions, but instead she said, "Have you seen the ACI?"

"No. I thought you were looking for him."

"I'm trying, but passengers keep stopping me and asking me questions. What about you, Kim?"

"I saw him earlier. He was checking on fire extinguishers or something. I haven't seen him in a while."

For the first time, the captain looked worried. "He was asking for the manifest?"

"Yes. And seemed irritated that we don't keep a full passenger list. I told him we could call for it."

"What'd he say?"

"He mumbled something about everyone moving seats because of the pig, then told me my shoes weren't up to standard. Really weird."

"Did you check the bathrooms?" Danny asked the captain.

"Yes. All of them except the one that was occupied. Agent Tasler looked a little ill. Everything okay there?"

Danny started scraping eggs again. "I'll have to brief you on that in a moment."

The captain glanced up and down the aisles. "All right. I'm going to start checking seats. Keep your eye out for him."

Danny nodded. "Okay, Kim, hand me that tray." Together, they scraped their piles of eggs onto the tray. With Kim trailing, Danny made his way back to the central bathrooms, where three other flight attendants waited with trays of eggs.

"Should we pick out the carpet fibers?" one asked.

"It's a pig," said another.

"Who doesn't like tortillas, for crying out loud," said the third.

"Okay, listen up," Danny said. "We're going to use this bathroom." He pointed to the largest of the three, twice the size of the others and, Danny guessed, big enough to host a pig. "I want you to put the eggs in the far corner. Close the toilet lid and put them between the toilet seat and the wall. I want him to have to turn to get to it, because then we're going to shove him in and close the door."

GiGi signaled to him. Danny told the FAs to start dumping the eggs and joined her a few feet away from the bathroom. "She's asking for you. She wants to know what you're going to do."

"Anna Sue?"

GiGi nodded.

"Where's the pig?"

"About five bites away from finishing up the only eggs left on the floor."

Danny took a deep breath. "Okay, it's now or never. Get everyone to their stations." He rushed to Anna Sue's seat. "Hey. How're you doing?"

"What's happening? What are you going to do to him?"

Danny squatted. She seemed to take things better with him squatting. "Anna Sue, we have to get Chucky under control. We're setting a trap for him."

"A trap?"

"Listen, it's not going to harm him. We're going to lure him into that middle bathroom, the one that's really big that all the women fight over?" He grinned. Anna Sue didn't. "Anyway, we're going to give him some food and water, lure him in there, and shut the door."

"Then what?"

"Then, once we're on the ground, we'll let him out."

Anna Sue covered her mouth with a shaky hand. "You're going to keep him in there?"

"He'll have enough room to sit. Anna Sue, this is not what any of us want, but we've got to think of the other passengers. People are freaking out."

Through the cabin they heard, "He's going to kill me!"

Danny swallowed. "Um, see? People are really overreacting."

"He's the sweetest pig anyone could ever hope to meet! He would never hurt anyone."

"You and I understand that, but not everyone does. With the woman passing away, it's been a lot for people to take, you know?"

"You've been so kind." She squeezed his hand. "I'll trust you."

"Okay." He rose and hurried past the flight attendants. "GiGi, let's do it."

GiGi cleared her throat. "Ladies and gentlemen, thank you for your patience." Her voice, cool and smooth like she was about to announce the beverage service, gave instructions as Danny scrambled, albeit delicately, toward Chucky with a handful of cold, rubbery eggs. "We're going to lead Chucky down the aisle and toward the bathroom area. Once we get him there, we're going to allow him into the bathroom, where he'll have a nice supply of food and water for the rest of the trip." GiGi's voice took on a singsong tone. Danny liked the "allow" part, as if Chucky suddenly became a Gold Star flier and got a perk.

GiGi continued as Danny slowly approached the pig. He tried not to notice that all eyes were on him. All eyes except Chucky's. He was rooting around on the carpet, suddenly aware he was out of eggs.

"Chucky…"

Chucky's ears perked up, and he turned his head. His eyes locked with Danny's, and for a moment, Danny swore he saw recognition there. The pig's snout tightened as if to say, "You're the one who spiked my applesauce."

Danny gently threw down a few pieces of scrambled egg. "Here you go, Chucky."

Except Chucky wasn't looking at the eggs. Chucky was looking at Danny.

"Eat the eggs, Chucky."

"…and if you all could remain calm and quiet while we carry

out this task, it would be so much appreciated. Meanwhile, Amsterdam is reporting balmy, slightly cooler temperatures…"

"Come on, Chucky…"

Chucky took one step forward. Then another. Then another. He stepped on some egg, never looking down.

"Chucky, see? Egg? You love eggs. Exactly what you were eating before. Just more of it. Lots more of it where this came from."

"…and we'll announce which gate we'll be arriving at as soon as we get that information. For your convenience, there is a diagram of the Amsterdam airport in the back of your *Atlantica Sky High* magazine, located in the seatback…"

Chucky started moving faster, his hoofs thumping along the carpet and his beady, black eyes looking determined, despite the fluffy white eyelashes that lined them.

"He's not eating the eggs," a passenger whispered.

"Thank you, I see that," Danny said, still backing up. Either way, Chucky was following him. And now, following him rather quickly. Danny hustled backward, dropping eggs every three feet.

He didn't really know if Chucky could run, but whatever he was doing, it was faster than Danny expected. Sidestepping now, Danny tossed eggs from his hands and hurried around the corner to the bathroom, Chucky close behind. Danny could hear him huffing and puffing.

"Move!" Danny flung open the bathroom door. It was a split-second decision, but it wasn't hard. Chucky was not going to steal his job. He threw himself into the bathroom and climbed on top of the toilet seat. Chucky rushed in after him. Just as Chucky was about to put a hoof up and do who knew what—probably murder him with his snout—Danny grabbed the sides of the bathroom door, heaved himself over Chucky, and cast himself out of the bathroom. Agent Tasler slammed the door and flung her back against it, her arms spread wide.

"Lock it!" she ordered.

Danny grabbed the tool they used to lock the bathroom in case of an emergency or if the toilet was broken. Inching it into the small opening, he shoved it sideways, and they heard a click.

The door now read Occupied.

A collective round of relieved laughter came and went. Danny listened for Chucky attempting to get out, but he heard nothing except his own breathing and GiGi's announcement asking everyone to use the bathrooms in the back of the plane.

"I think he's okay," he said.

Nobody smiled and agreed, but nobody disagreed either. They waited awhile longer and heard nothing.

"I think he's okay," Danny said again. He turned to Kim. "Go tell Anna Sue he's fine. Don't forget to smile and use a light voice and positive reinforcement."

Kim nodded and rushed off.

The agent slid upward to a complete standing position and lowered her arms. She handed him a Bic pen.

"It's time to get Leendert."

Chapter 22

Every time Jake tried to ease back in to watching television or staring out the window, something shook him up, like a squeal, a scream, a bitter comment from Mrs. Kilpatrick, and now Hank "the gentleman" sitting back down in the seat across from him.

From the looks of it, he'd crashed and burned with polka-dot chick.

"You okay?"

Hank rolled his head to the side. His look painted a good-enough picture.

"Dude, I'm sorry. She wasn't interested?"

"She decided to use another fake boyfriend."

"Oh. Dang. Sorry."

"You know, one of my younger sisters got married recently. It came easy for her. She met the guy, they liked each other, and that was that. It doesn't seem to be that difficult."

"That's a one-in-a-million chance."

"My parents made it look easy too." Hank looked depressed. "I really thought she liked me. But then, I have no business being

interested in a woman who doesn't believe in God. He's everything to me. That relationship could have turned out to be a mis-
erable thing."

"Yeah, man. You gotta have similar ideals. I once dated a
chick who hated music. It was so ridiculous. I thought it might
be cool to get to know someone with other interests, and she was
really hot, you know? But at the end of the day, we didn't have
anything to talk about."

A commotion ahead caused them both to pause and look, but
they couldn't see much of anything.

"Do you work for the airline or something?" Jake asked.

"Why?"

"I don't know, you just seem to be the person the pilots ask to
help them."

"I guess I was just in the right place at the right time." Hank
rose and moved forward a couple of rows. "Mrs. Kilpatrick, how
are you—"

"I don't know why you keep coming over here checking on
me," the old woman snapped. "It's irritating."

"Ma'am, what can I get you? Maybe I could check on the
remainder of the flight time."

"See, that's what I mean. You're standing there like we're best
friends."

"Mrs. Kilpatrick, if you were my mom and this happened to
her, I would want someone to take care of her."

Jake observed a quiet pause between them. If Mrs. Kilpatrick
had treated him that way, he would've hightailed it back to his

seat and never spoken another word to her or would have cussed her out or something. Of course, he wasn't certain he would've helped her in the first place.

Jake suddenly clasped his hands over his belly. He'd nearly forgotten about the diamonds. He could feel the pouch underneath his shirt. Soon he'd be on the ground, and then he'd have to make his way to Idya's house. It was the final leg of the journey, but possibly the most dangerous. Not that he could help it, but he tried not to sweat. That, more than anything, seemed to bring the most attention.

He closed his eyes and attempted some deep breathing.

"Young man," he heard Mrs. Kilpatrick say, "a word of advice on your love life."

"My love life?" He heard Hank chuckle.

"I heard you back there talking about a woman in polka dots. First of all, never trust a woman in polka dots. Secondly, don't compromise, young man. As much as you annoy me, I recognize that you're quite a gentleman, and you deserve nothing less than a proper woman."

"What is a proper woman?"

Jake opened his eyes and sat up in order to hear better.

"Someone your grandmother would approve of."

Perry listened very carefully for any movement or sound. Nothing since the loud-mouthed flight attendant returned to the cockpit a few minutes ago, ranting about the pig in the bathroom. If he was going to do it, the time was now. He opened the small door to the coat closet he'd hidden in and inhaled like he was surrounded by mountain air.

He'd been sitting in the closet for a while, trying to decide what to do. And what he'd decided to do was prove everyone wrong. He was a man capable of carrying out any plan, no matter what that entailed. Not only that, he was capable of being flexible, unlike his boss. Playing out a scenario that involved a gun he'd found in the cockpit would be a challenge, but he was up for it. He did wonder whose gun it was. Pilots didn't carry them. At least they weren't supposed to. Maybe it was the FBI agent's.

Either way, he had access to a weapon now, which ushered in Plan C.

Plan B had been to locate Van Der Mark, follow him off the plane, jump him—possibly in an airport bathroom—get the diamonds, and flee. He planned to restrain Van Der Mark, because he figured the guy would put up quite a fight. He had leftover zip ties from the batch he used to cuff Miles Smilt to the chair. However, his plan got complicated when he realized he had no way of telling where Van Der Mark sat, and that was problem number one, because that was how he'd planned to figure out what the guy looked like.

Perry glanced quickly toward the cabin, then knocked on the cockpit door.

Without hesitation, the door opened. James sat with an oxygen mask on his face, looking irritated. GiGi sat in one of the jump seats, her arms folded tightly against her chest. "Where is the captain?" she asked. "Did she get sucked into the Bermuda Triangle or something?"

"Laugh it up," James said in a muffled voice, the hiss of oxygen barely making his words audible. "When they find Amelia Earhart, remember who told you where she would be."

"Take off the oxygen mask," Perry said, shutting the cockpit door.

James turned. "Is this a trick question?"

"Take it off."

"I can't until the captain returns."

"I said take it off."

"The captain is looking for you."

Perry took the gun out of his waistband and aimed it at James. "Get the mask off."

The pilot tore off the mask.

"Put your hands in the air, and get out of that seat."

James's eyes cut downward, and Perry knew he was going to attempt to push the hijacking button.

"Don't even think about it," Perry said, waving the gun.

James slowly got out of his seat and stood next to GiGi.

"Is autopilot on?"

James nodded. "How did you get a gun onboard?"

"Yes, I'm going to sit here and explain everything to you. Listen up, jerk. Nobody is going to get hurt if you do what I say. But

as you know, one bullet hole through the plane and the discussion
is over, so don't make me fire this gun. I'm sort of jumpy, so don't
test me."

"What do you want?" GiGi cried.

"Just a man named Jaap Van Der Mark and some very valuable items he is carrying. Now, we are going to walk to the back
of the plane very calmly. Don't say a word. Don't look distressed."
He turned James toward the door.

The radio crackled. "This is the captain. Is Mr. Smilt in the
cockpit?"

Perry spoke through clenched teeth. "Say no. Now."

The pilot reached for the phone. "Negative."

"All right."

The pilot hung up the phone. "Look, we can work something
out. We can try to."

"Shut up. You first. The flight attendant will walk with me.
Let's go."

"You're leaving the cockpit empty," James said.

"That's what autopilot is for."

"This doesn't seem like a good plan."

Rage seized Perry. "Don't *ever* say that again."

For every tear she wiped, another soon replaced it. Lucy slid down
in her seat, trying to block out everything around her. It was useless. Neil kept looking at her.

"Come on," he finally said. "Give me a break. It's not like you even have a relationship with this guy."

"He was nice."

Neil snorted. "Yeah, well, I was nice enough to offer to help too."

Lucy turned away. "Just leave me alone."

"You owe me dinner."

"Shut up." Lucy closed her eyes, but no matter how much she tried, she could not stop the tears from flowing. She wondered if Hank would stay in the back of the plane for the rest of the flight. She wondered if she would ever be able to forget seeing Jeff and that other woman.

For about one minute, standing there with Neil nuzzling her neck felt good. But that feeling faded as quickly as it came, and the high she got off of stuffing it in Jeff's face couldn't match the low she felt knowing she'd hurt Hank's feelings.

She noticed Hank's notebook sitting in his seat and wondered what he'd been writing all this time. A journal? A diary?

Don't you dare. But her hand had a mind of its own. Slowly, she reached out and flipped it over. She leaned forward, trying to read his handwriting. It was a long list of words and phrases:

nice

willing

prompt

gracious

looked nice

very conscious of the temperature

outfit very appropriate
very nice, well-kept hair
makeup well done, some overdone
priorities in place
smiling most of the time
able to handle difficult situations

Lucy's hand went over her heart. He was making a list about her? She'd never had anyone say such nice things about her. Even when she dated Jeff, all he could talk about was himself.

Nice? Gracious? And, well, she had to agree her makeup was probably overdone, but with the airplane lighting, it was sort of a must. Also she did have a vague interest in global warming. It amazed her that he could sense that! Even more meaningful was that he thought she had her priorities in place.

Nobody had ever told her that before. Her mother kept insisting that no matter how many self-help books she read, she would have to actually help herself before they did any good.

Lucy's heart deflated a little at the idea that he thought she handed difficult situations well. That was probably no longer the case. She wiped her nose with a tissue and glanced toward the back of the airplane.

"I don't get you," Neil said. "All you can think about is your stupid ex-boyfriend, and now that you've put it to him, you're worried about what blondie thinks. I mean, which are you? The kind of chick who lies to get back at a boyfriend or someone who cares about a nobody?"

Lucy yanked off her seat belt.

"You go flying back there, and your boyfriend's going to wonder if we had a fight."

Lucy ignored him and the Fasten Seat Belt sign. All she cared about at the moment was apologizing to Hank.

Danny helped Agent Tasler pull Leendert back to his seat, reassuring passengers as he passed them. "It's fine, no need for alarm. He's disoriented and a little shaken up. We're just getting him back to his seat. He'll be fine. Thank you for understanding."

Danny wasn't sure how much of this was getting through over Leendert's loud insistence that somebody was going to murder him.

Finally, they dropped him into the backseat. The agent held her fist against his chest and looked mean. "Leendert, *shut up*."

Danny put a hand on Agent Tasler's shoulder. "Look, let's figure out what's going on. This doesn't seem like a ploy for attention or to break away. Where's he going to go?"

The agent stood, an exhausted look on her face. "Leendert, therapy is now in session." She gestured for Danny to step up.

"Tell me what's wrong."

"I have been!" Leendert protested.

"I know, but we've been very busy with the pig. Explain to me what you think is going on."

"I think not! I know!"

"Okay."

Leendert slowly turned his head and looked at the other side of the airplane. Hank, the mild-mannered passenger, sat with Mrs. Kilpatrick, and the man with the stomach condition watched them. Hetty was the only other passenger back there.

"That man over there," he whispered.

"The blond one?"

"No. The other."

Danny nodded, showing he understood.

"He is on this airplane to kill me."

Danny looked at him. He didn't look like a ruthless killer, but then, neither did anybody on *48 Hours*.

"How do you know this?"

"He looks like his grandmother. See the way his chin goes? It points. And the nose. I've only seen pictures of him as a boy, but I am certain it is him."

"Who is his grandmother?"

"The woman I stole from." Leendert's hand trembled as he grabbed Danny's shirt. "Why do you think he is back here sitting?"

"He's got a stomach condition."

"That's what they all say."

Danny stood, peeling Leendert's hand off his shirt. "Okay, what if…what if we relocate this man? Move him to the front of the plane?"

Leendert's eyes darted back and forth. "I don't know."

"That will keep him away from you. When we land, you'll stay on the plane until the rest of the passengers are deboarded."

"Okay."

Danny sighed with relief. The agent slid into her seat and eyed Leendert. "Enough out of you. Got it?"

Danny walked through the rear galley and over to the man giving Leendert fits. He looked perfectly harmless, but Danny still felt a sting of worry. "Sir?"

"Yes?" The man pulled off his earphones.

"I need you to come with me."

The man sat up. "Why?"

"We have a distraught passenger back here."

The man gestured forward. "She's just fine. That guy is talking to her."

"Not that passenger. Another passenger."

"She's dead."

"The one on the other side of the airplane."

"Oh." He looked across the way.

"Don't look at him! He's, um…he's…"

"Yes?"

"Paranoid."

"About what?"

"Look, it's not important. What is important is that I move you forward. We don't have much of the flight left. Is your stomach feeling okay?"

The man paused, then nodded.

"Okay, then let's go." Danny led the man up the aisle to an empty seat. "This should be fine."

"Oh no."

"What?"

"Hey, old friend!" said a man in the window seat.

"Great," Danny said. "You know each other. Have a seat."

Reluctantly, the man sat.

"Bubba, in the galley, now."

Danny turned to find the captain with a strained look on her face. He walked after her. "What's going on?"

"I can't find the ACI."

"You can't find him at all?"

"No."

A woman in polka dots breezed by. "Ma'am. Ma'am, you need to…" But she had already passed. He'd deal with her in a moment.

"Where's the pig?" the captain asked.

"In the bathroom."

"It can use a toilet?"

"That's yet to be seen. But it's secure, and Anna Sue seems to be handling all this remarkably well."

"Bubba, I have a bad feeling about this guy. How can a person disappear on an airplane?"

They were nowhere near the Bermuda Triangle. "Have you checked the cockpit?"

"Yes. I called a few minutes ago, and he wasn't there." The captain placed her hands firmly on her hips. "Something is very wrong."

Chapter 23

L ucy, what are you doing back here?"

Lucy slid into the seat across the aisle from Hank. "I wanted to apologize to you."

"For what?"

"For being a jerk. For putting my needs in front of your feelings. I mean, we had this connection, you know? We were sort of like kindred spirits, and then I go and do something stupid."

Hank reached across the aisle and patted her arm. "Lucy, it's fine. Really."

"Look, Hank, this is probably really forward of me, but I wanted to know if you would go out with me."

The smile slid off Hank's face. "What?"

"A date. You know, a date?"

Hank looked at his knees. "Lucy, this is complicated. I really like you. I feel that connection too. But we're very different."

"I know, and trust me, I don't normally dress this way." The old woman one seat ahead of Lucy raised an eyebrow, looking her up and down. "Really. I went overboard for the whole trip thing. And I can go without mascara if you prefer."

"Lucy, I'm not talking about your makeup."

"But you think it's overdone. It's okay, you can say it."

"No, I think you look wonderful."

Lucy took in a desperate breath. "It's just that when you see your ex-boyfriend taking a trip with another woman and you have nowhere to go, nowhere to run and hide, it brings out the worst side of you." Lucy blinked, studying his face. "But that's not what's bothering you, is it?"

"I think about my future wife a lot. I don't know her. Have no idea what she'll be like. But I picture us having a lot of children, and I picture us praying and going to church and building our life on the truth of the Bible."

Lucy twisted her bracelet around her wrist, trying to understand.

"The truth of the matter, Lucy, is that I'm not capable of being everything to you. That's why I have to find a woman who puts all her trust in God. That way I'm a bonus, not a guarantee."

Not a guarantee. There'd never been a truer statement about Jeff. He'd promised her everything and delivered nothing. She'd put every hope she had into him, and he ripped it away from her.

"There are no guarantees, right?" Lucy sniffled.

"There's one. You just don't know Him yet."

"Do you want to know why I don't believe in God?'

"I'd rather tell you why I do."

She looked down at her bracelet. *What Would Oprah Do?* Probably give away a car or something.

But right now, Lucy knew what she should do. Listen.

Perry stood in the middle galley with the flight attendant named GiGi and the pilot named James. He could hear the captain and Danny, the other first officer, talk in lowered voices about his disappearance, and he knew his time was short. He peeked around the corner and saw the captain and first officer move toward the front of the airplane, so Perry ducked out of their line of sight and headed toward the back.

"Show me where the FBI agent is." He pushed the muzzle of the gun into GiGi's side.

"In the back."

"Quietly, both of you. Don't make any sudden moves. No crying, nothing. Quickly."

Passengers noticed them, but nobody looked suspicious.

He shoved James and GiGi into the rear galley. Three other flight attendants were already there. "Not a sound. I will blow a hole in this airplane so fast you won't know what happened. I have nothing to lose here. I'd rather die than go to jail. So trust me, if you want out of this alive, you better cooperate."

"You have a gun?" a flight attendant whispered.

"Good for you. Now shut up." He handed GiGi a zip tie and

ordered her to bind herself to what looked like an oven door. Then he ordered the rest of them to tie themselves together by the wrist. "Hurry up!"

Perry pointed his gun at them as he stepped backward toward the other side of the galley, pulling the pilot with him. He would have to use the element of surprise to knock the agent unconscious from behind. She was the only one he worried about overtaking him. He figured the rest would comply, but there was no way an FBI agent would go down without a fight.

She sat in the very last aisle seat, so he could easily step forward and knock her on the head. However, he'd never knocked anyone unconscious, so he wasn't sure how hard to do it. He wasn't going to err on the side of light.

He rounded the corner and with one swift hit, she crumpled sideways. The old man next to her let out a frightened yelp. Perry reached for James. "You. Secure her. Tie her to his handcuffs. Hurry up."

Perry glanced around. Nobody was looking at them yet. Soon chaos would erupt.

"Hurry!"

The pilot threaded a zip tie around one of her wrists, then threaded another through the first one and then through one of the cuffs. Then he tied her other wrist to the first one. That would keep her from doing anything ridiculous, like trying to interfere.

Perry grabbed her keys, then James. "Flush these down the toilet." The pilot disappeared into the bathroom. Perry took off the pillow cover and tied it around the agent's mouth.

"Don't say a word, old man. I'm doing you a favor." He double-knotted it, and the toilet flushed. The pilot reappeared. "Okay, you're coming with me."

He wasn't sure what he was going to do, but he'd have to keep threatening to blow a hole in the plane. He wasn't sure if the other two pilots were even still in the cabin.

A million thoughts raced through his mind. Would it be better to have them there and not involved? Or use them as ransom one way or another?

And what, exactly, would he do once they landed?

Plan C.5 really needed to form. And quickly.

Perry kept the gun concealed as he followed James forward.

The pilot spoke. "I'm, um...I need something to eat. I have low blood sugar."

"Shut up."

"Just some juice. I'm starting to shake."

"That's because I have a gun in your back," Perry whispered.

They neared the middle of the plane, where the two other pilots had been talking just moments before. He paused and listened, ignoring the curious faces staring at him and the pilot. Things would have to move very fast.

Suddenly a loud cry came from the back of the airplane. "Help me! Help me!"

Perry froze, not sure what to do. He pulled James toward him, then saw the other two pilots race down the opposite aisle toward the commotion. With one deft step, he pulled himself and James into the bathroom area in the middle of the plane.

He sensed James about to call out to them, so he jammed the gun into his rib cage. James winced.

"To the front of the plane. Now."

Danny followed the captain down the aisle. Over her shoulder, he could see Leendert flagging them down with urgent gestures. Mrs. Kilpatrick and Hank looked distressed. "What's going on?" Mrs. Kilpatrick said. They slid through the center row to the other side.

Then Danny saw Agent Tasler slumped in her seat.

"What did you do?" the captain said.

"Nothing! It was not me! Look!" Leendert held up his wrist, which was zip-tied to the agent's.

Danny's attention darted to GiGi, who stood in the galley behind the agent, her hand over her mouth, crying. He could only see half of her.

She gestured toward the agent and said, "The ACI hit her with a gun!"

The captain hurried into the rear galley. "They're all bound together!"

Danny couldn't believe it. Four flight attendants were bound at the wrists with plastic zip ties and then tied to the plane.

"Danny," the captain said. "Listen to me. You have to get to the cockpit. Now. Be careful. Make sure you can get in without compromising the cockpit. We can't leave James up there alone."

Danny grabbed her arm. "No. Let me stay back here and find Smilt. You need to be up there. You're the captain. I can handle whatever is back here."

"He has James!" GiGi cried.

"James?" Danny looked at the captain. "There's nobody in the cockpit?"

The captain's flushed cheeks paled. For the first time, she looked unsure.

"Ma'am, you have to get to the cockpit. Someone has to fly this plane. That's all that matters right now. Once you're in, we'll deal with him."

She hesitated, regret flashing over her eyes.

"It wouldn't have mattered," Danny said. "He had full access to the cockpit anyway. You knew something was wrong, and you were right. Now go."

"I want you to stay back here until I call you from the cockpit. We don't know where this guy is, and if I don't make it into the cockpit, you'll still have a shot."

Danny swallowed as the captain rushed down the aisle.

"Is he going to kill me?" Leendert whispered.

As far as Danny knew, Smilt was going to kill them all.

At the front galley, Perry watched impatiently as James tied the remaining flight attendants together. The business-class passengers sat quietly, their eyes wide with fright.

"I'm not going to hurt you," Perry said, watching James out of the corner of his eye. "I want something that's on this plane, that's all. I'm not going to hurt anybody. See? I'm just tying them up. I have the pilot, he's safe and sound. Everything is going to be fine."

He sounded ridiculous, he knew, saying all this while waving a gun back and forth between them, the pilot, and the ceiling of the plane. He'd drawn the curtains, fairly certain the passengers in economy hadn't clued in to what was going on.

Then he heard the captain's voice getting closer. "Stay calm. Stay in your seat. That is an order… I know, I'm handling it. Stay there. Now. Stay in your seat."

Her voice stopped. He expected her to rip open the curtain, but she didn't.

"Miles?"

The last of the flight attendants had zip-tied themselves. They stood strung together like popcorn on a string, crowded into one side of the galley.

"Miles! This is your captain. I want you to answer me. Now."

Perry held his breath. For all she knew, he could be in the cockpit. But a passenger ratted him out. "He's here! Holding a gun!"

Perry pointed it at the passenger, then at the ceiling, which drew a round of screams. He yanked James backward just as the curtains parted and the captain stepped forward. Her fierce scowl caused him to steady his gun in her direction. She held up her hands as if surrendering, but her expression didn't change.

"What do you want?" she demanded.

"I don't want to harm anyone. I just want something that is on this airplane."

"What?"

"That doesn't matter at the moment. What matters is that I speak with one of the passengers."

"All right. We can do that. If you'll just let me into the cockpit—"

"I'm calling the shots." He swung the gun around, causing more than a few people to pop their hands up too. He tossed the captain two zip ties. "Tie yourself to the leg of that seat."

"You need me to fly the airplane."

"I've got two other pilots. But not for long, if you don't do what I say. I don't want to get crazy here, but I've come this far and I'm not stopping now. I'm going to finish what I started."

The captain picked up the zip ties. "You're not an ACI."

"It doesn't matter what I am. All that matters now is that I get what I want. And I'll die trying." For effect, he pointed the gun at the ceiling. He wasn't sure if he would die trying or not, but a gun could make it look that way.

Several of the passengers turned toward the captain, their eyes desperate and pleading. She glanced at them and then back at Perry. "You think you're going to just walk off this plane with whatever it is you want?"

"Nobody knows we're in distress yet. We land, I get off this plane, and by the time James here alerts the authorities, I'll be on my way out." It suddenly hit him that people could use cell phones to call the authorities. They probably couldn't get a signal yet, but it wouldn't be long. "Get those zip ties on!"

The captain looked at James.

"I can handle it," James said, "especially if I can get a candy bar."

The captain looked torn, but finally she complied. Perry inspected the ties from a distance. They looked snug. He turned to James. "I want you to make an announcement that we'll be coming through collecting wallets and cell phones."

James looked at him. "What?"

"Now."

"But how—"

"Do it."

James grabbed the intercom. "Ladies and gentlemen, this is First Officer James Lawrence. We have a situation onboard at the moment. We need your complete cooperation. We need you to surrender your wallets and cell phones. Please do as we ask."

"Tell them I have a gun and not to attack me, or I'll put a hole in this airplane."

"A man has a gun. Do not attack him, or he'll shoot a hole in the airplane."

"Tell them their lives depend on it."

James paused, his chin quivering. "Your lives depend on it. Stay calm. Do as I tell you."

Murmuring started. Perry grabbed a beverage cart, shoved the contents onto the floor, and ordered the pilot to push it down the opposite aisle. He waited impatiently for everyone to empty their pockets.

"Don't try anything! Get them out here! Pass them down the rows!" He thought it impressive that he thought to ask for credit cards too, so they couldn't use the Airfones. He was better at this than Miles gave him credit for. He scanned the group of first-class passengers, some of them juggling early morning alcoholic beverages while checking their pockets. "If I see anyone using a cell phone, I'll blow a hole through this ceiling! I swear it!"

They made their way through business class and into the main cabin, where a hundred pairs of terrified eyes locked on them. "Hurry it up! Don't try anything crazy! I've got your pilot and you're going to need him!"

He watched as passengers passed their items over. Anyone who didn't have a cell phone he stared down and asked questions.

"The only hero we need here is this pilot! You need him to get on the ground. Do you hear me?" Perry looked through the crowd for the other pilot. He had to be in the back of the plane, but it didn't hurt to make blanket threats at this point.

Perry swiped the sweat off his brow. He needed to secure James, and then it would be time to find Jaap Van Der Mark.

James eyed him. "Is this a cry for attention?"

"Shut up." Perry shoved him forward. "Let's go."

Chapter 24

D anny stayed in the back. Leendert tried to rouse the agent while Danny listened for the captain's call.

"I can't believe this!" GiGi said.

"Just stay calm. Are you okay? Can any of you break loose?"

They all shook their heads. GiGi said, "They're on too tight."

"Try using your collective weight to pull on the one attached to the handle. Maybe it'll snap."

GiGi offered a small smile. "Thanks for the 'collective.' But we don't have enough room to pull."

The zip ties weren't particularly thick, but needed something sharp to break through them. And thanks to 9/11, there was nothing like that on the plane. Not even a pair of scissors. James was on the intercom, instructing people to pass over cell phones and wallets. Danny wasn't sure what that meant, but he hadn't heard from the captain yet, so he assumed she hadn't made it to the cockpit.

He patted down the unconscious agent. Surely she had a cell phone. He felt a rectangular lump in her pocket and pulled out a phone. He turned it on, trying to muffle the power-up jingle it played, and hoped the FBI gave its agents international calling plans.

All five bars came up, indicating she had full power, but there was no signal.

"I don't think so."

Danny looked up at the voice. Miles Smilt pointed a gun at him while nudging James along with a beverage cart full of phones and wallets.

"You're going to be a problem, aren't you?"

Danny dropped the phone but kept a fearless expression. "What do you want? What is all this?"

"I'll do the talking. You shut up. I only need one pilot to get us on the ground."

Danny looked at James. He was pale and sweaty, looking like a zombie as people handed him stacks of wallets and phones. A hint of acknowledgment flashed through his eyes as he glanced at Danny, but then he concentrated on the phones and wallets.

"Fine," Danny said. "Use me, then. I'll get you on the ground."

Miles smirked. "I've got other plans for you."

"Look at him. He's a mess. He can barely pilot a beverage cart. You're talking about landing a 767, a hard thing to do on a sunny day with prime conditions."

James's head shot up, and his attention fixed on Danny. "I'm fine. Fine. I am." He stuttered through an attempt at another sentence.

Miles seemed to consider him for a moment. "What's wrong with you?"

"I'm fine. I have a gun... I mean you have a gun... It's looking...pointing at me. That's all. I could use some chocolate."

Miles nodded toward Danny. "I don't trust you."

"All that matters is getting this plane on the ground. Where's the captain?"

"Tied up at the moment." Miles smiled.

"If you tie me up, you've got one pilot left, and I don't think he's going to be able to pull this off." Danny looked at James, hoping he would sense that a transition in pilots could give them a window to do something. What, he didn't know, but even putting some hesitation into this guy might help.

"Shut up."

"Listen to me. If you tie me up, I'm stuck back here. If something happens to James, there's nobody to fly this airplane."

"Then I guess nothing better happen to James."

James pushed his sweaty hair to the side. "I'm perfectly capable of flying the airplane."

Danny sighed. This wasn't a personal insult. Why couldn't he play along? Maybe he thought if he was flying the airplane he was the least likely to get killed.

Suddenly Miles pointed the gun at the young man who'd helped move the body earlier. Hank sat next to Mrs. Kilpatrick, who clung to him like a brooch to a blouse. Another woman, young and in bright red polka dots, sat across the aisle.

Hank kept his cool, slowly raising his hands. "What?"

"Stand up." He stood. Miles threw him three ties and nodded

toward Danny. "Tie one around his wrist, then tie him to the leg of this chair."

"You're making a mistake," Danny said. "You need two pilots!"

"James here seems to disagree."

"I…I didn't… I mean, it's better to have two." James looked at Danny, who tried to convey an entire litany of ego-boosting exhortation through an eye blink while also hinting that James could dig a little deeper here and help out. "You should have two. It's…it is better."

"Hmm. Two against one. I don't think so." Miles waved the gun at Hank. "Do it. Now."

Hank slid through the center aisle to where Danny stood. "Give me your wrist."

"Try to do it loose," Danny muttered under his breath.

"Don't try anything," Miles said. "I'm watching."

"Where did he get the gun?" Hank whispered.

"I don't know," Danny said.

"It's the FBI agent's," GiGi whispered. "He said so."

Hank glanced at the agent. She was starting to come to but had yet to open her eyes. "Are you sure?"

"It makes sense," Danny said. "I don't see how else he could get a weapon onboard. It was in the cockpit."

Hank locked eyes with Danny. "Okay. Then you're going to have to trust me."

Danny watched as Hank pulled a zip tie through the one he'd put on his wrist, then anchored him to the leg. He didn't know what Hank meant or why he said it, but for some reason he trusted him more than anyone at the moment.

"Now," Miles said to James. "Get me over to that intercom."

The small guy with the pencil-thin mustache waved his gun then and moved to the back of the plane. Jake tried not to engage. So far he hadn't said a thing about diamonds, and Jake reassured himself that he was probably just a crazed maniac.

Then he wondered if he should try swallowing the diamonds or hiding them under his seat. However, that would take a lot of work. They were duct-taped to his belly. More importantly, to his belly hair. That thought had crossed his mind as he wrapped himself in duct tape, but he figured it was a painful problem he could solve in the future.

Right now he needed to lay low and assume this wasn't about him.

Blimp-My-Ride Eddie was beside him, talking a mile a minute. "I mean, I think we need to take this guy, you know? I mean, just take him down."

Jake shook his head. "He's got a gun. He could blow ten holes in the airplane before we even got to him. Besides, I'm not sure there's even a pilot in the cockpit. One passed us. I saw another one go to the back a while ago, and he hasn't come back since. And everyone says the captain is up in first class, chained to something."

Eddie's chest inflated. "I can fly this plane. I know I can. I can fly an airship, for crying out loud. This thing would be a breeze."

Jake wanted to argue that a breeze was more likely to help a blimp than a 767, but there was no need to make Eddie feel small. He already felt small, it seemed, which was why he boasted about ridiculous talents, like being able to fly a 767.

"I think we need to just lay low. Let's not draw attention to ourselves. The crew knows what they're doing. Flight attendants are trained to handle things like this."

"It had to be an inside job," Eddie said.

"What are you talking about?"

"How else do you get three pilots out of a cockpit?"

Jake considered this. He didn't want to be an unwilling costar in *The Dutch Job*.

The intercom clicked on. "Attention! Everyone sit down and shut up! I have the pilot, and we're all going to land safely if you do what I say. I want one thing on this airplane. Jaap Van Der Mark, stand up."

Miles stood a few feet away with his gun pointed at James and his other hand holding the intercom phone. "Jaap Van Der Mark! You can save the lives of every person on this plane by showing yourself. You know what I want! Stand up and walk to the back of the aircraft with your hands up."

"You're killing me."

Danny looked up to see GiGi with her free hand on her hip, looking Miles up and down.

"GiGi, shut up," he said.

"Listen to him," Miles agreed.

GiGi ignored them. "It's just that you've gone to all this trouble, and it's ridiculously unplanned. I mean, any woman in her right mind would have this very well thought out."

"I've got the entire crew tied up except the one I need," Miles said. "That's not well thought out?"

"And what, exactly, do you plan to do once you're on the ground? Elude the bazillion police officers waiting for you? Ask for a getaway 767 that James here can fly—who, incidentally, is probably going to need a case of Snickers."

"GiGi…" Danny tried to catch her eyes, but she deliberately looked away.

"As a matter of fact," Miles said, "the ground doesn't know anything is wrong. Some air-traffic controllers may be trying to contact us, but as soon as I get James back in the cockpit, he's going to radio in that everything is fine. We'll land, I'll deboard, and by the time you can alert the authorities, I'll be on my way."

Leendert's hand suddenly popped up. "I…I can help."

"Shut up, old man," Miles said. His voice blared through the cabin. "Jaap Van Der Mark! I know you're on this airplane! I'm not taking this pilot to the cockpit until you give me what I want."

"I help." Leendert gestured with shaky hands.

"Shut up!" Miles yelled. Leendert cowered in his seat.

Danny suddenly put it together. The man Leendert said wanted to kill him was Van Der Mark. The old man had said something about him looking like the woman he'd stolen the diamonds from. Maybe this guy had brought the diamonds onboard.

Danny had taken him to midcabin earlier.

Hank stood up. "I'm who you're looking for."

Chapter 25

J ake had always wondered what he would do in a life-threatening situation. He'd once been at a friend's house when he was eight, and his buddy's dad cut off his hand with an electric saw. The mother flipped out and couldn't do anything, but Jake's friend ran to the neighbors to get help.

He'd never been in a situation that rivaled that. He'd not been in a serious car accident or even seen one. He'd never been near someone who had a heart attack or started choking on a piece of food. His bandmate passed out drunk once and dry heaved for the next twenty-four hours. That was the most he'd experienced, and all he could offer was a couple of wet washrags.

This, though…this rested on his shoulders. It didn't hit him hard, like a slap in the face. It felt more like a distant memory pulled forward by a sight or a smell. He knew what he had taped to his belly might be the key to delivering everyone home safely, but he was having a hard time winding his mind around it.

Maybe it was because Eddie couldn't stop talking.

"Eddie, can I ask you a question?"

"What do you want to know?"

"Do you have a grandmother?"

"Two of them, one on each side. Both still alive and kicking."

"Which is your favorite?"

"Grandma Mildred."

"What is the most valuable thing she owns?"

Eddie thought for a moment and then smiled. "I would say it's her 1952 Cadillac, but she would say it's me."

Jake couldn't help the emotion that washed over him.

"You okay?" Eddie asked.

Jake pictured Grandma Mildred listening with complete fascination as Eddie droned on about life as a blimp pilot.

"I think my grandmother would say the same thing." Jake stood.

"Where are you going?"

"I'm a Van Der Mark. Jaap Van Der Mark."

Lucy had never chewed or bitten a fingernail in her entire life, or at least since the age of thirteen when she was allowed to start having manicures. But the bright red polish she'd dared to wear for the trip was now cracked and peeling, with bits falling to the floor—and she suspected some bits stuck to the corners of her mouth.

Hank had told her something, something to do, but she couldn't remember what it was. He'd been very specific. "Do you understand me, Lucy?"

She'd nodded but now she'd forgotten everything. Every single thing.

He'd been talking about waiting. "We have to be patient. We have to wait for the right time."

She'd nodded to that too. She didn't know what the right time would be, but she kept nodding.

Then he said, "This is it. I've got to go. Remember what I said."

Lucy watched it all unfold in front of her. Hank leapt up and said he was the guy that the man with the gun was looking for.

Lucy nodded, but she didn't know why. She couldn't stop.

Now the bad guy was smiling.

"So, here you are," he said. "Didn't take you much time to make the right choice. Glad you're thinking with your head on. Hand them over."

"Not so fast," Hank said. "First, you get the pilot to the cockpit."

"I'm calling the shots. The guy with the gun calls the shots."

Lucy tried to tune out the scene in front of her and remember what Hank told her to say, but her mind was totally blank. All she could focus on was Hank, his hands in the air, his face more serious than she ever imagined it could be.

She couldn't believe he was willing to be shot. She wanted to crawl under the seats and hide. Her hands trembled so badly she could barely get her fingers in her mouth to chew.

"Are you ready?"

Lucy glanced back. Mrs. Kilpatrick was whispering to her.

"What?"

"Are you ready?"

Lucy shook her head. "I can't remember what he told me to do."

Mrs. Kilpatrick, for once, didn't look irritated. "He said when he looks at the ceiling, you should jump up and yell."

Lucy blinked. Was that what she'd agreed to? "Jump up and yell?"

"Give me what I want!" The bad guy's voice boomed through the cabin.

"Not until you get him to the cockpit," Hank replied.

"You're in no position to play games!"

"This is no game."

Mrs. Kilpatrick whispered again, pulling Lucy's attention away from Hank. "He said that as soon as the guy looks at you, he's going to knock him down and get the gun away."

"But…but…"

"He said it has to be the right timing, because he can't risk the pilot being hurt."

"But…"

Mrs. Kilpatrick reached across the aisle, her fingers beckoning. Lucy took her hand.

"You can do this," the old woman said. "You have to do this."

"I don't know if I can." Lucy began to cry. "What if…?" She couldn't even say the words. She'd never thought much about death. It was more important to think about life. That's where the energy was, what caused the world to go around.

But now that she faced death, she realized it was just as real as life. They were equally real.

And the man she'd befriended, the one who thought she was gracious and smiled a lot, stared death in the face, willing to give up his life for every stranger on this plane. He was willing to give up his life for her.

"Remember?" Mrs. Kilpatrick said. "He asked if you trusted him."

"What did I say?"

Mrs. Kilpatrick looked confused. "You nodded."

"I nodded. I nodded. That I trusted him?"

"Yes." Mrs. Kilpatrick looked at the scene behind Lucy, the one she could barely stand to watch. "I think he's trustworthy. He seems trustworthy."

Nobody had ever held her life in their hands until now, and she couldn't think of a better person to trust her life with. She looked at Mrs. Kilpatrick. "Okay. I'm not religious. Are you?"

"Only when it's convenient," Mrs. Kilpatrick said, with a plaintive look.

"Would this qualify?"

"I think it would."

"Then pray, okay?"

"Okay."

Lucy watched the two men face off. The bad guy pointed the gun over the pilot's shoulder. His eyes had a crazed look about them. Hank, on the other hand, looked calm. He inched closer to the man, taking one small step after another.

Lucy noticed the old guy in the back row with an unconscious woman slumped over in his lap. He fidgeted, his eyes darting back and forth, his hand popping up and down like he wanted to insert himself into some interesting debate on politics.

She tried to concentrate only on Hank and do exactly what he told her—stand up and yell. She trusted him with her life. How she could trust a stranger with her life, she didn't know, but something told her he'd die before he let her die. Maybe it was because, as he explained to her earlier, he believed that one Man's sacrifice saved his life once.

Hank jerked his head upward and stared at the ceiling.

Lucy grabbed the front of the chair and was about to hoist herself up when a man walked past her and yelled, "I'm Van Der Mark, and I have what you want!"

Jake kept his hands raised. The crazed guy yanked the pilot back, his gun pointing toward the man who'd crashed and burned with polka-dot woman. Jake couldn't fathom why someone would volunteer to step in harm's way, but there was no time to think about that now. He had to show the guy with the gun his duct-taped belly.

The man swung the gun around and put it to the pilot's temple. A collective gasp rose from the passengers. "Then show it to me."

"No. You release the pilot first."

"Not this song and dance again! I don't know who to believe. Maybe neither of you is who you say you are."

Hank looked at Jake. "Let me handle this."

"I'm Jaap and you know it," Jake said. It sounded weird using his birth name.

"Look, I've got what he wants, and I'm willing to give it to him," said Hank.

Jake was definitely going to have to show his duct-taped belly and maybe sacrifice an entire circle of body hair if this guy wanted to rip it off him.

The old man sitting in the back pointed toward Jake. "That's him!"

"Would you just *shut up*?" The crazy guy waved his gun.

The old man said, "You want the diamonds, right?"

"How did you know that? That I want diamonds?"

Behind him, the flight attendant with the fire red lipstick spoke up. "He's the diamond thief. He stole the diamonds in the first place."

Jake stared at the old man. *This* was the guy who robbed his grandmother?

"He's being extradited back to the Netherlands," explained the flight attendant. The agent, her eyes now open but her mouth still bound, nodded. She looked at Leendert, trying to get him to remove the gag, but he ignored her.

"He is Idya's grandson," the old man insisted. His English was far worse than Idya's. "I would recognize him anywhere. She displays pictures of him all in the house! He is brought the diamonds back to return. He is your man!"

Jake lowered his hands. "What are you talking about? What pictures?"

"It is true," the old man said. "All over the place. Any picture, big or small, she has a frame on it. You look as if her. As if her!"

Jake looked at the guy holding the gun. "I'm Ja—"

"It's made with a *yah*," the old man said, pronouncing it with his Dutch accent. "*Yaap.* Idya would not approve of you saying your own name wrong."

"For now," Jake said, focusing back on the man with the gun, "you can call me Jake."

"All right, Miles," said the pilot bound to the leg of the chair. "You've got what you want."

"I want to see the diamonds!"

Jake sighed and lifted his shirt. Another round of gasps. "The five diamonds are in a pouch underneath the tape."

Everyone turned their attention to Miles, who looked unsure and increasingly unsteady. The gun waved back and forth.

"Okay, look," Jake said, wincing at the thought of it, "I'll rip the tape off. Show you the diamonds. Will that satisfy you?"

Miles nodded, but Hank stepped into the aisle where Miles stood. "Don't move!" Miles said.

"It's time to get this over with," Hank said.

"Hank!" the bound pilot said. "What are you doing? Stop! We can't risk him blowing a hole in the airplane!"

"I'll do it!" Miles said, pointing the gun toward the ceiling. "I'll do it! Don't take another step toward me!"

But Hank kept moving forward.

"Stop! I'll shoot!"

"Stop!" the pilot commanded, but Hank kept walking until Miles pointed the gun toward him.

"I will shoot you!"

"I have no doubt you'll try."

Hank reached toward him, and Miles fired the gun. Jake squeezed his eyes shut but opened them again when he heard nothing. He saw Hank grab the gun and try to wrestle it away from Miles, and he hurried through the center row to help.

Hank's face was red as he clawed at Miles's arm, trying to reach for the gun. "Get the pilot away! Get him out of the way!"

Jake stepped between the pilot and the fight just as Hank slammed Miles's hand against a seatback. The gun dropped to the floor, and with one full punch from Hank, so did Miles.

The pilot on the floor said, "Get him secured! Zip-tie his hands behind him! He's got those things in his pocket."

Miles moaned, barely conscious as Jake felt in his pockets. A handful of zip ties fell out. Jake grabbed two and secured Miles's hands behind his back.

A small stretch of silence was followed by a round of relieved sighs.

"Get the gun secured," the bound pilot ordered.

"It won't go off. It's not loaded," Hank said.

"How did you know *that*?" Jake asked.

"I've been around law enforcement some," said Hank. "And one thing I know for sure is that a law-enforcement officer would never, ever hand over his or her gun loaded. They're very safety conscious."

They all looked at the FBI agent, who could only nod in agreement.

The bound pilot said, "James, get over here."

Jake stepped aside to make room for James to move through.

"James, are you okay? Can you fly this plane?"

James looked down at him. "Danny, you worry more than my mother."

"Are you hurt?"

"No, I'm not hurt. I'm fine. I was just getting ready to put my elbow into Miles's rib cage when this guy went for the gun. I was trying to time it right so I wouldn't get myself shot, you know, because I have to fly the airplane."

"You look pale. Do you need some water? some juice?"

"Danny, relax. Let me handle this, okay?" The pilot took a deep, albeit shaky breath and said, "Okay. I need to get to the cockpit."

A moan drew their attention to the back. At first Jake thought it was the FBI agent. Then he thought maybe he was moaning out of pure relief that he wasn't dead.

The realization dawned a moment later, Jake thought, for all of them.

The dead woman under the blanket sat up.

Chapter 26

B efore Danny could comprehend what he saw, what they all saw, a loud thump caused him to jump. James lay beside him, unconscious.

Screams filled their end of the cabin: the familiar, high-pitched sound of Mrs. Kilpatrick and then the girl in polka dots.

He couldn't believe it. The dead woman he'd carried to the back of the plane and covered with a blanket was sitting up and asking for coffee.

"Mama!" Mrs. Kilpatrick cried. "Mama! You're alive!"

"What?" Hetty asked. "I can't hear with all the commotion."

As fast as an old woman could rush to an even older woman, Mrs. Kilpatrick made her way to Hetty. "We thought you were dead!"

"What?"

"Dead, Ma! Dead!"

"Fed? No, they haven't fed me. Did I miss it during my nap?"

"But...but we didn't find a pulse."

"A what?"

"Your pulse!"

"No, the doctors never can find that thing. Why?"

Danny shook off his shock and concentrated on James. "James!" He slapped James's cheeks with his free hand. "James! Wake up! Help me get him awake, Hank. Get some ice water."

James moaned. Hank hurried over with cups of water and poured them on the pilot's head. James's eyes flew open, and he struggled to sit up. "What happened?"

"You fainted."

James blinked. "I don't faint."

"You just did."

"That's ridiculous." James stood up, water dripping off of him. He looked down at Danny. "Why am I wet?"

"You fainted."

James growled. "Look, it's probably the low blood sugar. I need some orange juice or a candy bar or…" His eyes wandered to his left, grew big, and his mouth opened wide at the sight of Hetty.

"James…no, no, no, look away. Just look away! Don't look at…"

Thump. James fell again, this time hitting his head hard against the corner of the seat before collapsing to the floor.

A passenger screamed. "We have no pilots! We have no pilots!"

Chaos erupted as people scrambled out of their seats.

Danny looked at GiGi. "GiGi, can you get on the intercom? Can you reach it?" She nodded. "Tell everyone to get in their seats!"

"Folks, we need your full cooperation. We're working on getting the pilot back into the cockpit…"

She continued to address the cabin as Danny got the attention of whatever his name was. "You. Jake?"

"Yeah?"

"I need you to go to the front of the plane. Tell me where the captain is and what state she's in. Can you do that?"

"Yeah." Jake rushed off. Danny continued slapping James, who came in and out of consciousness. The FBI agent was in no condition to help, since she was zip-tied to Leendert.

Suddenly a passenger appeared, shoving another passenger in front of him. "Hey! This guy is a pilot!"

Danny sat up a little taller, trying to look at him across the middle row of seats. "You're a pilot?"

"Well, um, I'm a…yeah, I mean…I'm a…"

"I was sitting right in front of him," the other passenger said. "I heard him say he could land a 767!"

"Is that true?" Danny asked.

"Well, uh…it's…uh…"

"Can you or can't you?"

"You're our only hope!" the passenger said.

"What's your name?" Danny asked.

"Eddie."

"What kind of airplanes do you fly?"

"I…an airshi…a blimp."

Danny blinked. "A blimp?"

"Yes. A blimp."

The only thing it had in common with a plane was the ability to lift off the ground.

"We've been asking everyone," the passenger said. "Nobody is a pilot except this guy."

Danny looked at Eddie. "Can you do this? I can talk you through."

"I…prefer helium."

"You're our best chance."

The man pressed his lips together, looking determined but also like he could burst into tears. "Okay."

Jake returned. "The captain is okay but in your same predicament. She's tied to a chair. They're trying everything to get her loose, but there's nothing sharp onboard to cut the zip tie, and they can't get the chair unbolted."

"Everything on this plane is bolted securely, and we'll be lucky to find something sharp enough to cut through plastic." Danny looked at Eddie. "Okay, Eddie, go tell the captain you're going to the cockpit. She'll talk you through what you need to do. Okay?"

Eddie headed toward the cockpit. Then Danny called Hank over.

"Listen, I need your help."

"Tell me."

"I need you to go up there with Eddie and do your thing."

"My thing?"

"That calm thing. That thing you do with your eyes. Keep him calm, assure him he can do it. Help him get the instructions from the captain right. Just keep him calm and focused."

"Okay."

"Tell the captain I'm working on getting James conscious, but it doesn't look promising. Tell her she's going to have to talk Eddie through this."

"Okay." Hank turned to the girl in polka dots. "Lucy, come with me. I need your help."

They disappeared up the aisle, and Danny nudged James. He was out cold, a huge purple lump on his forehead. Miles remained slumped in the corner of the galley, his face bloody, his hands tied behind his back, and one eye swollen shut.

Danny tugged at the zip tie. He kicked the tray table with his knee but couldn't get it loose.

Then something occurred to him. *No. That's stupid. That's ridiculous. That's...*

It was a stretch, but at this point he was betting everything on a nervous, helium-dependent pilot, so he really had nothing to lose.

"Jake, I need you to find a woman named Anna Sue. She's the one who had the pig. Do you know what she looks like?"

"Yes."

"Bring her to me."

"Okay."

Jake rushed off, and Danny turned to GiGi. "GiGi, can you reach some jelly?"

"You want orange juice to go with that?"

"GiGi, focus. Can you?"

"Yeah, we can reach the jelly."

"Get me as much as you can."

Lucy followed Hank closely. Adrenaline shot through her body, but for Hank, she kept her cool and tried not to think about the fact that the airplane was flying without pilots.

Hank made his way through the thick crowd of passengers trying to help the captain and stooped next to her.

The captain said, "I already met Eddie."

"I was sent to help Eddie, and Lucy is going to help us both by delivering your instructions."

The captain glanced toward the cockpit, where alarms sounded.

"What's that?" Hank asked.

"It means we're getting too close to another aircraft. We'll have to hope the air-traffic controllers are doing their jobs. First things first—we need to contact the tower."

Hank looked up at Lucy. "I'm going to help Eddie get situated. Then we'll be ready. Lucy, you'll convey the instructions to us, okay?"

Lucy nodded as Hank cleared the passengers and headed to the cockpit, and the captain ordered everyone to their seats.

"First we're going to make an announcement for everyone to fasten their seat belts," the captain said.

Lucy stood and yelled, "Everyone! Fasten your seat belts!"

"We have an intercom system."

Lucy smiled. "This was faster." She glanced toward the cockpit. "They're getting ready. Can I get you anything? Water?"

The captain shook her head and leaned against the seat she was tied to. "This is my fault."

"Your fault? A madman is onboard."

"I should've never left the cockpit."

"You couldn't have known this was going to happen."

"Nobody ever knows anything is going to happen. That's why we have protocol." She looked at Lucy. "This is my final flight."

"No, don't say that. You're going to get us down safe and sound. You hear me?"

The captain looked toward the cockpit. "You ready, Lucy?"

Lucy saw Hank sitting in one of the pilot's seats. She watched him place a hand on Eddie's shoulder. There was a real guy. Not because of a Rolex. Not because of fancy shoes or spiky hair. Not because of anything except his character.

"I'm ready."

Danny watched Anna Sue make her way to the back of the airplane like her feet were made of lead. She clutched the seatbacks so hard her knuckles turned white.

"Anna Sue, focus on me," he said. "You can do it. Just look at me."

She nodded and locked eyes with Danny, stepping slowly but surely. Finally she reached him and dropped to the floor.

"Anna Sue, I have to get out of these plastic zip ties and get to the cockpit."

"Okay," she said, her voice trembling.

"I need your help."

"What can I do?"

"You told me that Chucky likes to chew on plastic. He's always chewing up his plastic toys, right? And eating them sometimes?"

"Yes."

"Do you think you could get him to chew on this restraint?"

Anna Sue gazed at the zip ties. "I-I don't know. Maybe."

"We have grape jelly. We could smother it with grape jelly as an incentive. What do you think?"

"He prefers strawberry."

"Anna Sue, work with me here."

She nodded. "Yeah, yeah. I think so. I think he would do grape."

Jake reappeared, out of breath. "The captain wants me back here, helping you. She's going to talk Eddie and Hank through it all, but she wants me to try to get you undone."

"All right, Anna Sue," Danny said. "Go get your pig."

Nervousness stirred in the air.

"Danny, are you sure this is a good idea?" GiGi asked in the kind of tone that already said it wasn't.

"No. But unless you've got wire cutters on you, it's all I can think of."

"What if he goes crazy?"

"He's not a crazy pig!" Anna Sue said. "I swear it. He's a good pig. I don't know what got into him."

"Anna Sue," Danny said, "I know he's the one who's supposed to be helping you, but I need you to help him. Soothe him. Make sure he's feeling good, and then bring him back here."

She looked at the plastic restraints. "He usually likes them if they squeak, like a dog toy."

"Let's give him the benefit of the doubt, okay?"

Anna Sue nodded and pointed behind her. "Now?"

"Yes."

She crawled up the aisle and eventually reached the bathrooms. They could faintly hear her talking to Chucky. Soon, they heard the heavy breathing of the pig as it rounded the corner and faced Danny's direction.

Danny braced himself, but there was something different about Chucky's demeanor. He waddled like he had nothing better to do—like a regular pig. Anna Sue went to her seat and got his leash, then hooked it on to his collar.

"He doing okay?" Danny called.

"I think so."

"Okay, bring him this way."

They both walked slowly, Anna leading, Chucky following with the manners of a trained dog. Danny shivered at the thought of looking this animal in the eye again, but as he did, the pig blinked back without animosity.

In a gentle, steady voice, Danny said, "All right, now, Anna Sue, do you think you can get him interested in this plastic around the steel right here?" That was a better pick than the one around his wrist. He couldn't fathom having a pig nibbling at him.

"You can't make it squeak?"

Danny sighed. The closest option was having Mrs. Kilpatrick get hysterical, but he figured that was pushing it.

Anna Sue said, "Okay, but I need to turn around."

"Turn around?"

"I think it's better that I face the front of the plane."

Danny tried not to look irritated. After all, she was doing very well for being an emotionally challenged woman. She turned and gripped the seatbacks on either side, then nudged the pig toward Danny. "Chucky, look! Squeaky toy! Look!"

Danny waved his hand and smiled.

Chucky blinked, not amused.

"Come on, Chucky," Anna Sue urged. "You love plastic. It's okay. You're not going to get in trouble this time. I promise."

Chucky just stood there.

"Okay, what about jelly?" Danny asked. "What if we smear the jelly all over it now?"

"We could give it a try." Anna Sue glanced over his shoulder. "But I think he's full."

"Excuse me?"

"He ate all those eggs in the bathroom. I can tell by the way he's walking that he's really full."

"Anna Sue, he's a pig. Surely if there's anyone prone to overeating, it's a pig."

"That's a myth. They eat just like any other animal—until they get full. Also, they're not voracious or dirty." Danny had about had his fill of pacifying the woman, but he tried a small smile. She smiled back. "We can try."

"Great. Thank you." Danny couldn't believe his life depended on whether or not a pig liked jelly. "Jake, get those jelly packs. Open them and start smearing them on."

Jake took a handful from GiGi, who was using her one hand to fish them out of the cabinet. "You um…want me to smear it all over your…uh, body?" Jake asked.

"No! No, just on the plastic and maybe my hand. Maybe part of the seat. The idea is to get the pig interested in chewing through this zip tie."

"Right." Jake peeled open the first packet. "Here we go. Smuckers, don't let us down."

Chapter 27

L ucy had an awful lot of information to convey back and forth—particularly considering she nearly flubbed a rather simple coded plan earlier.

She had the good idea of running back to her seat to get Hank's notebook and pen. That way she could jot down notes from the captain.

As she grabbed it, Jeff stood. "Lucy."

She looked at him. Maybe it was because her adrenaline was at an all-time high, but she felt nothing as she stared at him. "Yeah?"

"Do you know that guy? That guy you were sitting with who's up in the cockpit?"

This would've been the perfect opportunity to announce he was her boyfriend had she not already used Neil.

"He's just a great guy," she answered honestly.

"Wish him luck, okay?"

"He's got more than luck on his side." Lucy rushed back to the captain. "Okay. I'm ready."

"Tell them to turn on the speaker switch," the captain said. "It's located above them. Look at the approach plate. It will have the frequency they need to dial in to contact the tower."

"Okay."

"Tell them to contact the tower. Say: 'Schipol Tower, this is Atlantica Flight 1945. We have an emergency onboard. Do you read me? Over.'"

Lucy nodded. "Got it."

"Go. Then come back."

Lucy wrote as legibly as one could with chewed-up fingernails and the sense that life could end very soon. Running into the cockpit, she felt overwhelmed by the enormity of her surroundings. Hundreds of switches, lights, and sounds threatened to swallow them all. Eddie and Hank turned, awaiting their instructions. Lucy read from her notepad everything the captain had told her.

Eddie's fingers twitched as he keyed the speaker. "Mayday, mayday. This is Atlantica Flight 1945. Over."

Lucy was about to interrupt and explain the right way, but the radio crackled overhead.

"Nineteen Forty-Five, this is Schipol. Where have you been?" The English was proper, with a Dutch accent.

"Um…this is… My name is Eddie. I'm, um, I'm a passenger. The pilots were…well, there was a man…a gun…"

Hank set his hand on Eddie's shoulder and said, "This is Hank Hazard. I am a passenger on the flight. We've had an incident onboard. All three pilots are incapacitated. Two are conscious but restrained. They're trying to wake the third pilot up at the moment. We had a man onboard with a gun, but he has been restrained and we are safe. However, we've got to figure out how to land this plane. The captain is able to speak with us and is giving us directions, but she said we need to make an emergency landing at the airport."

Eddie nodded. "Yeah."

They could hear talking in the background. Then: "Nineteen Forty-Five, stand by." There was a long pause. "Are you declaring an emergency?"

"We just said that!" Eddie said.

"Stand by. You are going to squawk 7700 on the transponder."

"Okay." Hank patted Eddie on the back. "You're doing great."

Eddie laughed weakly. "This is when that 'God is my copilot' bumper sticker would come in handy."

"Yes, well, I think in this case we need Him to take over completely," Hank said.

"I believe so." Eddie's laugh faded.

"Do you see the throttles?" the controller asked.

"Yes," said Eddie.

"Follow them down, past the two black rectangles."

"You mean the ones that say DISCH?"

"Don't touch those!"

Eddie's hand flew straight up, and his other hand grabbed his heart.

The controller said, "They shut off the engines and shoot fire retardant into them. Don't touch the fuel control either." They heard some whispering. "Okay, tell you what, don't touch anything on that throttle quadrant. Just *under* the two black rectangles is a digital number. There are two round pegs that you turn to change that number. Turn the pegs so the number reads 7700."

Eddie's hand shook as he turned the numbers. "All right."

"Now we need the number of souls onboard."

"Souls onboard?" Eddie looked at Hank.

Hank turned to Lucy. "Lucy, find out how many passengers we have onboard, okay?"

Lucy returned to the captain. "Okay, we've contacted the tower, and they want to know—"

"Two hundred and three souls onboard." The captain held up a hand. "Don't write. I'm thinking out loud here."

"Okay."

"We've already programmed the runway into the FMS. We're on a short runway. I know the airport, and this is not a long runway."

"Okay…"

"Autopilot won't be able to stop the airplane in time, especially on a wet runway. It needs a long runway. They're going to have to set the…"

Lucy felt like she needed to write something down.

The captain glanced up at her. "Okay. One step at a time.

They've got to manually put the flaps down. This is to slow the airplane down to landing speed."

Lucy started writing.

"First, they will need to find the Autopilot Speed Select knob."

Jake's seat belt stretched so tightly across his lap that his legs were going numb, but he hardly noticed. He was more interested in talking with the old man—Leendert—who thought Jake wanted to kill him. Judging by the guy's expression, he still thought his life might be in danger.

"Look, I don't want to hurt you," Jake said. "I'm just curious about something."

"Why would I do such thing? Because that is who I am. Every time I have a good opportunity, I blow up it. I began eying your grandmother, and I liked her very much. Then she told me of the diamonds, and my old ways got the best of me." Leendert paused. "I am much happy she is having them to return."

Jake tried to tune out what was happening all around him, because it was just too weird. He'd smeared jelly on the pilot's zip ties and wrist, and now the pig woman tried to coax Chucky into licking the jelly and chewing the plastic.

If this was his best chance at getting off this plane alive, he wasn't optimistic about it. In fact, he was pretty sure he was going to die, so he figured before he went, he'd like to know more about Idya.

"You said she had pictures? Of me?" he asked.

Leendert's eyes brightened. "Everywhere! All over the house! Any small picture. School picture. Whatever your parents were kind to send."

"But she doesn't even know me. I mean, we've talked a couple of times on the phone about getting the diamonds back to her, but…"

Leendert smiled. "Oh, young boy. Listen to Leendert on this. I know I am a thief and a liar, but I tell you the truth of this matter. She does no care about these diamonds. If she did, she would no have put them under mattress. When she learned they were in America, she knew it was her chance to get you to come over the ocean to see her."

Jake looked down and smiled to himself. He knew it. It hadn't been about the money for her, and it wasn't for him either.

"You will enjoy her," Leendert said. "She has a sense of funny, and has very interesting stories to tell about the World War. She barely escaped the concentration camps herself because she was hiding Jews."

Jake put the back of his hands to his eyes. He had no idea. About any of it.

"He's licking! He's licking!" the pilot said. Sparse clapping came and went.

"I need a pen and a piece of paper." Jake tapped the seat.

Leendert shrugged. "I can't help you."

Jake looked at the agent, who still seemed dazed and barely aware she was on a plane. He reached over the seat and lowered the gag.

"You have a pen? Paper?" he asked.

"What?"

"Pen? Paper?"

She nodded. "In my blazer. It's over by the undead woman."

Jake found them and wrote the date at the top of a sheet of paper. Then he wrote, *I love you, Idya. My Oma. —Jaap*

He folded it and pulled out his wallet, then stuffed the note between a credit card and a McDonald's gift card one of the guys had given him on his birthday. He figured it had the best chance of surviving a fire there.

Beside her, Sandy, Kim, and Gloria clung to each other, crying. GiGi didn't feel a single tear. She watched with half interest as the pig licked Danny up and down his arm, taking his sweet time about it.

Ordinarily that would've brought her great delight, but she felt nothing. Not even glee at a pilot being licked by a pig.

So this was how it would all end for her. Three marriages, three divorces. Nine months from retirement with nobody to look forward to spending time with.

What a completely ordinary, ridiculous life. She tried to think of some good memories, but nothing came to her. Her childhood was too long ago, and besides, her parents had divorced, so after the age of six, all she remembered was hoping they'd get back together.

And this is what her job gave back to her: a retirement package cut in half thanks to 9/11 and now death in a fiery crash while zip-tied to half her crew.

If she'd had access to a cell phone, she wondered who she'd call. Her friend Cora, maybe, but she was probably at the gym. Maybe her neighbor who always watched her dog. If her other friend Lynn hadn't died from breast cancer last year, she'd call her.

GiGi smiled a little. She was probably going to meet up with Lynn real soon.

Except…Lynn told her heaven wasn't a guarantee. On her deathbed, moaning from pain and too frail to grip GiGi's hand, Lynn told her there was only one way to heaven.

Now the tears came. GiGi covered her face with her free hand. She couldn't remember the prayer. Her friend had told her what to pray if she decided she needed it. A year ago, she sat by her friend's bed and thought to herself that if that's what her friend needed to say to comfort herself before death, who was she to discount it? She'd pretended to pray with her, just to give the situation some much-needed peace, but she never meant it.

Now she couldn't remember it. Now she was staring death in the face just like Lynn.

She had nothing, nothing to cling to. No hope of anything beyond being erased from this earth.

Suddenly a voice came through the cabin.

"Ladies and gentlemen, this is Hank, one of two temporary pilots up here. We're in contact with the tower at the airport, and Captain Brewster-Yarley is giving us step-by-step directions on how to get this plane on the ground. But there is no guarantee we're going to pull this off."

Crying swept the cabin.

"So while we're awaiting further instruction," Hank continued, "I'd like to talk to the two hundred and three souls onboard."

Chapter 28

D anny opened his eyes. He always thought that if he was about to die, he'd repeat the Lord's Prayer. He knew it only because his grandmother used to make him repeat it before every Sunday lunch. But this was the sinner's prayer. Danny looked at James, still unconscious on the floor. Maybe in his own way, this was what James had been trying to say. He was a sinner. Sin had consequences. Sin was death.

Danny thought of Maya. Maybe he'd messed her up. Maybe she'd never felt secure. They lived together, but there was nothing keeping him from walking out the door at the drop of a hat. At least from her perspective. Danny loved her, but he didn't cherish her. He didn't do what was right.

It was hard to admit moral failing. And even if Maya had been his only mistake, she was still a mistake. Yet his life was marred by mistake after mistake—big ones, small ones. All were there.

He'd failed by leaving the cockpit. He was responsible for every person on this plane, and he'd failed them all. He could hear them crying. He could see Mrs. Kilpatrick holding her one-hundred-three-year-old mother, rocking her like a baby, having already lost her once, about to lose her again.

It suffocated him. It buried him. Even though he sat on the floor of the airplane, his back felt tired from the burden. His name, once released to the media, would become synonymous with failure. They would listen to the black boxes and find out he made the fatal error of deciding to the leave the cockpit. If there had been two or three pilots in there, Miles would've had far less opportunity to do what he did.

Danny looked at Miles, who sat in a corner of the plane where a jump seat normally folded down. Blood trickled from his brow and nose. He looked scared.

Was Danny so different from Miles? He would never kill anyone, but he wasn't above personal gain. He wasn't above feeling the need for revenge. Restitution. Smacking James upside the head.

The man who'd been swinging the gun around and barking orders now looked like a frightened, weary child, huddled in the corner with his knees pulled to his chest.

"My name is Perry," Miles said.

"What?" Danny asked.

"Not Miles. I'm not Miles Smilt. He's tied to a chair in his house. My name is Perry Watts. I worked for the FAA, but I got fired. Because I wasn't good at planning things out." The guy looked down. "I'm sorry for all this." He didn't look back up.

Danny suddenly noticed that Chucky had stopped licking him. He turned his head to see Chucky nibbling on the plastic.

"Anna Sue!"

Anna Sue, who still stood in the middle of the aisle, turned her head. "Yes?"

"He's doing it! He's eating the plastic!"

"Good boy, Chucky. Good boy. You're not going to get in trouble for this, I promise!"

"Anna Sue, I want you to sit down and get your seat belt on, okay?"

"Okay."

"How fast can he chew through plastic?"

"I don't know. Sometimes he chews it up in a matter of minutes, other times he takes his time about it."

"Any way to get him to hurry?"

"I don't think so."

The plane seemed to slow. Everyone cried out, and panic stirred in the air.

"GiGi!" Danny called.

"What?"

"They've put down the flaps! Get on the intercom and explain what's happening, talk everyone through this. Tell them the plane is slowing down so it can land. This is a good thing."

Danny was surprised to see her wiping tears. "You okay?"

"Tears of laughter. This is better than watching a pig fly." She got on the intercom.

The girl in polka dots appeared, squeezed past the pig, and sat in the seat to his left. "The captain needs to know something."

"What?"

"She said the…the…" She glanced down at her notes. "The FMS computer or something is already set?"

"The Flight Management System. It has the entire flight programmed in."

"Yes, that's it. She said you guys were set to land on the shorter runway in Amsterdam."

"Yes, that's right." They all dreaded that runway. It made every pilot nervous. The airport had been promising for years to make it longer, but so far nothing had happened. It was within regulation, but barely.

"She doesn't think it's a good idea to have them try to change it," the girl said. "A lot could go wrong."

Danny nodded, trying to process it all.

"She said she's going to have them arm the autobrakes, but she's going back and forth between Maximum and Medium."

Danny thought it through. The knob had four settings: Off, Min, Med, or Max. Normally it would be set at Min for landing. The Max setting made your eyes water. Danny had heard of guys blowing tires on Max on a dry runway. Usually, the Max setting was only for snow-covered or icy runways. The Med setting was normally used for wet runways. They were landing on a short runway with two guys not familiar with the procedures. Set it on Med and risk running off the end of the runway? Or set it on Max and risk blowing all the tires?

Danny took a deep breath and tried to block out everything around him. It was second nature to him, all of this, but trying to tell someone else how to do it seemed nearly impossible.

"Okay, write this. Tell her I think we should go Max, but we have to make sure they keep the engines at the same EPR and—"

"EPR?"

"Engine pressure ratio. If not, they'll slide sideways, and that can be disast—problematic if our tires blow."

Lucy wrote quickly. "Okay, I'll tell her."

She turned to go, but Danny said, "Wait."

"What?"

"No. Medium. Tell her Medium."

"You're sure?"

"Yes. That runway can handle it if winds are light. Yeah. Medium."

Lucy paused after scratching out her notes and rewriting them, and Danny urged her on her way. A few passengers' stares caused him to second-guess himself again, but he closed his eyes and told himself he knew what he was doing. He repeated it over and over to the sound of Chucky chewing plastic and making wet breathing noises through his snout.

He really loathed this pig. He wanted to yank at the plastic, kick against the metal bar that held him, anything to hurry this along, but that might distract Chucky, and the pig was, to Danny's dismay, his best hope. To say he was growing irritated was an understatement. His life hung in the balance, his career was likely shot, and he was chained to a chair with a pig licking him.

Then, like a shooting star across the sky, a thought flickered through his mind.

No. No, no, no. No!

Yet as he attempted to talk himself out of it, like a compulsion, his hand disobeyed.

He reached out and started stroking the pig.

"This is going to cause the throttles to retard and the airplane to slow down. It will not slow below the minimum airspeed for the flap setting, so as it slows below the maximum speed for a flap setting, you are going to step the flaps out incrementally. Flaps 5. Flaps fifteen. Flaps twenty-five. Flaps thirty. Do you understand?"

Lucy looked back and forth between the men. Neither nodded. Neither acknowledged anything that the tower said. "Hank?" she asked.

Eddie said, "Um…can you… Can you repeat that?"

"Lucy!" The captain's voice sounded urgent. Clutching her notepad, Lucy raced out of the cockpit and toward her. The captain had pulled herself into an awkward position to get a better view of the cockpit. "Tell them to tell the tower to instruct them to set the speed command to the ref speed. That's the approach speed. Tell them it's going to be easier to put out flaps as we reach each maximum flap speed. Go."

Lucy was still jotting down notes as she raced back to the cockpit. She repeated everything the captain said.

The Dutch voice on the radio said, "Okay, listen. The flap handle is to the right of the throttles and is shaped like a small airfoil."

"What's an airfoil?" Hank whispered.

Eddie shrugged, but they both seemed to be looking at the same thing.

"It has detents at each of the appropriate flap settings, and it must be lifted slightly to get out of each detent. The settings are marked on the console," the controller explained.

Lucy watched and listened as Hank followed the instructions. The invisible person on the ground spoke softly, calmly, as if the quieter he spoke, the more they would have to strain to listen. If there was a God and He had a voice, maybe He sounded like a Dutch air-traffic controller.

The airplane slowed as Eddie turned the knob and Hank opened the flaps. Thirty miles out. Twenty miles out. Fifteen miles. Ten miles.

Suddenly the craft turned. Eddie's hands flew up, and he yelled.

"Don't panic," said the voice. "The airplane is lining itself up with the runway."

Lucy held on until she felt the turn end. An unexpected turn, but they were still on course.

"All right," the voice said. "It's time to put the landing gear down."

"Lucy!" the captain called.

Lucy ran back to her. "Yes?"

"What's happening?"

"We're ten miles out. We've slowed the airplane. Um, they're getting ready to put the landing gear down."

With tears in her eyes, the captain smiled. "That's the easiest part, that landing gear. Three green lights—it's all you want to see."

"Okay."

"Lucy," the captain said, grabbing her arm.

"Yeah?"

"There's a seat up there. It's called the jump seat. Sit in it. Buckle yourself in, okay? Don't forget to buckle yourself in. Put it over your lap, not on your waist."

"Okay."

"And I want you to watch it all. Watch every moment of it. There's this really cool moment where you come through the clouds and the tiny specks on the earth become buildings and houses. You know people on the ground can hear the engines roar. You can feel your belly tickle, because really, we're not supposed to be up here, you know? That's for the birds. But here we are, flying like we were made for it all along. I was made for this. I always knew it. Ever since I was a kid. This is my last flight. And I need you to be my eyes, okay? I need you to tell me everything you see, what it feels like, okay? Can you do that?"

Lucy nodded, choked up at how vulnerable the captain looked, chained to the floor and unable to even look out a window.

"Okay. You've done a great job, Lucy. We're going to be okay."

"Yeah. We're going to be okay."

Lucy walked back to the cockpit, sat down in the small, black seat and buckled her belt over her lap like she was supposed to. She pulled it tight for the first time, and listened to the voice.

"We're at two hundred and fifty knots," Eddie said.

"All right. This is going just fine. Now, I want you to punch the ILS button. It is located on the console. Do you see it?"

Hank pointed. "Right here. Got it. What is it?"

"It's the Instrument Landing System. The instruments are going to read the data from the airport. Okay?"

"We can't see anything. There are clouds everywhere. All we can see are gray clouds!" Eddie's voice climbed with every word.

"It's okay, the airplane will do all the work."

Hank put a steady hand on Eddie's shoulder. "We're going to have to trust even though we can't see."

"Fly by faith, not by sight," Lucy added.

Hank looked back and smiled. "Exactly."

"Two hundred and forty knots," Eddie said.

"Perfect. Everything is going very smoothly," said the voice. "Just trust me, do what I tell you to do, and you're going to be fine."

"Two hundred and thirty knots. We still can't see the ground," Eddie said.

"You're fine. There are some low clouds, that's all."

Lucy gripped the edge of her seat. It felt like they could crash into something at any moment, like flying blind. They just had to trust the voice.

"It's time to punch the Autoland button. Do you see it? It's located in front of you, on what you would call the dashboard of your car."

"Got it."

"Now we're going to arm the autobrakes. The spoilers are to the left side of the throttles on a large handle that sticks up about even with the throttles. You arm them by pulling the handle up."

Eddie pulled it up. Lights blinked. Computers beeped. Somehow, Lucy had a good feeling about it all. "Got it. Our pilot said to turn the knob to Medium. That the runway could handle it."

"We concur."

"Oh. Good." Eddie took a deep breath in and popped his knuckles. He looked like he'd just stepped out of a pool.

"All right. We're looking for you coming in from the north. Stand by."

Hank smiled. "Waiting's always the hardest part."

Danny considered the pig. It chewed like a cow on cud. He had never been around pigs much, except the elementary trip to the farm, so maybe he had the wrong idea about them. Maybe everything he knew about pigs was wrong. He'd always imagined pigs eating very quickly. Scarfing it down. Eating everything in sight.

But Chucky seemed to be a nibbler, at least when it came to plastic.

As Danny sat, feeling the airplane slow, turn, line up with the runway, and descend, all the while stroking Chucky's back, he thought it was awfully ironic that he was chained to an airplane. He'd been afraid of losing his job, and here he was, chained to it. He couldn't lose this airplane if he wanted to.

And now, in the midst of facing his own mortality and his own morality, separated by a mere letter in the alphabet, none of it seemed to matter. He liked his job, but it didn't define him. He made a mistake, but it wouldn't ruin him. Like a camera with autofocus, his life suddenly became clear. He felt whole again. And it was an odd time to feel whole, surrounded by a pig, a passed-out pilot, a prisoner, and four millimeters of plastic.

He looked at Anna Sue, sitting, clutching the seatback. He felt sorry for her. If ever she'd needed Chucky, it was now. A sense of admiration came over him. Here was a woman who only wanted to get from one place to another. Who knew what kind of teasing and discrimination she constantly felt for having a pig and being emotionally challenged. The world was not a kind or understanding place.

But here she was, hanging in there like a trooper.

"Anna Sue?" he called.

She turned. "Yes?"

"I'm proud of you."

"What?"

"I'm proud of you."

"Why?" Tears worked their way out of her eyes. "Chucky and I have caused a big mess."

Danny paused, wondering if it was appropriate to discuss her disability. In their predicament, appropriateness could probably fly out the window. He wanted her to know something.

"You know, Anna Sue, we've been on a wild ride, and I don't know how you're doing it, but you're holding up."

"Don't be too impressed. We still have to land."

"Yeah. But Anna Sue, your disability isn't easy to live with. There's a lot of stigma attached to a person with emotional challenges."

Anna Sue raised an eyebrow. "Did you say emotional challenges?"

Danny nodded. *Uh oh.* Maybe he'd crossed the line.

She laughed and shook her head. "I'm not *emotionally* challenged. I'm *motionally* challenged. I get carsick. And train sick." She looked forward. "And airplane-wreck sick."

Danny laughed. Then he laughed harder. He laughed so hard people started to stare, but he didn't care.

Anna Sue chuckled and shook her head. "What'd you think was going to happen? I was going to go crazy or something?" Danny could hardly catch his breath.

James moaned, then turned on his side and opened his eyes. He rubbed his head with a shaky hand. "What happened?"

Danny prayed he wouldn't glance to his left again.

Snap.

Danny gasped. His hand was free. "I'm loose!"

"Go!" someone yelled.

Danny scrambled to his feet. He ran down the aisle, holding on to the seats, focused on getting to the cockpit. The only thing he could think about was that he should have gone with Maximum. Medium would have been fine if they had the possibility of using the thrust reversers.

Maybe he could get there in time.

He passed the captain, her eyes lighting up as she saw him. "Go!"

Danny stepped quickly, steadily right into the cockpit.

"It's the pilot!"

Hank started to unbuckle.

"Stay there! Stay buckled in. Sir," he said to the other man, "go ahead and sit back here, and buckle in."

They exchanged seats. The airplane, as always, felt like it was floating to the ground, no matter what the speed indicator showed.

He took a quick glance at the instruments. The landing gear was down. Everything looked perfect. The only thing out of order was the fact that his copilot was a passenger.

"Schipol, this is Atlantica 1945. First Officer Danny Mc-Sweeney here. I'm in control of the aircraft."

Cheers from the tower echoed through the cockpit.

Danny watched the instruments, just like always, and tuned everything out. He smiled at the thought of the sterile cockpit rule.

They were flying through "zero-zero" weather, or "the goo," as pilots called it. It meant visibility was zero and the ceiling of the clouds was zero too. The goo had caused many accidents over the years. Lots of guys had flown into the ground obeying what their inner ears told them instead of the airplane's instruments.

Behind him, the passenger in the jump seat sounded nervous. "We can't see anything! We can't see!"

"It's okay. Everything's fine," Danny said. "We have to trust what we can't see." And every mechanic who had ever touched this plane. He knew the plane could land itself. Now he just had to believe it.

"But shouldn't you…?"

And then they broke through the lowest clouds right as the wheels touched down. The tires made that skid sound that let you know you were back on earth. Danny reached to the front of the throttle, which upon landing retarded to idle, and pulled up on the reversers until they were above the throttle and past the detent.

The engines spooled up again and reversed the thrust. He turned the EPR up to 1.4, careful to keep the engines equal. The last thing they needed was asymmetric thrust problems.

The airplane slowed to sixty knots, and Danny eased the reversers down to the detent and then carefully stowed them.

"This is McSweeney. Flight 1945. We've come to a complete stop. Over."

The fire trucks and ambulances waiting in preparation for a disaster surrounded the plane as if it were on fire. Danny smiled. They were just doing it like they'd been trained.

Just like Danny.

But this time, he'd done it with a little help from above. And a pig named Chucky.

Chapter 29

B ob Worton closed the folder and set it on his desk. "Well."

"Sir? Is something wrong?"

Bob shook his head. "No. Hank, this is a very thorough report."

"Yes sir. You told me you wanted it that way."

"Yes. I did say that, didn't I?" Bob leaned back in his chair. It creaked like it was about to pop a spring. "So, you had quite a ride."

Hank smiled. "Yes, we did."

"You know, news reports are talking about a guy named Hank. A guy who helped a blimp pilot land the plane. A guy who disappeared."

"I didn't disappear! Here I am, sitting right in front of you."

"You weren't in any of the news reports."

"I figured I'd let Eddie take care of that."

"What was it like?"

Hank looked thoughtful. "It was amazing that such an enormous machine could virtually land itself. I remember the tower said, 'Just let go. It will land by itself.' And for a second, Eddie and I looked at each other. We couldn't believe it. But it did. It was like a hand carried it all the way to the ground."

"I heard there's going to be a big story about it in *People* magazine. About the pig, the woman who came back to life, and some lady who says she now believes in God." Bob chuckled. "I bet she does."

"What about the pilots? What's going to happen to them?"

"I don't know."

"The captain was going to retire, I heard," Hank said.

"Yes. I heard she's finally going to tell her story about what happened over Bermuda."

"And the other two pilots?"

"The other two pilots will go under review. It's mandatory. They got two hundred and three souls safely on the ground, though, so I'm sure that will play heavily into any decision that's made."

"Good."

"You have some very complimentary things to say about the flight attendants."

"They did a wonderful job serving drinks and, later, keeping everyone calm during a stressful situation."

Bob sighed, reaching behind his head and clasping his hands together. "Maybe this will shed good light on everything. Help get our name out there."

"The report?"

"The coverage. You know, the fact that it wasn't engine failure helps. And thank God it didn't end in a ball of flames."

"Yeah. Thank God."

"So, Hank, I guess you're finished with this whole flying business?"

"Finished? No, in fact, I think I'm going to learn how to be a pilot."

"Really?"

"Yes. I think that's what I want to do."

"I guess you have a nice résumé started. Most people start in a simulator."

Hank laughed. "I guess so."

"Well, Hank," Bob said, rising and offering his hand. "It's been a pleasure knowing you."

"Thank you, sir. Best wishes."

"And Merry Christmas. I guess I can say that. It's not too far off. A couple of weeks. Plans for the holidays?"

"I always spend it with my family and at church."

"Oh. Good for you."

"Merry Christmas to you, sir. And may God bless you."

Hank walked out the door, and Bob sat back down. He lifted the sleeve of his shirt and rubbed the nicotine patch. It had occurred to him for some strange reason that more important than getting an entire airline out of its rut was getting himself out of his rut. It was something about the way the kid looked at him the first time they met, like Bob was the only thing important at the moment. Bob couldn't remember the last time anyone had looked at him that way. Maybe somebody would again if he could get out of this rut.

It was going to take more than olives on a salad. Bob smiled. Maybe he'd attend Mass this Christmas Eve. That sounded like a good place to start.

Hank thought if you happened to peer in the window, which was cold to the touch and frosty around the edges, it might've looked like old times. Like when their parents would sit by the hearth, his mother reading about Saint Nick and his father reading from the Bible.

Things were different now, but not too different. The story being told at the moment, though not related in any way to Christmas, still held the attention of everyone in the room.

Hank smiled, taking in the scene. They were all there, sitting near a sparkling Christmas tree, its branches heavy with the weight of too many ornaments. Nearby, a fire crackled in the fireplace. Hanging from its mantel were stockings, decorated especially for each person.

Hank studied the picture in front of him. Mitch and Claire cuddled on the couch, their children next to them with their feet tucked into the cushions. Hayden and Ray sat on pillows on the floor near the Christmas tree, like they were guarding the gifts.

Holt and Avery sipped apple cider while sitting on the hearth. And Mack stood at the front window, her hands on her hips, staring out into the white snowscape.

"Mack, get over here!" Hayden said. "You're missing all the fun."

"I can hear it," Mack said. "Did anyone mention to Hank we're having a *ham* this Christmas?"

Everyone roared with laughter.

"Uncle Hank! Tell us about Lucy again!" squealed one of his nieces.

Hank blushed. "Oh, I think once is enough."

"Didn't anyone ever tell you never to trust a woman in polka dots?" Mitch laughed.

"Yeah…I think I've heard that once before."

"I just can't believe you landed the plane!" Hayden said.

Hank held up his hands. "Okay, listen, for the tenth time, I didn't land the plane! It landed itself!"

"That's not what the news said!"

Ray laughed. "Yes, well, sometimes you have to take those reports with a grain of salt."

Hayden stood. "Mack, please get over here. You're missing all the fun."

"I just don't understand where she could be. She was supposed to be home thirty minutes ago."

Mitch said, "You know Cassie, Mack. She probably stopped at the drugstore for a makeup sample or something. She's fine."

"It's just very snowy. I know there's no ice, but Cassie is not the best driver, especially when she's emotional." Mack turned to the family. "Which she's likely to be if she didn't get the job."

"I don't understand why anyone would have a job interview on Christmas Eve," sighed Claire. "That's seems ridiculous."

"Cassie said they're short staffed. Two girls quit last night. I don't know," Mack said. "All I know is that I'm about to go out there and find her—wait! Here she is!"

Headlights shone through the window and bounced off the walls. Mack closed the curtains as Cassie came bounding through the door.

"I was worried sick," Mack said. "You should've called."

Cassie grinned like it was…well, Christmas. She handed Mack a sack as she passed. "It was incredible!"

"Did you get the job?" Hayden asked.

"Yes! Yes!" She danced around the room, throwing sacks into people's laps.

"What's this?" Hank asked.

"Samples. I get *samples*!"

"Of what?" Hank peered into the bag.

"Don't worry, Hank, I didn't get you lip gloss and mascara. They have aftershave and skin cream for men."

Hank raised a skeptical eyebrow, but he had to admit it smelled good.

Mack held up a tube of lipstick. "What, exactly, am I supposed to do with this?"

Cassie giggled. "Wear it, silly."

"It's called Gothic Grape."

"Might come in handy if you ever go undercover again," Mitch suggested.

"Or when you're napping tomorrow on the couch and I feel like being ornery," Mack retorted.

"You wouldn't," Mitch said.

"Oh, I would." Mack smiled.

Cassie finished spinning around the room and stopped in front of Hank to give him a big hug. "I'm so glad you're safe!"

"I can't thank you enough for your help on the plane, Sis."

"It was my pleasure." She lowered her voice. "So...?"

"So what?"

"Anything happen with Lucy that I should know about?"

Hank smiled and looked down. "No. She's a nice lady, though. I wish her the best."

"Well, don't give up."

"I'm proud of you."

"Me?" Cassie asked. "Why? I didn't land an airplane."

"No," he smiled. "But you're doing something you love. You didn't give up on your dream...even if the rest of the family doesn't understand it."

Cassie grinned. "I can't even describe it! Standing behind that counter, smelling all those perfumes, getting to see the spring colors before Christmas!" She hopped and clapped her hands. "It's incredible!"

Mitch slid up next to them. "Congratulations, Cassie."

"Thanks."

"It's good to know you'll have a steady job and money to pay the bills." He patted her on the back. "You want some cider?"

"Sure."

Mitch left, and Cassie's face dimmed.

"What's the matter?" Hank nudged her.

"Well…it doesn't exactly pay the bills."

"What do you mean?"

"It's part-time."

He arched an eyebrow. "Oh."

"I'll have to find another job to pay the bills."

"Well, that's okay, right? Surely there's something else out there you'd like to do."

Cassie shook her head. "Nothing. Nothing at all."

"Then look at it this way: the other part-time job will allow you to do what you really want to do. And who knows? Maybe sometime soon you'll be manager of the cosmetics department or something!"

"True." Cassie grabbed him by the arm, and they headed to the kitchen. "Come on. I have to tell you about a new pore minimizer they're making in the men's line!"

Acknowledgments

I didn't know how little I knew about airplanes until I began the journey of writing *Skid*. If it takes a village to raise a child, it took a good-size town to write *Skid*! This book wouldn't have happened had God not brought some really terrific people onboard.

First I'd like to thank Dave Belton, who tolerated endless questions about his profession as a commercial pilot. Thanks also to his beautiful family, who took me in for a couple of days and let me borrow Dave. Dave, it was truly fun to work with you.

I'd also like to thank Sam Ward and Bob and Marci Burke for their willingness to share their knowledge and to tolerate my not-so-bright questions! And thank you to Ron Wheatley for great technical advice.

A special thanks is extended to Doug Troy and Delta Airlines for allowing me the privilege of touring their headquarters and flying their 767 simulator. (Sorry I broke it! Obviously, I have no future as a pilot!)

I'm also indebted to Pat Pedley, Ginny Oxford, Ellen Warren, Chris Lambert, and Melinda Lysiak for sharing their experiences as flight attendants. I had such a great time listening to their stories, some of which ended up in my book! I'd also like to thank Micki Keiser and Deb Orcutt for their graciousness in responding to additional questions about flight attendants.

Last but certainly not least is the team at WaterBrook, who continues to support my vision and make every book the best it can be. You are all so talented! Special thanks to Shannon Hill and Laura Wright for their editorial skill, wisdom, and encouragement.

As always, thanks to my family, who tolerated research trips and some long hours at the computer. I love you! And thank You, Lord, for the blessing of the process and all You teach me through it.

About the Author

R ene Gutteridge is the author of fourteen novels, including the Boo series, the Storm series, *My Life as a Doormat,* and the Occupational Hazards series. She has worked as a church drama director and has published over fifty short comedy sketches as a playwright.

Rene is married to Sean, a musician, and enjoys raising their two children while writing full time. She also enjoys helping new writers and teaching at writers' conferences. She and her family make their home in Oklahoma.

Please visit her Web site at www.renegutteridge.com.